# Red Gifts in the Garden of Stones

## A tale of grief and ghosts and at least one small dog

P. A. SWANBOROUGH

# RED GIFTS IN THE GARDEN OF STONES

To Winston, and Queenie,
and all
small dogs of great character

# Glossary

*Glossary of Welsh terms used in the story:*

*Bach:* little one; a term of endearment to anyone of any age, size or gender; also used in casual speech by shopkeepers and publicans to their customers.

*Blodeudd:* [name] Flower

*Blodeuwedd:* [name] Woman of flowers; flower-face. Blodeuwedd in Welsh legend is the goddess of flowers and owls; emotions, transformation and betrayal.

*Bore da:* Good day (used for both hello and goodbye)

*Cariad:* sweetheart, beloved

*Cwtch:* noun:1, the small room/cupboard under the stairs; 2, a hug.

*Cwtch:* verb: to hug, to cuddle, to tuck in/away together.

*Da:* father

*Dwt:* child

*Ffwc:* an approximation of 'fuck'; *'y ffwc'* the fuck

*Hiraeth:* the heart's longing for home, even a home one has only known in story or rumour, or dream (there is no adequate English equivalent)

*Hen Nain:* great-grandmother

*Ie:* Yes (exclamation)

*Mam:* mother

*Mamgu*: grandmother

*Nage:* no (exclamation)

*Os gwelwch yn dda:* please

*Rhos*: meadow, heathland

*Ty Merched*: The Women's House

*Ydu:* Yes (agreement)

There are other Welsh words in the text, but their meaning is deliberately unstated.

# PROLOGUE: Sunrise

The house rests in the folded hills like an old woman abed this spring-dawning morning, blinking her window eyes at the first light. The sky cups its cloudy fingers over a pair of hen harriers as they fly their courtship race: rocketing from shade to light as they soar above the hamlet, the road, the chapel, the graves in the dewy damp. Above the blue sky's curve, a man is preparing to walk on the Moon, but down here it's a very special morning.

Lizzie lies deep in the folds of her bed that was her mother's before her, and mother by mother before that. The yellow ceiling hasn't been recoated for more than her hundred years; her mother gazed unfocused on that same paint the night Lizzie was conceived, pressed into the same feather mattress, and probably had the self-same quilt tangled round an ankle as she arched her hips up to meet the body of her husband; both relicts of former marriages and well into the enjoyment of the sacramental gift.

But Lizzie doesn't think of old Gwenllian and Dafydd, tupping away with grins of mutual delight. She's smoothing her own body, her gnarled old fingers spidering their way round under her bedclothes. No-one touches an old woman intentionally, so she strokes herself, reminds her skin and nerves of pleasure, of where she starts and ends, of her edges and shapes. Inside her head there is no much-patched bedding or soft yellow welkin: it's hot and crowded...

*Mmmm, warm, the soft belly of me. I'm an old cat I am in the sun, love my belly scratched... Love the feel of soft skin even the old girl I am. Ach, an' it's my birthday oh god.*

Lizzie shifts in the depths of her bedding and the Spring sunrise catches in the corner of her eye. A sunbeam gilds the dressing table, a cut-glass bowl throws a reflection onto the wall, a snippet of rainbow curves across the corner of a picture frame: a monochrome couple in their best Sunday clothes pause seventy-eight years on chapel steps: he tilts his head and smiles out askance; she frisks, smiles, on the brink of a laugh. The girl's veil is a frozen blur in a breeze that never let go.

*William, oh my own dear man, but you left me alone to bury our sons. There's right for a father to die before his boys but ach,* cariad, *the grief of it ... they're by you now in the hill; do you chat, in the dark or in the noon? Where are you now, William* bach, *with your poor health, and your beautiful smile like the fox, like the wolf, like the hungry moon rising over Panteg?...*

The orbit of her thoughts tracks its yearly path, back through loss to gain and from need to want, from adult dis-appointments to childish plans. Duty and harness, cleaving to and cleaving from. All the past sits at her bedside.

*Come round me you blessed ghosts you all,* canu penblwydd hapus a fi: *sing a hundred happy birthdays to me; sing and blow out the candle of me. Happy births and deaths and teas and suppers and beds and graves for all of us. There'll be cake and beer; I will squeeze this day for all the milk and honey it will give me...*

Lizzie shifts again, aware of her full bladder, fumbles the bedclothes away from her skinny legs, feels the cold dawn, smells the old stones of the house.

'Bugger' she mumbles as her left foot misses the rug and taps the chilly floor; she gathers the fuggy nightdress round her knees. It is Lizzie's birthday. No gazunder for her; she heads towards the new-fangled bathroom down the passage, where she is going to flush the indoors toilet.

Out the window, frowning low under the sloping roof, she can see the valley as it's always stood: rocks and hills and sheep, and neighbours.

'Bugger you and all' she mutters. She has long ago stopped caring for the neighbours; she doesn't even care that it's mutual.

Her feet stir dust along the corridor, where rag rugs hold the cloths and scraps of decades, knotted and flattened and staring up her skirts as she ages and sheds the years like flakes of grey and lacey skin. Memory whispers round her like a fog. A nothing-hand tickles at her from the brass handle of an old dresser lining the hall, tugs a greeting. Moths stir awake inside a bunch of dried flowers, nudging another petal into silent dust. In the bathroom, the eyes of a porcelain jug watch protectively as Lizzie's soft backside hits the cold toilet seat with a quiver. She rubs her feet in cloths that layer the stone floor like geological strata.

Through the window the garden is a frosty grey. Inside, the dawn fills the dusky room with a loamy damp. On the lip of the basin is an orange sliver of coal-tar soap; its heavy-handed odour soaks through everything this end of the house, over-riding Myfanwy's rose geranium soap in the blue bowl on the windowsill. But here next to the toilet the two scents meet with a vengeance that annoys Lizzie's nose.

She opens the window, watches disinterestedly as the pink soap arcs down into the garden shadows. It might have been an accident. The sharp air of the open window sets the furnishings muttering with alarm. An irritated curtain flicks itself; a towel skitters sideways. The small ribbon looped through the bathroom door key glances about anxiously.

The chill follows Lizzie back up the hallway as she returns to her room, closes the door against the silence of the house. After a pause, the bed creaks under her returning weight.

Throughout the house, breathing slow, the other women are still asleep, their eyes shut and their doors ajar. Down the hallway, Lizzie's granddaughter—feckless and frightened despite her nearly forty years—Sarah Maud curls round herself and dreams in beat and rhythm and span of low-grade, self-conscious verse; her thoughts are dancing in gloomy candle-lit rooms feverish with hangovers. In sleep, she tangles her hands in a withered flower garland that fell from her fair hair during the night. Sarah Maud needs both her names to hold her up. With the nervous strength of a thoroughbred filly, but mind-light and starved of everything good, Sarah Maud knows life as a string of shattered nights and unendurable days, her eyes only work when she's half-asleep. As her feet move through the habituated steps of an old jazz riff, Sarah Maud accidentally kicks the grey cat that owns the foot of her bed.

The grey cat resettles to his dreams of wind and warmth and bats in the eaves.

Above the kitchen, forever clay-footed from the day she was born some seventy-six years and a few months ago, stolid Myfanwy dreams of her mother Lizzie; over and over she dreams of burying her mother. *Is she dead?* asks the dream vicar, leaning over the bottomless grave, but Myfanwy does not want to answer.

Myfanwy has been wanting, and not wanting, to bury her mother for a very long time. *What's being dead got to do with anything?*

Behind the kitchen stairs, in the child's *cwtch*, ten-year-old Jenner, dark-haired, birdish daughter of Sarah Maud and the fourth in line for Lizzie's bed and the yellow welkin, visits a place of leaves and feathers and wordless unclothed creatures, in her sleep. The ghosts lean by Jenner's bedstead, watching and caring for her solitary soul as they have done all her little life, for no-one else is taking enough notice of the child.

This: the morning dream state of Ty Merched farmhouse. The house so cluttered the walls recede to infinite distance. The house so full of ghosts, the living have no need to talk to each other.

Lizzie hates the epithet she is known by, Lizzie Ty Merched, Lizzie of The Women's House, for it reminds her that regardless of her grip on those chapel virtues of wealth, and pride, and determined work-boots, of her good bones and the sacrifice of her family's blood to Welsh soil and old wars, this one thing is all the neighbours want to know of her. Her family's story, in the minds of her neighbours, is only this: that all the men she loved or should have loved—father, brother, husband, sons— are dead, and what's more, died prematurely, died younger than they ought to. Yet here she is, surviving beyond love, beyond those loved bodies' graves. Her grip on life provokes people.

*But who'll look after things arightly if I go? Myfanwy is no farmer for all her bulk and broad feet, and Sarah Maud is ...'* Well, Sarah Maud will always be the unwed mother of Jenner— that *flightful* child! —but otherwise ... who can say what Sarah Maud is.

There will be no letting go. For who would catch and who would fall? Lizzie sleeps on, dream-wandering, and in her sleep a ruby necklace slips through her fingers, to be caught just before it drops away.

The sun rises further above the valley.

# Chapter 1

# Dydd Gwener
# (Venus's Day)

In Myfanwy's dreams, a pink soap falls past her watchful long-ing into the dark of the open grave. She briefly smells rose geraniums.

'The beggar! She's done it again' Myfanwy wakes with a shout. Lies back looking at the low sloped ceiling of spidery cracked daub, breathes deeply of the lavender sachets and potpourri pots filling her bedroom, opaquing the smell of old woman that creeps upstairs in the nights. 'The beggar!' she repeats hopelessly. And struggles her heavy body out of bed, already planning—for she is reliable as well as bitter—the day's tasks: cooking, smiling, cleaning. How dare her mother live a hundred years and cause all this fuss and work for her, and not a spit of use to help her. The beggar. Myfanwy clambers down the narrow stairs into the kitchen.

In the cwtch below-stairs, Jenner's dream turns and runs out a door. Sarah Maud in her own bed reaches for a glass in her sleep.

Lizzie's room is growing into chaos. Camphor sparks the air and tissue papers rustle in the quiet. This is her special day: the photographer coming from Pontardawe; the old farming neighbours; the vicar and the doctor. That will do. Her thin hair has been dyed in strong tea, and now the soft gold threads of it are pinned into the style of another era. She has pulled and lifted and shaken and held up two, three dozen bits of skirt and dress and blouse last seen in pattern books and draper's shop windows two, maybe three, decades ago. The scents of another generation fill the room: cedarwood, mothballs, *Narcisse Noir* perfume.

Lizzie is well past the age of hating her body's shifting shape and failing functions and is comfortable in her pleated skin and encrusted joints. The increasing tendency to farts and constipation, the drying womb, falling hair, softening cartilage, hardening knuckles, are mere irritants as long as she feels she can still haul a lamb from its mother's belly, dig over the potatoes and harvest a good bargain from a neighbour. Work and the thought of work have kept her alert, and for that she has worn the clothes remaindered by her long-late husband: heavy trousers, thick jerseys, fencing wire latching a worn belt. Today, however, she wants to look like a woman who gets a telegram from the Queen, and not just for her tenacity.

Only, the gowns and blouses she's preserved so carefully simply don't fit in the right places anymore. Quality can only endure, it cannot adapt. Gloves and shawls and hosiery, beaded reticules and bridge jackets; camisoles and girdles and hair nets, all near-perfect; all wrong. Lizzie looks at herself in the cheval glass, naked except for various pieces of underwear and a heavy necklace of rubies. Her hair needs re-pinning, but she focuses only on the necklace.

She remembers wearing it to hunt balls and Christmas parties when this small valley was richer in wealth and life, flirting with cocktails and whispering behind the epergne as hard-mouthed relatives tut-tutted at displays of affection between a married couple; she remembers dancing alone, when that old war was over, the ruby necklace like wet blood at her throat.

The shantung and guipure, the grosgrain and petersham are shovelled back into their boxes and drawers. A pair of long black gloves is pulled out again.

At the other end of the house, in the kitchen, Myfanwy tightens an apron over her cautiously pastel frock and stares at a list scribbled on a scrap of envelope: apple cake, pickles, sliced oranges with mint. Arsenic sandwiches, sausage rolls, henbane salad. A fruit punch, beer for the men; tea, and scones with cream. Nightshade jam. She knocks on the door post of the cwtch.

'Jenner! Are you awake, bach?' A pause. 'Jenner!' Myfanwy goes into the room and shudders the mattress. Jenner, silent on the pillow, turns her eyes to Myfanwy. Myfanwy tips her head towards the door: dress, breakfast, help me with the housework. Jenner turns her eyes away.

Myfanwy pockets the envelope and returns to the kitchen to light the boiler and get out the bowls, the spoons, the nutmeg grater. Soon the house is creaking with the warming pipes and the sin of pride: a cosy house in daytime to afront the neighbours. Myfanwy is doing her best.

An instinctive physicist, Myfanwy knows time and mass and gravity are her enemies. She hates the light in the mirror, the mathematics of reflection, the atrophy of muscles and joints. Dust and entropy, weakening and decay. She shrugs. Work done is still work done, whether it has any effect or not.

Across the hallway, Sarah Maud turns in her bed and turns in her bed and turns again; she is not here and then she is and then she is not. Sarah Maud wakes to find the pieces of her crushed garland, picks them out of the sheets as if they might be made of gold, or mouse-droppings. Her mouth is dry, and she needs a cigarette, but the first thing Sarah Maud does is reach for a pencil and notebook on the floor by her, begins to write feverishly, words leaping down the page in time with her whispers. Words and words and words fill the book. They are poor words, clumsy and ugly and uninspired, but she must get them out of her troubled head.

Jenner passes Sarah Maud's doorway silently on her way to the bathroom; she hears the whispering woman, her muttering mother, in the shadows within. On the way back to the kitchen Jenner hears her mother moving, and scampers on.

Jenner soaks bread in milk, takes the bowl out to the garden and sits on a stone by the gravel path in the morning sun. The path and the sunlight win her attention. She drops the bowl into the grass and takes up a trowel and a brush. A pattern of pebbles and leaves begins to form under her hands, creeps across the swept gravel in arabesques. Time moves.

In the kitchen, cakes rise and sultanas swell, orange slices oxidise and mint pings the air. Myfanwy has gone into the front room to polish and shake and organise, but the furniture, too, questions her authority. Myfanwy has always been in-effectual; even the ghosts sometimes ignore her despite their bottomless need for attention. Only the kitchen bends to her will. She recalls a moment of dream, and bustles into the bath-room. The open window mocks the hot radiator.

'The beggar.' Myfanwy stomps out the side door, planting her feet on the stone flags as if laying down cash at an auc-tion. Below the bathroom window, she lifts the soap from the broken pieces of bowl in the garden bed, that lie atop a pile of older, muddier, broken china. She has more soap dishes in the shed. She will not be beaten over soap. Lifting her head, she sees Jenner bent over the front path, working at something.

'Jenner! Come and –'

Jenner ducks through the hedge and away up the hill.

Myfanwy picks grit from the perfumed block in her hand. Inside again, she leans to polish the bathroom window with her sleeve, and sees that, below in Sarah Maud's strange garden, west-facing and still in shadow, her daughter is making a wreath of fresh-pulled daffodils. The sap is trickling into Sarah Maud's hair. Myfanwy continues to clean the window until her sleeve catches on the window clasp.

If Myfanwy understood her life's grief, she would be crying enough to drown old Swansea town. The ghosts would hug her if they could.

-oOo-

Relatives, having compared the rarity of the occasion against the remoteness of the valley and the tenuousness of their connection, are underrepresented at the party: a single cousin from over Ammanford way has made the winding journey, alone except for his small brindle dog now tied to the gatepost.

The front room is full, nonetheless, for it's rare if not down-right suspicious for anyone to reach a century in years in this hard life. The village is here in what passes for finery; old neighbours niggling against each other: negotiations of status on this tiny stage, at this extraordinary event. There is a prick-ling expectation; for some, this is the first time they've seen the inside of Ty Merched though they've lived nearby for half a century. The ghosts are here: in the scent of attar by the win-dow, the draft down a frowsy neck and up a sepulchral skirt. Their chill fleshless fingers tap the cake crumbs apart, hunting for poison. The heating has lifted the scent of wax and horse-hair from the chairs and mingles it with a rustic rankness; a spill of local brew adds a tang of hops.

The room is dark, the windows obscured by the wall of coated neighbours crammed into the bay. Myfanwy hovers in the doorway, ready to greet, feed, observe, deny. Sarah Maud is feeling sick again and, oppressed by the unfamiliar noise of visitors in the house, shuffles stiffly around the kitchen. In a crumpled cocktail dress and mis-buttoned angora cardigan, she has the air of an overlooked doll just lifted from under a child's bed.

When the camera appears, the guests press forward to be in front of the shot, closest to the cake and the punchbowl.

'Bugger off' mutters the diminutive Lizzie as she's engulfed by larger bodies, but she smiles at the man from the paper as he brings her front and centre again. Jenner is called for, to stand by her great-grandmother. But the crush of people is stifling. Jenner is wanting to run—away and away and away.

Lizzie has decided to wear clothes after all. One future day, some random researcher in the National Library will smile and shake his head at the page he's stumbled across: the centenarian, surrounded by fusty old worthies as she proudly holds a letter in her black-gloved hands, a sharp greyscale necklace peeking through the open collar of the man's work shirt she wears. Just before he moves to the next slide, the researcher's eyes will snag on the other old woman, staring askance and accusingly at the birthday celebrant. A blurred shadow of a young girl is disappearing out the edge of the frame. The researcher will move on, already forgetting what he's seen...

Jenner wriggles away from the camera and in doing so, she backs into the vicar's side. The air cracks; short, sharp, acrid. Jenner startles in reflex as if struck. The vicar is completely unaware that for a moment his eyes flash yellow, his body rumbles in a monstrous sub-audible slavering. The ghosts flee the room, and in the vacuum they have created, the vicar clears his bland throat. Conversations continue to ramble.

'Did you hear, butt, she went to Llanelli Crematorium!'

'No!'

'Yes!'

'But why not Morriston Crem? She lived just by there.'

'Ah well, she'd paid into a funeral plan for a coach and black horses, the works, see, and wanted to get her money's worth.' The listeners nod their heads sagely: it's a fair point.

Jenner has gone outside in her emerald cardigan and amethyst dress, soothing herself with distance from whatever was snarling in the front room, and taking the Ammanford cousin's small dog to sniff round the yard. In the room, the guests' old jaws, tough from the grinding of mutton gristle and now underemployed in the presence of Myfanwy's good cake, chew over each other's news. The monster in the vicar's belly sleeps again. The ghosts creep back in from the chilly rooftop, shivering and rubbing each other's long old bones.

Sarah Maud is – nominally – handing round a plate of sandwiches. Purblind with migraine, she feels the chatter bounce round and round in her head, spinning like a fairground ride. She is very pale. Her hands shake.

'... and they thought it was an old carpet on the compost heap, turns out it was his brother, died a few years past and the only one of them who could drive. So, he just...'

The mood reminds Lizzie of her own mother's time: of afternoon teas and the neighbour women always in and out of each other's lives. Kindly, or pinning each other like a butterfly on the village rumour board, as the mood took them. Against her expectations, Lizzie is enjoying herself. Until. The vicar clears his throat more loudly, k-hem, k-hem; taps the teacup with a spoon, chick chink.

'... and the tree we used to play in? Only dead. Last winter, yes!' No-one talks about the dead as much as the living do.

Vicar eyes the last speaker coolly. 'Ladies, gentleman, dear old Lizzie...' he begins with such sureness. Then falters when he catches sight of Lizzie's baleful eye. She has had two serves of the fruit punch and is no man's fool today, her almost-good mood is gone again. He struggles on; the growling DNA of his puritan ancestors resumes its millennial-long slumber, and he is once again, and most thoroughly, the prosaic vicar of a small community. In all major respects of appearance and height the vicar is notably average; hovering on the borders of overweight, middle-aged, beige, and bald, he clings to the belief that he's young, spry and – an interesting possibility, still to be explored – evangelical.

Lizzie watches the neighbours steadily working their way through the food with grim focus, and the ritual is deemed appropriate. She could have no more refused to celebrate her age by inviting the whole '...*gossipy rabble...*' of her neighbours, than the village could refuse to attend on '...*the old snob...*'. No-one could be allowed to ignore the day, no matter what anyone wanted.

Myfanwy too is eyeing the table, calculating the quantities, and adjusting for the dryness of the vicar's speech. Should she put the kettle on again? Unless she lets the kettle stay cold, and the guests must go early and dry-mouthed. That would serve her mother right, Lizzie with her thoughtless longevity. Every day is an affront to Myfanwy's repressed anticipation of the yellow-ceilinged room and the bank account. Myfanwy has never even had a doctor's bill in her own name. Lizzie has cast a long shadow.

The vicar continues like wind in sycamores, hypnotic words come spinning down on everyone's heads. He is finding his stride, warming to his subject – although he'd be as hard-pressed to say what it was as anyone else present. His voice is washing over Lizzie; the room recedes, as if she's losing hold of something important.

Jenner, in the garden outside, runs past the windows and all eyes track her, from window to window and gone.

Sarah Maud, turning to face the wall, trembles away the dampness on her forehead. '*Doom doom the boom/ of the room and the gloom,*' she rolls the endless words around in the fog of her thoughts '...*don't they won't they lie down and be still in the chair and the hat and the shoes of them, you chomping teeth and mumbling jaws and you glassy eyes staring, you dry old dead, let me out, I ...*' Sarah Maud doesn't feel her hand fail or the plate slip, watches disconnectedly as the sandwiches tumble into the empty fireplace...

Lizzie is just bringing her attention back to the room; something unspoken has made her anxious and she wants to find that something and squeeze it. She turns her eyes away from the window, in time to see Sarah Maud tumble a plate of sandwiches into the fireplace.

The vicar is interrupted by a gasp, and the ripe bloom of tomato floats on the stuffy air.

'Sarah Maud? Are you alright?' Myfanwy's puzzlement pecks at the sudden silence.

'Well, what else could we expect?' someone mutters.

The Ammanford cousin, on alert for the unknown dynamics of strangers, leans well back. The ghosts of Ty Merched lean forward; this is the very meat and drink of their stomachless, throatless, existence.

'Drunk again' affirms a voice behind Lizzie.

'Was that you, Dai Pentre?' she calls over her shoulder. 'Was that you calling the kettle black, Mr Dai Pentre The Pot? Was that you, telling us it takes one to know one?' Lizzie has been losing patience for some minutes now. 'You drunk old bugger!' she finishes.

'I'd say not drunk enough,' from Zipporah Barry, 'she's got the shakes. I'd say she's got the shakes from not drunk enough'. Murmurs of agreement from several of the women, their husbands all dipsomaniacs of long standing. Mrs Barry has the acknowledged status of someone who had once been all the way to Abergavenny, and today she is not satisfied with her portion of cake. She will have her say.

Lizzie pivots in her chair, the ruby necklace flashes; the long black gloves are off. Any excuse to stare these old crows down is welcome; her early brooding has left a sour feeling, and now she's too easily provoked by the requirements of being a host.

'You'd know, would you? I've known you all from babies, from when I sat with you while your mam and da were staggering poor and my mam gave them our spare scraps to keep mind and body together. And you're still got your feet under my table' Lizzie stabs the air with a finger. She stands, bumps the table; the sugar bowl tips a spill of crystals across the embroidery. Lizzie looks at it a moment, contemplates throwing the whole table over...

But she knows her rage is fake, and she would never waste food. Certainly not in front of such a judgement of neighbours. Her main irritation is a need for the toilet again. Still, the big gestures are always tempting.

Lizzie sees that Sarah Maud is swaying in an invisible breeze by the mantlepiece, hair damp and face pallid. '*Du, du*, the vicar's turned Sarah Maud into the walking dead with all his talk. I was half-way there myself.'

Sarah Maud stumbles away up the hall. They hear her open the side door and be loudly sick in the garden.

'Killed off the men, now she's starting on her women,' came from somewhere in the room. Lizzie can't at first believe she heard correctly. Myfanwy blanches at the suggestion of poison. Jenner flashes away past the window again, raising muttering in the room as if she'd run through a drift of autumn leaves.

Lizzie's indignation which had so far been feigned, flares up, then falls into shame. The ruby necklace didn't protect her after all. For they all think this, that she has bought her long life with other people's deaths. And so does she. At some level.

'Oh heavens, no, surely...' the vicar attempts an appeasement, flapping his hands; but in the dark of his mind, at the base of his skull, an itching silent glee is rising to a smothered laugh.

Lizzie stands. 'Have you had enough of the free meal? It seems you have. I think...' Lizzie draws herself to her full five-foot two-inches height, 'I think we have run out of tea.' she finishes with conviction.

Even in this forthright community, where a spade only ever has one name, such an unequivocal statement of dismissal is rarely heard. The message is not misunderstood.

The cousin from Ammanford way shuffles to the door, turning his hat in his hands, reaching for his coat. He is the first out the door. The vicar is last, mumbling an attempted appeasement a few seconds later. The exodus would have made an Olympic speed trail had such an event existed: the 100mt Breaking Up of Tea Party Sprint, the Team Clearing of Front Room Relay.

Lizzie and Myfanwy look at each other over the empty room, the skewed furniture, the spilt sandwiches. They have nothing to say. It's a kind of caring, surely: arrogance and distance and poisonous pride?

'Go and look after your daughter' Lizzie tells Myfanwy.

'She's an adult' Myfanwy replies, 'she can look after herself.' But they both know this: no she isn't, no she can't.

Out in the garden, Sarah Maud has finished being sick—a purging brought on by accidentally eating some of the berries on her sleeper's garland, not a failure of liver—and wanders around to the front of the house to peer wetly at the ground. The gravel path is scuffed and scoured, and Jenner's arabesques of leaf and pebble have retreated to the shadowed edges, where they begin to glow under the overhanging grass.

Sarah Maud moves as if wading in a pool. Aware that the party has broken up, she steps back towards the open door, lifting from a pocket the forgotten gift she'd carefully wrapped the day before and taped over with crocuses and wood anemones. But the briar hedge of her family's boundary from their neighbours is echoed to a nicety in the barriers that formed between the inhabitants of the farm itself, and Sarah Maud cannot figure out how to reach out an arm, offer the gift to the old woman, recite the birthday formula of love with an embrace, for all that she constantly, deeply, feels the need to connect. She falters, and turns, and steps against the slope, follows the rising path to the lane and away to the pub. Her heels slide out the back of the ornamental slippers she wears. Her gift is left on the gatepost, above the spot where the small dog from Ammanford way had left a wormy turd. There is a footprint halfway crossing the dog turd.

Lizzie alone in the front room, looks at the disappointment of her day; shuffles the dirty plates, bends her old joints to pick through the sandwiches on the floor and stack them loosely in the hearth. One pile is for the hens. One pile is for the ghosts. One pile is for Jenner's supper.


-oOo-


Myfanwy hasn't found Sarah Maud, but that's because Myfanwy hasn't been looking. Myfanwy is tamping angry. Myfanwy is voiceless and alone with her compliant kitchen. Her pink soap and her heavy shoes. Her beating heart and her grating thoughts. The day was neither right nor proper, neither a success for Lizzie nor for herself and all the pointless baking. There was no bloody song and what is a Welsh party except cursed when there's no bloody song. The ghosts agree.

Myfanwy pours hot water over the soap in the scullery sink, and under her stomping hands the dishes rattle in fright. She chips a rare jug decorated with harebells and stops to scowl at the damage. She can hear Lizzie moving about the front room, the clatter of crockery and the rattle of chairs and fire tongs. Myfanwy does not care for Lizzie and does not care for the fire tongs or the crockery. Myfanwy barely cares for breathing, only to fuel her seething beating insides. She is utterly, pointlessly, furious. It doesn't even matter with whom. It's probably herself.

Her stubbornness broken by the chipped jug, Myfanwy starts to cry. A low wail of unidentified, immeasurable frustration. Alone in the front room, Lizzie hears and, without a thought, joins in; a thin keening whine from shrivelled old airbags escapes her birdcage ribs. The ghosts urge caution, but no-one listens to them; they shuffle anxiously, cover their soundless ears with fleshless hands, wail 'lalalala' and 'happy birthday to us' to muffle their fears—old scaredy-ghosts—as the crying women reduce themselves to nothing but breath and noise, the exhaled sounds of grief rising and rising until two old women, alone in their separate rooms in this ancient house, are roaring.

Were this a long-haul space cruiser, heading into the future with its crew trapped together for life, such a careful selection would have been made. But this was a family, child pulled from between the legs of mother, thrown into each other's arms willy-nilly, parented by choice or despite it but in any case, in every case: random, random, random, and only luck pertains.

Lizzie had truly loved her William, loved him like breath; but her babies—the tiny new girl now old and clumpy, the gristly squabbling boys now buried on the hill—they were drawn from her without consideration for what else she had wanted to do instead, without consideration for her nature and aspirations.

She never resented the boys. It was too late by then.

Myfanwy, for her part, only sees an absence when she looks at her single and strange offspring, Sarah Maud.

And Sarah Maud? Sarah Maud has no clear idea about her baby Jenner, no experience of love to lean into...

The ghosts look after Jenner, for no other beggar does. They fear they will not be enough.

# Chapter 1B

# Dydd Gwener, After the Party

The vicar is making his way up the lane, slowly behind his flock, bringing up the rear of the exodus from Ty Merched and Lizzie's party. '*Flock*' is exactly what he thinks, but not for the Christianity of the image. He's a farmer's son—although a family tradition of second sons has led him to this ecclesiastical path—and the sight of those broad backsides on the path ahead takes him back to the days of judging rams as a youth at the Pont Senni show. He pockets his right hand to stop himself from reaching forward between Dai Spuds's baggy-trousered thighs and hefting the old man's bollocks, critically marking them out of ten.

'Four' he mutters unconsciously.

Jenner flashes again across the near horizon ahead of the vicar, emerald cardigan and amethyst dress forming a bright flag against the cloudy sky. She leaves the graveyard by the top gate, vaults the drystone wall, is over the ridge and away, down towards the quarry below Panteg in a moment. Beside her runs a small dog, red tongue flying.

'Vile' thinks the vicar, 'I can smell its wormy arse from here'. He steps into a puddle and glances down. Words such as he speaks now, should not be heard by any congregation. He sloshes his right boot in the muddy water, wipes it on the muddy grass, leaves a smear of dogshit, thinks of the cost of a new pair of boots. He is not a very godly man of God.

Jenner. And the small dog. Surely it was one or other of them who laid that stinking trap for his beautiful footwear. He moves into the Old Testament of his soul. He needs revenge, like Jenner needs the sky, like the small dog needs worm tablets.

'Mrs Barry? May I walk with you a moment?'

Mrs Barry smiles her most saccharine accedence: yes, he most certainly may walk. Their heads bend towards each, their feet stamp the ruts and ridges of the lane in conspiratorial rhythm.

'Oh, Vicar!' The Misses Perry are not to be left out, and join in, one on the vicar's left and one on the right flank of Mrs Barry. 'We were just going to say...' But they weren't just going to say anything until they had heard who the subject under discussion was. Of course, it's—

'Jenner.' says the vicar, and the women agree with the Reverend Twdr Morgan, still a bachelor and most recent post-holder of the long reign of Morgan clerics in the valley. The Morgans are an old family, and Twdr shares the same bony forehead of the missionary ancestors that hammered their way into the pagan lives of the old tribes, drained the sacred swamps, uprooted the sacred trees and shattered the world order; and the same round belly of the Calvinist ancestor who proclaimed against the English church as if the very Devil himself had come amongst them to buy a round for the opposing team on Darts Night.

Vicar-by-inheritance doesn't guarantee a deep commitment to God, however, and the past Reverend Morgans have varied widely in the depth of their otherworldliness or faith. There have even, long ago, been Rumours of Exegesis...

The current Reverend Morgan has a fondness for stylish shoes, and these ones are ruined. Reverend Twdr Morgan regularly hears words raining down from the angels above; today they're calling for retribution.

'Jenner!' he proclaims in a voice that needs no pulpit to aid projection. Several close-by parishioners sidle up to the small group, swelling its numbers like frog spawn collecting in a small river's eddy. Round and round they swirl as they lean in, one ear each into the centre, one ear waving free to the hills around and above.

The walkers further up the hill, noticing that something is afoot, turn and dawdle back down the lane. The party may have broken up early, but that does not mean the afternoon is without further entertainment.

When he is being honest—an event always held in private —Reverend Morgan does not like being the vicar of Gwrhyd Chapel. He does not like the land, he does not like the people; he does not like the way something restless flickers inside him at the feel of the ancient stones and heathen bones under his feet. But he can soothe that restlessness by playing the villagers like a harp, a performance for the watcher in his head, and he has come to enjoy this modest power. 'For their own good...' the angels remind him.

'Jenner!' A pause, to collect his thoughts. 'Jenner needs controlling!' Rev Morgan announces. 'Jenner', he continues, 'Jenner is a Mischief.'

'Oh now, it's true!'

'I thought she'd been at the hens and now I'm sure she has.'

'That girl, what hope has she with that family' says the elder Miss Perry.

'Oh, and what about them?' askes the significantly younger Miss Perry. Younger Miss Perry had been enwarded in the TB hospital for most of her childhood and is still trying to catch up. Her sister gives her a glare, around the reverend's back, that she knows to interpret as 'wait until we get home'. She fizzes with excitement; old gossip is still gossip for all that. Elder Miss Perry scowls again across the reverend's back: the excitement will send Younger Miss P to her bed in an hour, and her duties will remain undone for the day. Still, gossip is gossip.

'I wouldn't be surprised if she came to a worse end than her mother' says one of the men, late arriving and a little breathless. Several mouths draw a gasp; the mother had indeed come to the very definition of a bad end; for reasons no-one could pin down considering her promising start, but all the same: a bad end.

'Oh, the mother!'

'Oh, but oh the grandmother!'

'And oh, but oh, but oh, the wealthy old witch, that great-grandmother; oh!'

'Oh!' says the Reverend Morgan, and he glances again at the stained side of his boot, 'Oh, but Jenner!'

The crowd can't help but agree: oh, but Jenner. The absence of any firm details about Jenner, her failure to fit the behavioural norms of the village children, have always allowed the villagers to make things up with impunity. Today, their collective imaginings pile the accusations of Jenner up into the blue arching sky until her fabled mischiefs disturb even the soft-hearted clouds, and provoke a light rain.

Jenner herself is by this time sitting quiet under the sycamores and ash trees on the riverbank below Panteg, utterly unaware of the conversations of adults, humming along with the song of the brook, weaving a crown of ramson flowers and leafy simples for the small dog, who curls round her hips in adoration. When he chews the crown, later this night, Jenner's herbs will cleanse his gut like a dose from heaven. On the A4073, the distant cousin from Ammanford way is driving slower and slower, trying to remember what it is that's missing; it's not until his untidy pantry is visited by the rat, that he will recall his small dog. The small dog, however, will have turned his small back on Ammanford and its ways forever.

Jenner is neither mute nor stupid; Jenner is of the valley like no-one has been since the first Reverend Morgan pushed the pagan spirits out. She has no human friends. The other children, learning how to close their minds at the hands of their chalky teacher, find her too close to the wild ways; they go to her when they feel sick, or when they want to appear sick; they'll use her but keep their distance. Jenner is happy with this arrangement. School makes her feel bruised in a way her recipes and herbs cannot cure—the brutality of the children, the brutality of the exams and textbooks and hard splintery benches. School is a base punishment; like rain and cold summers, it's a thing to be dodged and endured.

It has registered on the collective mind of the valley residents that animals, both wild and domestic, and—impossibly—the plants and streams all seem to alter their behaviour when Jenner passes. The collective mind hasn't decided if it approves.

The afternoon is dimming into a chill spring evening and the small dog begins to shiver. Jenner knows where an old blanket waits. She turns towards home.

The Misses Perry are sitting at their low cottage window, the one that looks along the top road and sees everything on the eastern flank of the valley. They see Jenner. They see a small dog wearing an emerald cardigan.

'Hens!' Elder Miss P snaps, and Younger Miss P leaps to the yard door, to shoo and fluster and terrify the hens into their coop before Jenner can pass. The hens are thinking they might stay out a moment to say hello to their friend, and Younger Miss P is yet again shown to be hopeless at the simplest task, until Jenner leans over the gate to chuck-chuck at the poultry.

'Chuck-chuck' reply the hens, and only then will they waggle their feathery skirts and settle their feathery shawls, wittering their way in, to perch and preen and nestle in the coop. Younger Miss P nods dismissively at Jenner who in fact hasn't even seen her. Jenner's world is as occupied by shades as by neighbours and she no longer bothers to distinguish them, other than the ghosts are usually friendly and the neighbours are usually scary. Jenner continues down to the old home in the crook of the low lane. Everything is still, no-one is crying now.

Myfanwy catches her when she enters the kitchen. 'Where the living god have you been?' For Myfanwy has been in the valley long enough to know there's something in the air—and who it's aiming at—just by the way the light reflects off a soap bubble, the way a door creaks when no-one's there, the way her ears itch when she turns in the hallway. And she was outside Jenner's bedroom door when she felt a jab under her left shoulder-blade.

Myfanwy's voice is croaky and dry. In a minute or two Jenner will slip some different leaves into the pot of Myfanwy's tea before disappearing outside again. Having an instinct for care, but a learned chariness of being noticed, Jenner will do this so quietly that Myfanwy won't even know anyone has lifted the teapot lid. Myfanwy will feel better.

Down the hall in the yellow-ceilinged bedroom, Lizzie is packing away the clothes and jewels and face powder of the morning; she pushes another drawer closed. She is in as much disarray as the room. She takes petty revenge on Myfanwy by refusing to eat any dinner. She has not thought why she needs revenge, but she knows in her bones that she does. Another box is wrestled into place.

Up the Rhiwfawr Road, Sarah Maud is sleeping by the pub fireside. Her stomach is empty, and a couple of glasses of rum and blackcurrant cordial have been effective.

'Another one, before I call time, Sarah Maud?' Gwyn the publican waves a glass in the air above the beer pumps and advertising placards on the bar.

'Oh god, is it that late already?' Sarah Maud lifts her head, but not enough to see the low sun outside; it is not that late already. 'I... no, no I'm ok.'

'Righto' says Gwyn the publican and adds another rum and black to Sarah Maud's slate behind the bar, safe in the knowledge of these past years that Sarah Maud's tab will be paid without anyone checking. His wife wants a holiday, this time in Fort William of all places, and while Gwyn never questions the source of Lizzie's apparent wealth, still he's confident that the tab will always be paid without question. 'How was the day? Old Lizzie had a good time? I saw the Newspaper was there and all!'

'Oh god, it was. There was. Sandwiches though.' Sarah Maud frowns in effort, clears her throat, sits up straighter, smooths her clothes. 'Sandwiches' she offers again. 'And the doctor'.

'Right. Great then.' He winks at the few drinkers at the bar. 'Send her our best wishes, will you? And did you want another one, before I call time?' He marks the slate: another rum and black, as Sarah Maud sleeps again, in the corner. None of the regulars keeps a slate in Gwyn's pub; his father was just the same.

The door opens softly, and a short breeze blows a man inside. He's maybe thirty years old; jacket and boots and hairy face have something of the earth about them. He leans in the door, nods an acknowledgement to the room in general then glances round to find that Sarah Maud sleeps in her usual place. The few drinkers study their pint mugs, their knees, the fire.

Gwyn polishes a glass. '*A beth fydd hi, Llundain Ioan? Peint felly? Neu efallai ddim...*' he puts the glass down with a crack, leans forward over the bar.

It's known that John arrived from London a few years past and doesn't speak Welsh. Neither do most of the valley now. That he and his woman have found a friend in the '...*crazy... arty...*' Sarah Maud is bad enough. But 'Llundain John', London John, lives in a caravan by the old rail line, has no normal job, buys no beer. Gwyn keeps his language loose in its scabbard for just such a customer.

'*Tramorwr!*' Gwyn confides to no-one. No-one nods agreement.

John crosses the room, lifts Sarah Maud to her wobbling feet, slips an arm round her and helps her homeward, muttering quietly to her now and then. The wind hits them as they cross the ridge and John gives Sarah Maud his jacket to cover her shivering.

Behind them, Gwyn adds another rum and black to the slate.

-oOo-

Jenner from the East and Sarah Maud from the North, both are drawn back down into the curving valley; the sun flashes on the peaks of the eastern ridge, sinks, and vanishes. Dusk draws in, draws everything home, fills the cup of the valley with a smoky tisane of supper and night. Around the banking ridge, and down in the folds of wood and pasture, small lights come on here and there; some belong to human dwellings, some do not. The lone streetlamp at the crossroad shines a light that just reaches the front gate of Ty Merched. Long shadow-fingers stretch beneath the picket gate and up the path, to tap the front door with darkness.

-oOo-

Myfanwy occupies her kitchen. The fire sighs and crackles. The kettle purrs and the electric light dims and brightens according to the wind outside. The whispering radio cradles a male voice choir, where every man in his own pitch is missing a girl with bright eyes. Myfanwy has eaten her supper alone, is missing no-one. Her old teeth grind, and her thick old hands clench the plate and the spoon. Before her on the table sits Sarah Maud's present to Lizzie, retrieved from the gatepost at dusk, its wrappings soggy with dew. After a moment's hard stare, she pockets it into her flowery apron, carries on chewing as if the well-made cawl were nothing but gristle and bones. The ghosts hold each other for safety, count their parts one more time. Myfanwy is certainly thinking of someone's gristle and someone's bones.

Over the decades Myfanwy has solidified into an unappealing stubbornness; the brief chilly girlhood soured immediately into late middle age before she had the daughter, even before she was married off—both willing, for the status, and bitter, for the choice—and given a brief freedom from Lizzie's dominion that ended too soon when the old husband fell over and died in a field and her marital home was taken by the son of his first marriage. Myfanwy has never felt she had any beauty to mourn the loss of, but inchoately hankers after her lost youth, for this very reason: she can't remember it ever happening. She cradles a *hiraeth* for her unlived past. Her nature and body are a battleground between plodding duty and the crystalline distortion of bones and joints, between her determination to control and the aching uncontrollability of her flesh and hormones. And then the final, tediously drawn out, difficult drying up of her womb; the appearance of dark hairs on her plain face, of thickening hands and ankles, mottling skin; unruly bladder; awful hair. Like cake going stale, aging has both softened and hardened Myfanwy in unwelcome ways.

Upstairs, she readies for sleep. Glancing in the mirror, Myfanwy only looks at the reflections that are not hers.

Jenner has shared the ashy sandwiches with the small dog, out in the shed by the night sky. She hauls out a blanket to make a bed and finds a name ready-made for the small dog; but Smalldog is away into the shadows and just outside the circle of light from the kitchen windows. Defeated in her plan to sleep out, Jenner goes inside to her own bed. Which is exactly what Smalldog has intended: for her to be indoors.

Sarah Maud has slid into her crumpled bedding, fully clothed and quite empty; for she had been sick again on arriving home, John carefully holding her at arms' length while she spewed and giving her water when she'd finished. She will smell bad in the morning, but her head will be better.

Lizzie, in her green quilt under that yellow ceiling, nibbles at a biscuit she's found in a coat pocket and dozes again. Soon, all the women of Ty Merched are sleeping, here and there about the house.

Smalldog sits on guard and snacks on the occasional mouse. He may be late, but he's here now. The ghosts have a night off.

# Chapter 2

# Dydd Sadwrn
# (Saturn's Day)

Lizzie lies late in bed; she's one hundred years and one day old. She sees too little to look forward to, and too much to look back on.

*When did I get to be the oldest person I know?*

A creeping shiver starts in the centre of her spine, travels up and over her shoulders, down her belly and through her legs, only to turn round her toes and shiver its way back up her thighs, torso, spine, shoulders, scalp, and down again. For fully five minutes Lizzie's muscles tremble and shake like tiny earthquakes across an island the size of an old woman.

*I thought I was better than this. Oh, William bach, bugger this...*

One of the problems of planning for the future is you're so damn old when it arrives. Lizzie is caught, wondering when life became that closed door, all those beloved faces in the dirt. The world once seemed to be full of babies to hold. Now it's all old people: ugly, jealous, pained, sagging. Lizzie hates old people; doesn't make any exceptions. She especially doesn't make any exceptions for—

*Who lives here, in this house? What are we doing, why do we hang on...?* She'd overheard at the party, someone asking when Lizzie would 'give over' to Myfanwy. She had managed to appear deaf while the words hung in the air between them but hadn't turned away fast enough to avoid the look in Myfanwy's eyes.

Choosing not to find any answers to these new and disquieting thoughts, she clambers into the old moleskin trousers and flannel shirt, rubs her aching knuckles, laces old boots. The garden needs tending. That's something to get out of bed for, at least. Spring: pride and produce demand that old leaves be cleared, the last of the leeks harvested, soil turned and left to warm. She leaves the house by the sun-washed side door, doesn't see Jenner moving darkly up the hall behind her. Smalldog has hidden himself away, sleeping off his night watchdog's shift. Lizzie spends a good 30 minutes moving round the shed, turning things, and moving things from side to side, unsettling things.

*Day after? Who thinks about day after? My birthday. That was the end of it all, my birthday was all...* she cannot even think about ... she makes her mind a blank place rather than think about ...

Myfanwy comes outside to throw party-food scraps into the chicken run.

*'On purpose'* thinks Lizzie, watching from where she's crouching over the last winter vegetables. They catch each other's eye. Of course, it's on purpose. Lizzie's conviction of authority has required she ignore Myfanwy's silent moodiness even as she ignores Myfanwy's frumpy fondness for floral dresses and rosy perfumes. Lizzie wonders for the first time, when this had started, and trawls back in memory looking for a time of closeness with her firstborn...

*It doesn't matter.* Lizzie peremptorily dismisses a momentary feeling of loss.

It begins to rain, faint grey threads slipping through the ghosts on the washing line. Myfanwy says nothing, looks at no-one, goes back to her kitchen domain. The light rain eventually rinses her distain from the air.

Lizzie slowly follows her. Lizzie says nothing. Myfanwy at the sink says nothing. The ghosts, well they can hardly shut their mouths for chattering.

Lizzie goes to her bedroom and closes the door, locks it, and returns to bed fully dressed. She is the dragon under the castle. She will not move again. She closes her eyes and leans back into the pillows. She will stay here until she turns to compost. She is still wearing the ruby necklace; her stiff fingers took so long to clip it in place yesterday she's decided never to take it off again, alive or dead. *Let Myfanwy deal with that if she doesn't like it.*

Only, there's a noise from the closet.

The closet is one of several clothes presses banked along the bedroom wall, all the different shapes and tastes of past generations: a museum of clothing is in there; forgotten things whose owners were laid by the chapel long since; deeds and papers; special things, dull things. Not a place for noises. Yet there it is again.

*Mice?* Lizzie jumps to grab her boots before anything can occupy them that doesn't wear socks. The noise has frozen in mid-air. Lizzie waits.

A breath, as quiet as it could be without suffocating, from the closet. Lizzie thinks this doesn't sound like any rodent she's ever heard before. She grabs a forgotten walking stick from the clutter in a corner; a long-ago present from Sarah Maud, it has a carved wolf's head for a handle. Lizzie gets good purchase on the wolf's head, pokes the ferrule end in through the hanging gap of the closet door, rattles it about.

A hand traps the stick in the dark. Jenner's face peers out from between the hanging coats. 'Don't! Hurts!'

'Jenner? What are you doing in there?'

There's something in Jenner's hands, and she quickly hides it behind her back.

'What are you doing in there, I said. What's that you've got?'

'You should be outside; this's my place daytimes,' says Jenner as Lizzie steps back and motions her to get out of the cupboard.

Lizzie squints at the bundle of pages cradled in Jenner's hands. A dried flower has slipped to the floor, Jenner puts it back in the right place with proprietorial care.

'My book?' asks Lizzie.

'My book.' Not an aggressive possession, but as we might say 'my eye' or 'my breath'.

'No, I mean it was my book. You've got my book there. It's mine from old Elizabeth. Ah! It was her grandmother's before her. My book...' Lizzie feels the years fall: she's a girl at the end of her school years, yearning to study medicine, and then there's beloved William and then there's the baby Myfanwy and then there's no more chance to study ever again. 'The old herbal, fancy. I never remembered where it went to. Fancy.'

'My book.' says Jenner.

'No, dwt.' Lizzie takes the book—not much bigger than palm-sized, but so thick with inserted papers and notes and worn leather binding, patched and over-patched that it's al-most a cube—and sits on the bed, cradling it herself in her turn. 'No, look here, this is my writing.' She holds out a sheet of yellowed paper, covered in neat childish print. 'I took all the words from the Welsh, while old Elizabeth was still about to help me with it. She was my grandmother, bach. This is my writing. This is my book.'

'You wrote this?' Jenner sits on the bed too. 'My book?' she slides closer to the side of Lizzie. Lizzie has forgotten that Jenner doesn't talk to grown-ups; so has Jenner. They lean their heads over the words and the drawings.

'I wrote the English pages, dwt; no-one knew how old it was, even when I was your age.'

'I'm learning the old words.' Jenner points to a flower, mispronounces the Welsh name in three different attempts. 'This one, I uses it like this,' and lists its benefits, seasons, risks and dosages, when she's used it and where it's mentioned through the book. Lizzie thinks a moment, starts to talk, thinks a moment more, listens. The moments last until dinner time.

-oOo-

In her kitchen, where time spreads unmarked over years and years, Myfanwy doesn't notice that Lizzie has been gone all day for the first time since she can remember. She's looking at the chip on her harebell jug for an hour, and another hour. She's not seeing the chip, or the jug. She's seeing the boy who gave it to her, the boy who kissed her at the Eisteddfod in Abertawe when she was young and supple and thinking to head away from home and school and old people. The boy she wasn't allowed to marry, for he came from no valley family, brought no land with him, went not to chapel but to the Catholic church. Gregorio Esteban in Spanish Row over the next valley, immigrant miner's son. Gregorio of the dark eyes, Gregorio whose fossilising metatarsals, shattered phalanges, still hold the dream of her young heart close to his ribs, though his bones lie lost in Belgian mud under The Great Warpath. The ghosts agree: he was beautiful. And his taste in harebell jugs was impeccable; never mind that Lizzie had dismissed the jug as 'common.' Myfanwy holds the jug for the jug holds Gregorio. It is all she has of the boy she wanted to marry. No wonder she hates. No wonder.

Sarah Maud reminds Myfanwy every day of the man she didn't love, did marry. Sarah Maud has the family name of the man chosen for Myfanwy. Sarah Maud with the pale Welsh skin and the blue Welsh eyes of that respectable old man from the hill farm. No wonder Myfanwy hates, standing there in the kitchen with the more-than-sixty-years-old jug and its perfect harebells and its new, sharp-edged chip. It wasn't her fault she doesn't love. No-one asked her. She wasn't involved in the negotiations.

If space flight crew were chosen as if they were families, oh can you imagine the problems. Hah: lumped together for life with no care, no parole, no time out for good behaviour; random, random, random.


-oOo-


High above the earth, the man in the space suit goes about his daily tasks. He has seen twenty-seven sunsets and twenty-six sunrises since the birthday party.

If he looks down through the clouds and mists and fug of industry, what would he see but the talk of the neighbours, rising like farts over the houses.

'Oh Jenner!' they say, 'She's been in my woodshed causing mischief.'

'Oh Jenner!' they say, 'And then she came to my yard and put the hens off their lay.'

'Oh Jenner! Well! Then next it must have been she came to my yard and stole ... stole ... stole the washing off the line.' For the deeds need to escalate, there's status at stake here.

'Ha, the washing? She came to my house just by now and stole a cake I'd made for tea!'

The first speaker is already regretting that they started as low as mischief in the woodshed... but no matter. The rumour has been kindled, the sparks quicken, the tiny tongues of smoke curl up. By the time the news gets to the Reverend Morgan, that woodshed will be a pile of smouldering ashes in the telling. And the Reverend Morgan will taste, for the first time, the hot blood of power on his tongue as the congregation rushes to answer his call for revenge; he will wish he had called out louder and sooner, for the rusty taste is delicious, and soothes his fretful soul. But, he will reason to himself, there is still time. Oh, Jenner.

Oh, Jenner the beautiful girl. The stories they're preparing to slice her with, to cut her down from the sky and the trees and the wind.

'She's good with the animals, mind.' One recalls Jenner had done their house some good when the chills spread through them.

'Du, du, du; she's got a way with her I doesn't like, but!'

'I only thought... she knows the plants and things...'

'Oh! *Ydu*, she's a sneak. You can tell by looking.' And the good that was done is devalued. 'Knowing plants' becomes an accusation.

At home, Jenner is looking into the eyes of Lizzie with wonder. Lizzie is looking into the eyes of Jenner the same. Lizzie feels an awakening of memory, of fear and of falling when she looks at Jenner this time. For over the pages of the ancient herbal, they have found each other at last. The ones who want to heal, the ones who want to do no harm, the ones who know —with their fingers and eyes and nose and tongue and ears— what will work and what will not, what will harm and what will bring comfort, and what will offer easy release.

The century-old woman and the decade-old girl: what they know, and what they share, and what they fear.

# Chapter 3

# Dydd Sul (Sun's Day)

Lizzie stands in the chapel entrance, grinding her walking stick into the gravel in frustration. Myfanwy has already left; bustling grimly out the door as soon as liturgy allowed, she would be home by now. The last few members of the congregation slip past on the path, trying to slide backwards while appearing to walk forward, for their ears are aching with a peculiar thrill: gossip and the expectation of more gossip. Lizzie blinks, astonished; did someone just hiss at her?

The vicar puts his head cautiously out the door and is lassoed by Lizzie's glare.

'What did you mean by that? What actually did you mean? What? What...?' Lizzie's voice rises from a whisper to inchoate loudness as she struggles to keep her fury at the reverend's just-delivered sermon in check.

'I mean, Mrs Coombe, that she's been seen around the place. Seen.' Reverend Morgan lifts his weak chin and gazes unfocused across the valley before them, lying soft under the morning haze. He hopes he looks impressive; he hopes the few lingering parishioners can hear his authority, for it seems as if Lizzie is a bit obtuse in that regard.

'Doing what? What has she been seen doing? I don't under-stand you at all.'

'We don't know, Mrs Coombe. And that! That is precisely the thing; we don't know.'

'So. So you ... So, you name my great granddaughter from the pulpit for...? Hearsay? You moralise on the virtues of gossip?' Lizzie shakes herself, like an irritated hen. 'I don't see what point you want to make, Reverend. This is... Do you know what you're doing? Do you? Meddling; you're meddling in my family!'

'I'm sorry, Mrs Coombe, but she has been seen. I can't say it plainer than that. People see her. And they don't like it.'

'I see you, and I don't like it. She was with me all day yester-day. All day. Absolutely all day. I can promise you; all day she was with me.'

The reverend, guided by his ancestors, greets this inconve-nient evidence with silence. He is not that feeble sort who gets distracted by facts.

'Indoors. All day.' Lizzie leans on her walking stick, takes strength from the wolf's head; the once-neglected gift has re-surfaced, almost by chance, now that she needs it.

The reverend looks up at the sky, down to the gate, in the door to the chapel behind him. The angels are singing in his blood; he wonders if Lizzie might hear them too. 'Well, if that's all...?' He retreats towards sanctuary, drawn by his belly towards his tea and the fresh cake in the vestry. His authority over mortals fails to extend even to his own stomach.

Lizzie opens her pocketbook, hands the vicar five £5 notes. 'For the chapel fund,' she says, without intonation *This isn't a gift, it's a test.* This is equal to the vicar's weekly salary and Lizzie knows it.

*This isn't a gift, it's a slap in my face* thinks the vicar. None-theless, Reverend Morgan takes the money with alacrity, slips backwards inside with a mumbled nod; closing the door so fast his trouser leg is caught, and some awkward fumbling follows from behind the ancient timber. An unpractised snarl sneaks through his tight lips, but as response to Lizzie's trick, his own clumsiness, or the angels in his veins is uncertain. Lizzie would have been warned, alarmed, alert, had she heard it. But Lizzie has already turned away in contempt, walking the path away from the chapel door, down past the graves.

The grave styles vary according to age and fashion, and the wealth, or the rich love, of the relicts and children. But one thing all graves confirm: the dead can't be relied upon to stay in the ground on their own cognisance. The dear departed must be penned behind rusty fences or weighed down by sharp black granite and crumbling sandstone or watched over by tattle-tale cherubs and consumptive angels. The dead can't necessarily be trusted to stay dead, not here on this beautiful hillside with its sightlines like an alembic drawing the spirit off and down to Swansea Bay and the sea beyond the morning sun.

Lizzie sees from the corner of her memory, her mother Gwenllian sitting by the family marker, with her scrap of soft cloth polishing the lettering, seeking Old Elizabeth's dead council, or whispering to the shade of her husband, Lizzie's father. Lizzie sees herself, small and silent by her mother's skirts, practicing her reading on the tombstones. She feels the weight and boredom of her childish self, the button boots that hurt in one place on one little ankle, a fondness for the gloves she's growing out of, an impatience to be home with her books and a cup of weak tea, but happiness in her mother's company. It hurts. Lizzie feels her age now, her skin and spine, teeth and breath are a million years away from that young child in those ancient clothes, that candlelit life.

She stands a moment longer than she meant to, leaning on the wolf's head, then passes through the gate. She remembers family and neighbour pushing against each other over generations, for rights and pride, and a sense of worth despite grief. She feels the oldest thing on Earth, never mind the hillside scars of old industry, the ashlars of ancient dwellings now fallen into pavement under her feet. As Lizzie gets closer to home and sees the windows of her bedroom watching over the lane, she recalls the morning's sermon. The heat of words, the strange, strange accusations, the unexpected fervour.

'... *"the sins of superstition and stubbornness"? For heaven's sake, she just... that's not... pagan? The man must be... No, she's just not like the other children, that's hardly a sin; I was the same...ah...'*

So, the Ty Merched bloodline, running deep into these rocks, was an affront to the vicar and his newcomer ancestors. And this too: the neighbours were agreeing with him, enjoying it. Of course. For the first time since early widowhood forced a hardened assuredness on her, Lizzie is unsure of herself.

She's returned to a state of exasperation by the time she reaches her gates. Half the valley has seen her, wolf's head walking stick in hand, frowning at the lane before her as she makes her way down. She has seen none of them. Inside the cradling arms of the garden walls, the earth bank, and the clutter of sheds and coops, the house sits poised as if to back away from peril. Lizzie clatters in the front door, out the kitchen door: bang, bang.

Where is Sarah Maud? Where is Myfanwy? What is waiting in the still, chill kitchen, the silent cwtch, the empty closet? The echoes sound larger than yesterday.

Out in the yard, Myfanwy is bustling the hens. The hens are very annoyed. Myfanwy continues to bustle, regardless.

'You'll have soft shells tomorrow, or no eggs at all. What are you doing, child?' Lizzie's distracted use of the word 'child' —hearing her mother's voice in her own mouth as she looks up to peer into the closed eyes and flushed cheeks of her aged daughter—startles them both; the hens fall watchfully silent. 'Where's our tea? Where's the child? The fire's not even up.'

Myfanwy stands up, unconsciously mimicking the reverend's pose of defiance this morning; for it is exactly the reverend who has pricked her voice with tears.

'Tea's coming.' Myfanwy answers. 'I'm not...' she clears her suddenly dry throat, 'I'm not having it.'

'What? The tea? Suit yourself. I don't—'

'Not the tea! Not the tea, you stupid old woman! I'm not having the humiliation. Not anymore. No.' Myfanwy draws breath. 'Not having it.' The hens mill about her feet awkwardly. 'Stupid old woman.' She speaks the words as if she's said them a thousand times—which she has, inwardly—to the tiny woman, her mother. 'This is my farm; this is my valley. Du, this is the only life I was bloody allowed to have, and always you take it away from me.' Myfanwy begins the messy, ugly crying of old people.

A hen scuttles between them as Lizzie steps backwards, closes the wire door and pens in the birds and the sobbing woman. 'Me? You can't lay the gossip at my feet. None of us had the life we wanted. So you can stop gulping.' Myfanwy has had moments of sulky rebellion all her life, but this is jarring, coming after the morning's sermon. Lizzie would like to blame Myfanwy for something. And, annoyingly, Myfanwy seems to be blaming her. Lizzie turns back to the house, closes the door behind her impatiently. '"Take it away"? Pfft...' she snorts with exasperation in the empty kitchen.

Within the wire walls of the hen coop, Myfanwy sags wetly on an upturned tub; the hens crowd close, their eyes averted but their bodies warm. It's a two-way thing, keeping hens.

Again: *where is Sarah Maud? Where is Jenner?*

'Jenner?' Lizzie is suddenly full of the pleasure of yesterday, suddenly optimistic. She thinks to talk with Jenner about bee remedies; visit the hives in Sarah Maud's crazy neglected sculpture garden, talk about cures and cordials and poultices. She wonders about planting a physic garden... the coming days seem sunnier...

'Jenner?' The walls and the rooms and the empty spaces don't answer. The closet doesn't answer, not even to say there is no old book here anymore: no pressed flowers within waxed leather, no venerable Welsh nor childish English.

Lizzie looks in her closet and sees no-one. Lizzie looks in the cwtch and sees no-one. She looks in Sarah Maud's room, under the mess of bedding and twigs like a nest. She looks in the bathroom, she moves faster round the rooms in through the closets and up the front path and the side path and through Sarah Maud's garden and behind the woodshed and the potting shed. She sees no-one. She is by the chicken coop again.

'What have you done?'

Myfanwy doesn't answer. The hens know, but they all talk at once.

'Oh, for god's sake come inside,' Lizzie holds the coop door open and the old woman, her daughter, with hip joints stiff from the chill, struggles her bulk up off the tub, goes ahead into the kitchen and stirs the fire into life. The bright flame only highlights the chill of the house, where nothing is breathing unseen. Lizzie coming in behind, closes the door and stares silently into the crockery shelves, though the cups and bowls wink back at her in the thin morning firelight. The women move round the kitchen, unable to speak to each other. The butter makes more noise in its dish, the currants make more noise as they sit inside the waiting Welsh cake batter than these two bodies once separated by just a membrane and now facing each other over a gulf of mute silence.

'I can never go into chapel again' Myfanwy pours the tea into two cups. Lizzie has put out four, but Myfanwy only pours into two. 'I can't put my face in the shops. I don't know what I can do any more.'

'I don't know what you think it has to do with me,' says Lizzie, 'there's nothing but people's bored gossip out there. You're too old to be listening to that nonsense. Grow up...' She finishes lamely, for Myfanwy was born middle-aged and has had neither the personality or encouragement to grow in any other direction.

'She's the spit of you,' Myfanwy puts the teapot down on its trivet. 'If you're not running through Jenner like 'Llandilo' through rock-candy then I don't know what keeps her breathing.' Myfanwy sits, does not take a cup. Lizzie does not take a cup. 'Of course, it's something to do with you. You're not loved round here...'

Lizzie hurts in a deep place she had forgotten could hurt. *Here? Here the valley, or here the kitchen table? Oh...* But wasn't she better than this? No, maybe not. For she has forgotten to think about love and care: in this place; with this woman; with any of them.

She takes a cup of tea, to hide her face in its steam. 'And Jenner? What's happened to Jenner? And, oh, Sarah Maud too?'

'I don't know.'

The tea cools between them, the butter makes a golden moat round itself and the Welsh cakes on their griddle get harder, darker, in the heat from the ebbing fire. Indeed, Myfanwy does not know where Sarah Maud and Jenner are. But she knows why she doesn't know where. For, as she'd made her way home, mortified by the vicar's sermon, the thoughts and words had just piled up in her mind, so that when she opened the kitchen door a torrent of shouting flooded out of her, even as Lizzie was struggling not to shout up by the chapel. And Sarah Maud has gone running in fright to the woods, where John and his friends will have cider and nettle beer for her, yes and on a Sunday. Sarah Maud's head had been ringing from the words she felt rolling down the hill from the chapel pulpit, though she had stayed in her bed, under the covers, writing and shivering and listening and feeling. So, when Myfanwy started to shout, Sarah Maud started to run.

And Jenner, too, has fled from Myfanwy's anger. A cloud in the wind, Jenner has gone over the hills and far away.

Lizzie bumbles round the house all day. She's not alarmed by Jenner's absence, for she has barely seen the girl in the house for five summers or longer. But today Lizzie has run out of things to do in the garden; her tiny dry bones are itching with anticipation of the child's company, for the new pleasure of talk over the old book. Yes, Jenner must have been seen all over the valley for the last few years, doing and trying and learning; gathering plants, tending animals, learning the ways of the old places. Watching, seeing.

*But she's a child, it's ridiculous.* Only, Lizzie thinks she knows the valley people: traditional to the point of moribundity, close-knit to the point of claustrophobia. And they are the ridiculous ones. Sometimes.

Jenner doesn't come back at nightfall. Smalldog is also gone, but since no-one knew he'd arrived, this is not significant to anyone except Smalldog and a much-reduced family of mice.

Sarah Maud is brought stumbling down the hill in the starlight, by John and his friends. She's singing low, a pop song whose words she's muddling, and she smells of wood smoke and tobacco and safe company. John and Mich love Sarah Maud for all her bad poetry, her wild woody visons, her dreams of dark music and dark, dark loss; she's been a most welcome and welcoming kindred spirit in this generally guarded rural community. And Sarah Maud has found the friends she needs. But she has not seen Jenner all day, and the older women prepare for sleep unshriven.

Jenner doesn't come back at nightfall. Lizzie stays awake and listens out. But Jenner doesn't come back.

# Chapter 4

# Dydd Llun (Moon's Day)

Myfanwy immobile in bed, stares though the ceiling and the old rafters and slate and moss, clear through the clouds and the arc of the spaceman's journey. Of which she knows nothing; *Du*, he's not even from the valleys.

She has no heart for bustling, or scolding, or pushing and shoving everyone and everything. Pushing and shoving has been Myfanwy's role in the house since she first started to push herself into people's business, shove herself into the way of things. But she just knows that Jenner did not come home last night, and today she can't even push and shove herself. She feels sick and dull. The room is unfamiliar, alien; her hands are those of a stranger. For the first time in years, the old bed feels too big; the yawning gap of sheets is a tundra. She needs the comfort of another creature to tell her it's alright, to say she can go on as before; that the valley is still her home, that she still has a place and a chair and a day's work, and the neighbours will still nod sympathetic hellos and they will still understand her and how hard she works...

She needs to be angry at someone, to hear her own voice. But Someone has run away. And no-one else cares for Myfanwy like she needs – not even God, now the vicar's said his piece.

Growing up under Lizzie. It was always this way: *Mam and her acts and deeds and none of it allowed for me. No kindness, or a kiss-it-better.* Myfanwy reviews her scars, wounds of her own pride cutting back into her, trying to find her own place in home and school, be with the other children, and, later, the other wives and mothers; only, she is quite without an understanding of how they so effortlessly fit in with each other, and her on the edge always. *But they didn't have Mam as mother. And she didn't care what anyone else thought...*

Myfanwy tries to put her finger on the place she holds in the valley community, but she can't find it. She's looking now for the first time since her wedding, and she can't find herself in the valley at all; it's all covered by her mother's long shadow. If light years are something, as she's heard talked of in the news, then surely dark years must be as well. Lizzie and her shadow years, miles and miles of them.

*... Put no store by anyone's opinion. And here's me put too much, she'd say... Well, maybe as happens, I don't care for your opinion. What'd you say to that, Mam? What then?*

Myfanwy feels heavy and burdened, and at the same time almost non-existent. Where has Myfanwy gone, in her bed under the sloping ceiling and over the kitchen?

'Here. Here is me.' She speaks to Ty Merched directly. Under these eaves, above this hearth, is the breadth and depth of Myfanwy.

She is startled to hear Lizzie below her, raddling the coals of last night's fire. It's been forty years since Myfanwy has still been in bed when someone else is still moving around. Except Jenner. But day and night are the same to the twilit child; and Jenner carries silence in her pockets.

Lizzie has been awake all night. She is shaky from the lack of sleep. She can't remember Jenner staying out all night before now. This is not a failing of memory, this is not a thing that was once known and has now slipped from mind. She previously never even noticed whether Jenner was indoors or out. Lizzie is ashamed to realise this, that she has ignored the child for so long. *Regardless*, she tells herself firmly; *regardless of Jenner's precocious instincts for the healing book.* What else does the child do, what else is there to know about her?

Myfanwy pads down the stairs, to find the fire flicking up in the grate, and Lizzie hesitating at the cwtch doorway. The room is dark, hollow. Lizzie reaches for the light switch, enters, stands in the middle of the tiny space, and feels the absence of Jenner. Lizzie sniffs, and alongside the child smell of school bag and shoes and colouring pencils, something livelier, and, well, wild. The small clothes shelf built into the underside slope of Myfanwy's stairs has a sheet tacked over it, which Lizzie draws tentatively aside.

There are no clothes where clothes should be. On the shelves, old jars. In the old jars: leaves, twigs, berries of different colours. Fresher things, beginning to wilt, are spread out to dry on newspapers. Dried flower heads and petals form clouds of red and yellow and papery white, each in their jar. Labels carry drawings, not words. Coded pictograms in no style Lizzie has ever seen before. She stands still, puzzled by the arcane magic of the child's arrangement.

Myfanwy pushes her head in closer, breaks the stillness. Lizzie almost growls with irritation.

'What in the living god is this stuff?' asks Myfanwy, grabbing at the loose plants drying on the shelf nearest her. She goes to throw them out the door towards the kitchen fire. Introspection has made Myfanwy scratchy.

Lizzie stops her, a pre-emptory arm thrown out: 'Put it back. Now'

Myfanwy looks at Lizzie a long moment. 'What? Have you suddenly started to care for the girl? Leave me to get on.'

'Put it back now. Let go!'

'You let go! You never do, do you!' They struggle with clenched teeth, the plant stems fall to pieces within their grasp and Lizzie lets go abruptly, foolish and furious at her failure to keep the hoard intact.

Myfanwy pitches the plants out onto the kitchen floor, despite a smell of freshness and health that rises from the crushed stems. At her back Lizzie is longing to push her away into the kitchen and lock the door, lock out the things Myfanwy no longer holds back from saying. Only something has caught Lizzie's eye.

'Put the kettle on' she tells Myfanwy, in as neutral a voice as she can muster. She closes the door behind Myfanwy now, but softly, secretly. Turns, and in the dim light lifts an old Velvet Soap box from the lowest shelf. The label has just the one pictogram, but the gestures of the stick arms and stick legs, the tilt of the tousled head, the closed eyes and open mouth are unmistakable: Sarah Maud.

In the box, small paper bags. In the paper bags, measured amounts—all identical—of leaves and berries and something dried she thinks might be mushrooms, or bark. The box is half full; under the filled paper bags are folded empty paper bags. Jenner has been treating her own mother. For what? With what? Lizzie lacks the skill to understand the contents. She goes over what she can recall. Jenner admitted to working with the herbal for, what, maybe two years, a bit more? Alone, unguided; unnatural. In the child's untutored hands this could be dangerous, unpredictable. Has anything changed in Sarah Maud in the last two years or so...?

*Did Sarah Maud know?*

Lizzie sits on the little bed, hands collapsed in her lap, eyes closed. She doesn't know. She doesn't know what Sarah Maud has been like these past two years any more than the previous thirty-seven. Lizzie's neglect of family appals her.

The strength of will that's pushed her through ten decades without pause, now leans against the shame, shifts it away. *Oh William, bugger this!*

*Did you love me too much, cariad, that you forgot to love the children?* William's voice is ever close to her mind's ear.

*There's no such thing as too much, William.* But the thought makes Lizzie fall still.

Leaving the box on the bed, Lizzie covers the shelf again, pulling down the sheet and tucking it in at the bottom; she gets a chair from the kitchen and pushes it against the shelf, as clear a 'don't touch' sign as she can give to Myfanwy without alerting anyone else who might casually look in—the thought suddenly alarms her that someone else might look in. She finds Jenner's few jumpers and skirts on the floor, folds them tidily, tucks shoes under the chair as if ready for wearing, makes it look deliberate, permanent. Then Lizzie takes the Velvet Soap box to her room, pushes it in the closet where the herbal used to live. There was no box for Lizzie, thank the gods; and there was no box for Myfanwy.

Lizzie looks in on Sarah Maud now. What will change if she stops getting that amateur treatment? If Jenner doesn't come back? She has no idea; her family are as unreachable as specimens in jars, labelled with pictograms Lizzie never bothered to read. She'll have to rely on Myfanwy's blunt commentary if anything happens. Maybe the 'medicine' Jenner had devised was nothing much, just a herbal tea of no benefit. Maybe the book is useless, the *Materia Medica* is a myth. Maybe everything.

Sarah Maud is sleeping, again her bed is full of leaves and twigs, some dried flowers tangled in her hair are staining the pillowcase. The room smells bosky. *As if the old carpet were moss*, thinks Lizzie. And finds herself smiling at the idea.

When did the need for houses, for walls and permanence, make things so boring? Lizzie briefly scents the wild woods of her own childhood; and then wonders: what does her own room smell of: dust, or selfishness?

Making a fresh pot of tea now, she finds herself examining the tea caddy, sniffing, stirring the dry leaves, checking for things other than tea. Who knows what the girl was thinking of, where her untutored moral compass pointed? She imprisons an untamed thought—*witch?* —under the acceptable *wise woman?* Lizzie looks at Myfanwy's broad back, bent over the stove and diligently making porridge; she would know a change in Myfanwy, that is the one certainty. Would she know a change in herself? Probably not...

Lizzie had tolerated Myfanwy defending the child's wildness; was that a mistake? Lizzie and her daughter have one thing in common: they share a deep dislike of introspection. She turns her attention away, hears Sarah Maud moving up the hall to run a bath.

Sarah Maud will soak there until the water is cold, and her discarded clothes will be left dotted up the hallway for Myfanwy to collect. Sarah Maud, alert and optimistic in her early adulthood but lost to herself these past ten years, doesn't yet know that Jenner hasn't been seen for twenty-four hours. She's so used to the child running away from her she barely remembers the shape of Jenner's face, though once those wide blue eyes stared intensely into Sarah Maud's as the baby fed at her breast, one tiny hand stroking Sarah Maud's flinching skin... memory has slipped away into fog.

Lizzie will watch Sarah Maud with the same intensity. But more usefully, Lizzie will let Myfanwy watch Sarah Maud, for Myfanwy has always been the first to spot the many changes in Sarah Maud, though the causes always eluded them both. And Lizzie with watch Myfanwy. She starts by watching Myfanwy stir the porridge.

'Surely she'll be home soon. Jenner,' reasons Myfanwy, as the older women sit between the table and fire. *Surely*. In her own mind Myfanwy is retracting the anger she threw round the kitchen a day ago, downgrading the scale of her assault, blunting the sharpness of her words. Justifying herself.

'She must be told. She must learn she can't go round doing things. Being seen doing things. People don't like it. The old tales are still in memory, and...' Myfanwy has felt the draining away of her credibility all night, needs to keep talking. 'She has to learn, if she's going to be any use round here –.' The pause is filled with the noise of Sarah Maud singing a mangled folk song in the bathroom. 'If Jenner is to be any use at all,' finishes Myfanwy with a distinct emphasis.

'There it is, then,' Lizzie checks the teapot to see if a second cup is possible. 'Little Jenner must be made to be useful. Like a spade, or a teapot, think you? For all our acres, and the valleys stretching on to the sea, and the sea going to the edge and back again and the huge sky over, we're just come down to being useful in this one little place, here. We're here, and there it is.' How much she wants Jenner to come home, and how much she wants her to stay away. How much she wants to join her, lay her old bones in the bracken and stay there ... didn't she think something about her body on a compost heap, recently: yes, that feels the right thing. The flush of life that Lizzie felt yesterday, in Jenner's company, has slipped through the soles of her shoes today.

Myfanwy stares at Lizzie over the rim of her teacup. 'I was made to be useful.'

The things Myfanwy is saying these days. Lizzie doesn't know how to answer; she decides she doesn't need to answer... *bugger it.*

-oOo-

And where is Jenner, this breakfast time on a chilly spring morning? What can she find to eat, at this time of year, when it's too early for cobnuts, and the wild fruits are still green and bitter?

Smalldog knows. Smalldog is in a heaven of belonging, Smalldog is in a quandary of worry. They spent yesterday skirting the farms of Gwrhyd and taking the path down to the back streets of Ponty, haunting the shop yards for food, being quick and successful. In exchange for what she took, Jenner has left bunches of wild healing flowers as both currency and gift. A red-faced man set his brace of hounds on her; they ran straight to the unflinching Jenner and rubbed their scarred heads against her legs before returning to their astonished owner for a beating.

The night was fine and Jenner and Smalldog slept cosy together in the dry leaves under a rhododendron thicket. Today they are high up and crossing a hilltop bog. Jenner rides one of the wild ponies that have visited them in the dawn; she's clinging on to the thick short mane, her knees locked on the mare's hard flanks. The rest of the herd travel close. She's travelling over Fan Brycheiniog to the next little city, for food and shelter where no-one knows her. Like a wild fruit tree, Jenner will only become useful in her own time. Like a wild fruit tree, she's as likely be cut down; or uprooted.

It's very much on her mind that Sarah Maud will be unknowingly missing her daily tonic, and Jenner doesn't know what that will mean. She doesn't intend to be away long; but for now she needs some clear air and escape from the gossip stealing her breath away. There's little resentment; born into scandal, hard words from the village are all she's ever known. And she's always been running someplace, out a door or over a fence. Only, now she's having to run further. Like stones dropped across a brook, the gossips wish to dam her. Like a brook around stones, Jenner must ever find new paths.

She's running wild because her body needs to. Jenner doesn't understand revenge, or gossip, or the need to fit in; she couldn't even tell what 'in' looked like.

Smalldog is held tight against her stomach with one arm, for he wasn't up to the horses' pace. In her skirt pocket, the herbal is wrapped tightly in a scrap of oilcloth. Jenner has no plan. She ran from Myfanwy's frustrated anger: taking...*borrowing*...the book; borrowing a bit of space, a bit of time for herself. Jenner has never paid much attention to the neighbours other than to avoid them; but the child cannot process the mess of hurt and bewilderment she felt at Myfanwy's harsh anger yesterday. Hard though her grandmother always was, and loved nonetheless, this anger was different.

The randomness of unruly childhood is growing into a set of instincts, and Jenner is learning—after the injustice of Myfanwy's last tamping—to trust herself only. Adults just make walls.

Escape is euphoric, a level of disobedience, of independence, she'd never reached before. For all her running and hiding around the village, this is the first time she's left the valley. Jenner lifts her face to the boundless horizon and whoops, even as clouds are gathering.

Then she cries out in time with a lightning flash above. A moment's sensation: a knife-like chill slipping down her spine, a dragon's claw slicing her asunder. The fear is gone as soon as she's aware of it, but the thunder sounds like something ancient, sniffing for her marrow as it crawls around the grey mountains. Jenner holds Smalldog closer, and shivers as she clutches deeper into the pony's mane with her other hand, tightens her knees' grip on the pony's ribs. Jenner tastes adrenaline for the first time.

The roiling herd, white and brown and grey, carry Jenner and Smalldog north, into a rising wind and a dark sky. The horses take a gravelly path around the Lake of the Healers, high in the folds of the mountain. The dark waters watch them passing; thus, back at Ty Merched, the ghosts learn that Jenner is with the horses.

-oOo-

The ghosts try to get the message of Jenner's safety to the family, but Sarah Maud has gone back to sleep, sweet-smelling and damp from her bath. The hall furniture hears the news with relief, but furniture generally keeps its own council, as well they know who've ever lost something in a drawer. Jenner's bed cheers up a little but still, it can't help but feel neglected. Myfanwy never listens to the ghosts except when she wants to, when there's a chance they might be agreeing with her. She goes out at noon to feed the uneaten porridge to the hens, and sees they are still unsettled.

Myfanwy is unsettled herself; though she would rather chew her own leg off than admit it to Lizzie or anyone, she misses Jenner. She considers contacting the Ponty Police but draws back at the thought of more unwanted attention from her neighbours; the once-recurrent annoyance of her invisibility seems a lost treasure now, someone else's life. The familiar world—of sheep and neighbours, encircling kitchen and solitary sleep—is distorted, as if seen through water, or the telescope on Mumbles Pier: seeming close but in fact unreachable.

The upturned tub is still upturned, so Myfanwy sits with the hens awhile to take comfort from the warmth and distraction of their fowl business: feathery backsides and boot-beady eyes; chucks and pecks and querulous grumbles, the sour smell of damp grain and straw that needs changing. Dear old hens, how kind they are to Myfanwy. Sometime later, Myfanwy tells the hens everything that's on her mind. Myfanwy's bulk settles the hens likewise, and soon there's one announcing, astonished, that the miracle of an egg has arrived.

Lizzie, in her room, stares at the closet door for an hour seeing, not furniture, but the shadow-plays of a century. A number of uncomfortable 'ifs' are moving through her thoughts, and she takes to her bed fully clothed. The effort to press down on her thoughts, to stop the swirling sadness, is exhausting and Lizzie feels her every year and moment weighing down on her in leaden blankets. A moribund silence muffles her, ennui loosens the knots and strings of her limbs as the utter inability to act, to change the past and withdraw the mistakes – of pride, of arrogance, of mistaking tragedy for something meritorious – and rewrite the pages, clouds her heart.

Like old Gwenllian her mother, she had stood guard over this house of women, she'd fought adversity and prejudice, loss and bad weather over the long years. Unlike Gwennie, she had forgotten to distinguish between who she was fighting against and who she was fighting for, when to leave her weapons at the door. She struggles against her history, to find a path less thorny in the little time remaining...

Eventually Lizzie sleeps. And dreams of the vicar. The incommensurate vicar. No work will be done today in Ty Merched. The fire burns low in the grate.

-oOo-

Outside the day turns. The dimming sun is watching dark clouds pile up in the north after a red dawn. Grass twists in the sharpening breeze, trees set their buds on bitter stems. The white fingered blackberry rhizomes push relentless through the soil, gentle heather blurs the stony ground and peat forms a deceptive mat over the sinkholes and fissures of the amoral mountains. In his long old home under the hill, the vicar shivers by his mean electric radiator, cursing again the previous incumbent—Reverend Uncle Morgan Morgan—who removed all the fireplaces in an impulsive gesture of modernity.

The vicar has had a long day and struggles against the chill of his thoughts, which has nothing to do with the inadequate heating. A stream of visitors has tramped the gravel into his porch, across his mats and into his study.

'Oh, Jenner! Today, you'll never guess, Reverend. She was over by Cilybellbebil, stealing goats' milk. I heard it from my cousin. Very sad; starving no doubt. Something must be done for her.'

'Oh, Jenner! She's been seen again in Ystrad, twice today, Reverend, scratching the cars with a key. Bad, wilful child. Something should be done with her.'

*Child? She's no Christian's child...* thinks the vicar. *Something needs to be done to her.* He gets a whiff of punitive fire: ropes and ash and burning straw in a public space; looks guardedly at the little radiator. Sometimes he sees a golden future, sometimes a bedevilled ancestry, in its hot coils.

Jenner. In Cwm Giedd, leaving gates open. In Cwm Twrch, stealing fish and chips. Taking the children's lunchboxes, eating them empty and hiding them in poor Eric's locker so he's been in trouble, but we all know it's. Jenner. Leading all the dogs in Brynamman a-chasing the sheep across the hills. Down in Swansea she was, shoplifting at the market. Over in Neath all day ringing doorbells. She's made the Llantgiwg church bells ring and the Llanthony church bells fail to ring. She's made the pond flood and the brook dry up. She's made the children refuse their spelling, and the cats refuse to hunt. Up at Seith Maen she pushed the sacred stones flat into the ground, and by Carn Llechart she's pushed them all upright again.

Reverend Twdr Morgan may have sometimes doubted the effectiveness of his moral authority, but he is just now discovering a taste for, and an apparently willing congregation for, another kind of authority. The mean little radiator cannot soothe the goosebumps of his conscience over the child

Jenner; he feels culpable for starting something unpredictable, and that nagging doubt is chilling his bones.

Certainly, Jenner's way of disappearing like morning mist even as you think you've pinned her down, her untamed disregard for the ordinary expectations of the village, her total unpredictability—one moment she's focused like a hunting kestrel, the next, the world doesn't exist to her—make her an easy target for suspicion. Anything might be true of her. She moves round the edges of valley life like a hare on the run, fast and wayward.

But the congregation had sat up when he spoke. He was amazed to find conviction as he sermonised extemporaneously, the words flowed almost without him, and his people loved it. He shivers with the torment; he imagines a kinship with the anguished martyrs. The creature in his genes is stirring, craving light and air, wrenching at its weakening bonds. The radiator cannot warm his skin half as effectively as these thoughts of power warm his innards.

Once more the doorbell rings. It's Jeremiah Jenkins pushing his way into the study, late though it is. 'Jenner has a tiger!' he declares. 'I heard it roaring, after that birthday party of old Lizzie. We'll all be eaten alive.' He looks defiant, daring the vicar to contradict him. The vicar does not contradict.

Oh Jenner. The ghosts wring their hands over you.


-oOo-


By dusk Jenner has arrived at Llandovery's tattered edge, streetlights just coming on here and there. The temperature is dropping steadily, and the thin child is weary to her bones. The horses have slowed, crowded in close to her. Below the shards of castle on the town-side hill, in the park a few last picnicking tourists are packing up. Families pause, look up amazed at the shadow-eyed child and her retinue of ponies above them, backdropped by the stone tower as the dusk deepens.

A stallion of dappled grey moves forward, one loose-kneed step after another, towards a car of squabbling children and their fatigued mother packing things into the boot. She hesitates, a white and green Welsh tapestry blanket in her hands. The horse steps closer … step … step … step … echoing on the bitumen; puts its head down and snorts into the grass at the mother's feet, lifts its head and holds the woman's gaze. Lowers its beautiful huge head again, this time to lean one cheek against a foreleg … and places the hoof on the bottom corner of the blanket. Looks up at the woman again. Holds the blanket pinned. Looks at the woman. The squabbling children are transfixed…hesitantly, the white and green blanket is given to Jenner. And the last of the biscuits, crumbled in their packet.

The cars drive away. Jenner and the ponies remain.

# Chapter 5

# Dydd Mawrth
# (Mars's Day)

It has snowed in the night. Lizzie wakes just before dawn as the coldest air comes down. Myfanwy has been awake all night, listening to the roof slates shifting and the iron nails contracting and the rafters creaking, breathing the cold air almost liquid in her lungs. The stone in Myfanwy's heart is Lizzie. The stone in Lizzie's heart is Myfanwy. For it has snowed in the night.

They meet outside the cwtch door and see the bed inside is still empty. Lizzie checks the side door and yes it was unlocked all night, and the kitchen door too. Myfanwy is silent and furious at Lizzie's implication, and backs against the sink, arms hanging loose; like a challenger at a fairground boxing booth, she shifts her balance, poised for a fight she doesn't know how to win, or lose.

Lizzie stands stalled and uncertain in the middle of the doorway, bird-frail, an incumbent champion equally bereft of action. But being in the same room is intolerable. Lizzie hauls on her boots, grabs the oilskins and the wolf's head walking stick, and heads for the door. She has had nothing to eat for eighteen hours, but:

'The sheep need checking.' She closes the door behind her, faces into the glassy, fractured morning. She is too old for this weather, but she doesn't remember that now.

'I'm calling the police' says Myfanwy to the empty doorway. But she does not. She is in pain, and Lizzie's tacit rejection of food or tea has left Myfanwy without tasks or targets. She goes down to stand outside Sarah Maud's bedroom door but cannot say why. Away from the kitchen fire, carefully banked in case Jenner came home in the night, the house is as chill as the deeps of a mountain lake.

Out beyond the shelter of the clustered sheds, Lizzie sees the valley spreading like an upturned palm, spilling the snow downwards to the sea lying flat and cloud-grey in the thin light. The drifts below the house are thick, and make little deathly mounds of the bushes, turn the cowslip and celandine petals translucent, press down the daffodil heads. The hen coop is still; a ruffling and burring of sleeping birds is faint on the air. Sarah Maud's garden in the snow looks like a pencil sketch, black-lead scribbles of hedge and beehive, cinnabar dashes of still-leafless witch hazel stems, and the smudged charcoal of low plants rounded down by late snow on tender new shoots. Sarah Maud's bits of statuary—her passion, years ago, but abandoned before Jenner was born—look like huddled homeless rough-sleepers, and Lizzie imagines Jenner hiding under each frozen shroud. Everything is uncertain, unclear, across the valley. But Lizzie could find her way in the yard with her eyes closed, so familiar are the slate stepping-stones and gravel paths, and the muddy tracks of the farm vehicles.

The sheep are down from the hills, in anticipation of birthing but still outdoors yet. Lizzie heads up the lane and as she comes to a gap in the stone wall, the full cold of the morning hits her. Without the shelter of the garden walls, iron-hard crusts of ice cover the grass. The air at ground level is like a scythe across the fields. The sheep are huddling where the hedge and stone wall meet, their yellow eyes are alarmed. There is little she can do here alone, but the relief to be out and away from Myfanwy and the empty cwtch keeps her here. The house feels clogged with anxiety, and Myfanwy's need to blame her is undermining her own instinct to accuse Myfanwy. The mirroring of their responses to grief only highlights the barrier she feels, like silvered glass standing between them. Lizzie wonders if she were strong enough to break it, would she find Myfanwy taping it back in place again just as quickly. *What's happening to my family...* She falls into the past tense: *happened...*

She leans against the wall and makes useless soothing noises to calm the sheep. A few childish cries echo across the sharp still air, from the toboggan slope beyond the school. *Where is the child?*

The cold finally forces Lizzie to move.

She feels the need for warmth now, and retraces her earlier steps, showing black on the white snow. If only all paths were as clear. She stomps the slush of mud and snow on the doorstep, blusters inside, head down and forcing a chatter, faking a shiver.

'Is there tea? Du, du, du, but it's cold.' She stops, sighs, shakes her head. The kitchen is empty. What is she making all this noise for? She's not even listening to herself. She falls into a chair.

Myfanwy and Sarah Maud enter together and suddenly the room is crowded. Sarah Maud's hands shake as she pours herself a tea, adds too much sugar, gulps it down while still scalding and pours a second, repeats the scalding.

'How are the sheep?' asks Sarah Maud, reaching for her jacket as she clambers sockless into the nearest pair of boots. 'And where are they?' She doesn't wait for an answer but goes out into the wind and straight up towards the field. Her blue summer dress is wind-flattened against her trousered legs.

Lizzie cannot move from her chair. 'Did you call the police yet?' she addresses the wall ahead of her. To her left, Myfanwy lifts the porridge saucepan from the stove, and straightens up.

'No.' Myfanwy looks across the table at Lizzie's face in rigid profile. 'I don't know where to start, what to say. I don't want them thinking the worst of us. You can phone them if you want to. It's your fault, after all.'

'You're a cruel woman, Myfanwy.'

'I'm not cruel. I'm stupid. It's you that's cruel.' The sauce-pan drops onto the table. 'And selfish. Do you think no-one else cares for the girl? Do you think I don't care for her and look after, every day of her little poor life, and you there too busy with money and cleverness, and just too important for your own family? Me cruel? You don't know what it's like living with you forever and ever. By the living god I don't know what you want from us... Any of it... Jenner is ...' Myfanwy has run out of words, she has never spoken of what Jenner is, even to herself.

Her thin experience of family love—overlooked child of parents too devoted to each other, half-orphaned by a sickly father dying 'when he shouldn't have' as if early death showed a failure of character, and an etiolated adulthood in the shade of Lizzie's matriarchy; left to bring herself up when a child and treated like a child in her widowhood—is too narrow for Myfanwy to name what she is now feeling. A balance has been broken by the runaway child. Myfanwy's heart is at its rope's end for missing Jenner. She's ashamed of herself, and of her mother; it's all become a hideous jumble in her head. All of it: the shame of her daughter Sarah Maud an unwed mother, the shame of her sour marriage, the shame of her first love. The shame of the birthday just two days back. She could cover these old walls with words for a year and still not get to the end of her shame. Earlier she felt invisible; now she feels opened on an examining table for all the world, the neighbours, to poke and prod at.

But for now, Myfanwy has run out of anything to say. Falling silent, she spoons some of the near-cold porridge into a bowl, stands looking at the fire and eats her portion without tasting a bit of it.

Lizzie is still looking at the far wall. Lizzie's hands tremble as she cradles the teacup in her lap. Seeing this, Myfanwy returns the pan to the heat again until the contents are hot, scoops some into a clean bowl, places it near Lizzie with a spoon on one side.

'You better eat something. You're too thin,' says Myfanwy and leaves the room.

Lizzie takes up the bowl. For a moment it's poised in her raised hand like a shotput aimed at the wall in front of her: *'how dare she...'*. The burst of anger burns instantly into ashy collapse. Lizzie eats the porridge for she is truly empty. It's good, and hot.

*Dydd Mawrth.* Mars's day. Over the Dyke, in England this is Tiw's Day: the Vikings' god of single combat, victory and glory. But Roman Mars, so much more nuanced: yes, battle, but victory can only be prayed for, not guaranteed. Passion is a certainty, and energy, and endurance. Stamina, staying power. The Old Ones thundered over the limestone hills and crawled through the low marshes in defence of—literally and figuratively—home and hearth, swinging their soft bronze-tipped weapons against the iron-shielded invader whose language and writing they melded into their own, even as they yielded their native heroes to the foreign gods. Lizzie has the stamina of Mars in her narrow old veins, and it carries her yet.

Sarah Maud can be heard, now, in the yard. Sarah Maud lacks stamina. But she has an instinct for the sheep; indeed, it's the only thing she's good for, according to Myfanwy and the neighbours.

Lizzie goes out, swinging the old coat over her bony shoulders and thick wool shirt, cramming the shapeless felt hat back on her head. The ruby necklace glints inside her collar, flaring in the bright glare of the snow and the lifting sunlight. Sarah Maud has the sheep down from the field and they are just crossing the road into the yard. Lizzie scuttles over to the barn, opens a door and helps herd the ewes inside. She wouldn't have bothered since the thaw is probably due in a few hours, but...

'Best safest inside' says Sarah Maud, her voice purring in the cold air, and Lizzie nods; at least the sheep can settle into the new space in advance of lambing. When their time comes to drop, they'll feel more accustomed. Lizzie suspects Jenner has already added some herbs to the straw bedding; there are bunches of dried field flowers knotted to some of the nails on posts and rafters. Out of the cold wind, the flock trundle into the pens and begin to defrost, feed and socialise. They're slow and swollen with lambs.

'Jenner be needed soon.' Sarah Maud is still trembling; now her teeth are chattering as well. 'It's her favourite time, this, when the lambs come.'

'When did you last see Jenner?' asks Lizzie.

'I ... was it ... at your party? Yes, the party ...' Sarah Maud has a haunted look now; she finds time is just too slippery and she doesn't like to be expected to have a grip on it. But more than time, her thoughts about her baby Jenner have always been hard to grasp, tangled between love and distress and too many secrets. As she'd held the new breathing baby, touched the black hair and white skin and red birth blood with trembling fingers, she'd felt her own sense of self slipping out of reach. She'd not been able to grasp it back; alcohol helped to cloud memory, but alcohol was indiscriminate and took good as well as bad.

'Myfanwy hasn't told you, then.' A statement, not a question.

'Told me? No. She's not told me anything, *Mamgu*.'

Again, the use of a familial term—Mamgu, Grandmother—within Ty Merched sounds startling to Lizzie's ears; that the term now sounds strange in this old house of so many generations overawes her, knocks down a defence or two.

'Can you help me, Sarah Maud? I think I need your help, bach.'

Now it is Sarah Maud's turn to be startled. Her ability to help is seldom tested, never yet proven. 'Sure,' she says, but her voice is anything but. 'What can I, how?'

'If you were Jenner; let's say you were Jenner and you wanted to hide. Where would you go?'

'Oh now, Mamgu. There's a question.' Sarah Maud frequently wants to hide, and succeeds, if only from herself and the shadows in her head; but she's never looked at it from Jenner's view. 'Oh, now. Hiding. In the lake? Under a field? In a foxglove!' Sarah Maud nods her head affirmatively, yes indeed, for Sarah Maud would have hidden in a foxglove had it ever been necessary. Only, that one time they were needed no foxgloves were available... Sarah Maud's face falls; the bad thoughts are stronger today and she's frightened; she feels more her old, horrible, soiled self today.

Oblivious to Sarah Maud's turmoil, Lizzie smiles, almost laughs; it's amazing that Sarah Maud's mother was the stolid Myfanwy. And that farmer they found for Myfanwy to marry, after the rumours of the valley; God knows, maybe Sarah Maud's father had been touched by the fey folk after all. Or maybe it was just his old seed.

'Come and have some food, Sarah Maud. Then we'll go looking for foxgloves.'

There's no sign of Myfanwy inside, but the fire's good; a quick raddle gets it blazing. Lizzie pushes a chair close to the heat, puts Sarah Maud into it, serves her some of the reheated porridge. Sarah Maud heaps sugar on and gulps the sweet gluey mass down almost in one; Lizzie is reminded of a baby bird feeding. The police station will be open by now, but Lizzie doubts that is where Myfanwy has gone; the gossip would be horrendous. Myfanwy would do anything to avoid the attention if she could. And, worse, it would be an admission of someone's guilt; whose, Lizzie isn't sure. She only knows they agree on this: it's a family matter. Family will fix family.

Not that it has done so for a very long time, but then it's not been so undeniably broken for a very long time. Sarah Maud finishes her food, and Lizzie tends the fire.

'Let's go find those foxgloves, bach' says Lizzie gently. Sarah Maud looks puzzled, towards Jenner's doorway then towards the kitchen door. Lizzie has been increasingly mystified by her granddaughter these past years, and today is no different; she gets hat and walking stick again and slips a few slices of bread and butter into the poacher's pocket of her coat. Sarah Maud goes hatless but is now, as always, crowned by bits of flower and leaf in her hair. Today she wears frosted may-tree buds entangled from the hedgerow where the sheep had sheltered.

As they head out the gate Sarah Maud takes the lead, east to the small junction with the top lane, then turning up a narrow path, climbing west now, over the shadowy trench of the rail line and up towards a gully of trees near the ridge. The snow is deep in dips of ground, thin and glassy on exposed patches. Sarah Maud takes this path as if pulled by string. Lizzie follows as best she can. Suddenly Sarah Maud turns back to her:

'You breathe like an old man' she says. 'Or. Like a bad man.'

'I am old, Sarah Maud bach. But I'm not a man, I'm your mother's mam aren't I. And I'm not bad. Am I?' says Lizzie when she can catch her breath. They climb further up. *Why a bad man?* Lizzie thinks of the Velvet Soap box in her closet, promises herself that she'll speak to Myfanwy when they get back home. But she won't mention the box specifically.

Lizzie is aching by the time they reach the trees, and she pauses, breathless, to look back. They're at the top of the valley now, with a clear view south to the threading smokes of Swansea town, the Old Ones' burial mounds on Gower, and the sea beyond. To the west, the green waves of hills crest higher and higher until they break on the flanks of the Black Mountain. Over to the east, Panteg delineates the close horizon. The sky is clear above, but there's a nasty look to the clouds behind her and to the east, and she's anxious for Jenner and Sarah Maud and herself, all away from the house in this sudden bad spring weather. Where Myfanwy is, is only Myfanwy's business as far as Lizzie is concerned today.

Immediately below, almost under her boots, are the lichen-blushed slate roofs of Ty Merched and the barns, sheds and gardens. Someone, foreshortened so only the top of a knobbly head and a pair of highly polished shoes are visible, is walking up to the door of the house. It looks like the vicar and Lizzie wonders for a moment if he has news about Jenner, takes an instinctive step towards him. But no, he won't know that Jenner's missing; he'd be the last person Myfanwy would tell. Lizzie steps back, her foot hits a lump of ice and skids sideways. She starts to fall. A flash of panic, the fear of bones and blood; time slows, and she feels the ice take her boots away from beneath her. She goes rigid, tensing for the crash of her hips or spine on the iron-hard ground.

A strong hand grips her arm, nearly jerking it from her shoulder as another arm scoops round her waist to pull her upright. Lizzie steps backwards, stumbles as she tries to find solid ground behind her, slips again, is held secure against a body. Sarah Maud is yelling, somewhere behind her. Lizzie, poor old woman, slumps in the rescuer's arms. So vulnerable, again, she feels undermined. Life has become so much riskier this week. If she could, she would find it funny that turning one hundred has made her feel old, as if a few days could make all the difference. But just now she can't breathe. The arms hold her tighter. She can't even see who has her and wonders about spirits, or fairies, or the oaks themselves. Maybe she's dead, this could be what dead feels like: a freezing space, a squeezing entrapment, and nothing solid to stand on. But, no; Hell wouldn't have quite so much of Sarah Maud's screaming, would it?

'I. Can't breathe. Thank you,' Lizzie tips her head back, addresses the sky in lieu of turning to the person she's pinned against. The grip around her waist shifts a little, the hand on her arm adjusts its hold. She is lifted clear of the ground and spun round to land lightly on the flat gravel of the path; the arm round her ribs is removed and she draws a deep breath. Her torso, shoulders, one ankle, hurt: *but less than a plummet down the hillside. Oh, William bach!* 'Thank you,' Lizzie repeats.

London John is there, smiling and frowning at the same time. 'Are you OK? Like, really, are you alright?' Behind him a youngish woman and a large black dog stand just under the trees. Sarah Maud is shivering and hugging her ribs, she's got tears on her face.

'Oh, Du, thank you, yes I'm fine. Well, a bit shaken I am. But less than a plummet down the hillside. Thank you. I said that already didn't I. Sorry.'

'John it is, Mamgu.' Calls Sarah Maud from the trees. 'This is Llundain John, and Mish and Jessie, these are my friends, see.'

'It's lovely to meet you,' says Lizzie and does now laugh shakily at the misplaced formality of her words, in such a moment. 'No, I mean it really is. Du! How lucky. You were here.' She feels like her head is made of cotton wool; she's mumbling words that seem to make no sense. Just stop, just stop shaking, she thinks. She can't look into anyone's eyes, she's embarrassed, foolish; old. *Just wait a bit. Stop shaking!*

-oOo-

Way down below, the vicar has given up waiting for an answer to his knock on the front door of Ty Merched; guessing he has lost the privilege of going round to the yard, he walks away. Convinced that he has been deliberately refused entry, Morgan converts the foolishness he's feeling into something harder and darker and more acceptable. He is not a forgiving man. He never asks himself 'what would Jesus do?' because he knows enough about his faith to be assured the answer would prove to be inconvenient.

He has thought to come and warn the family about the mood of the neighbours; not that he'd put it that way. He has been practising the best way to put it but has come to no definite conclusion other than to deflect the blame from himself. He is certainly laying all the responsibility for resolving the hostility firmly at the Ty Merched door; not that he'd put it that way, either. *Old family like this, they should set an example. I go to the birthday, I deserve respect. Superstitions and wild men. They were like this long before I ... Really, the child is ... deserves what she... Like this before I...* What might happen to Jenner is a following thought; after all, he isn't an evil man.

But now his pride has been hurt by an unanswered door. The Reverend Twdr Morgan's pride is a bare, vulnerable thing, and today inflamed by doubt and inner debate. *Well, I did my best. Not home, not my fault. Out, all out... or pretending...* His momentary human instinct to redress the damage of his own making has been thwarted by his fragility; Jenner is without sanctuary. *Name in the baptism books but I never saw it. Well, now she is cast out... her actions, not mine.* Has she ever been cast in, really; who could say?

Myfanwy is not in the house. She has been. She was sitting, immobile with bitterness in the grim front room while Lizzie, and later Sarah Maud, ate porridge. Lizzie might arm her anger with words; Myfanwy uses silence as her weapon... a two-edged sword. She saw them leave, Sarah Maud leading on the path up the hill. Then Myfanwy wrapped up in two jumpers and two pairs of socks, and took a blanket, and now she is out in the barn. The house is choked with anger, and the hens had given her such comfort the day before. But the hen coop is cold, the old girls are all up on their perches, preening and crwwwing to each other, and they won't come out even for Myfanwy's sake. So, she has gone to the barn to sit among the sheep. She never hears the door knocker being knocked, nor the gate latch being unlatched. She never hears the vicar's self-conscious steps on the muffling snow of the front path. For she is only listening for a child's tread, and that would be at the back door.

In the house, the ghosts huddle round the dying fire. A piece of cold ash, the size of a walnut, falls through the un-cleaned grate and onto the hearthstone. They anxiously rub their hollow hands together. A second piece of ash falls, this time not so cold.

-oOo-

Jenner is far away from all these people, their falling and their pride, their loneliness. She is shivering, despite the blanket and Smalldog snuggling close, in an abandoned hardware store on the last of the shopping streets. The ponies were chased away by boys. She can't get home.

More than the hunger, and the cold in her fingers and toes, Jenner is thinking about her mother. Sarah Maud isn't getting the medicine Jenner would slip into the glass of water every night. And Jenner had learned through silent watching that Sarah Maud's pain had something, unstated, to do with her-self. It felt like a haunting, this scrap of grievous knowledge.

So then: Jenner could ease her own mind when she soothed her mother. But now: no.

Jenner sits all day, waiting for the shops to close and the bins to go out, so she can eat without thieving; without being seen. She could light a fire, the stove is still standing and there's enough rubbish around for some life-saving heat, but Jenner dare not risk the smoke being seen in this derelict part of the town. More than the cold or the hunger and thirst, she fears strangers. Soon it will be dark, and soon after that the shops will close. Jenner waits.

Her heart sinks when she hears rain on the roofs. She has no coat. And to walk around in the blanket would only draw adult attention.

-oOo-

Over the ridges of the Black Mountain, back in the oak forest, Lizzie has figured out which of the woman and dog is Mich and which is Jesse. Sarah Maud is drinking cider.

The women are in John's bus, fitted out with bed and cupboards and a few books and papers, parked in the lee of a ruined farmhouse. A basin outside collects rainwater for washing, says Mich. There's toilet paper hanging on a rope by the door, and a spade against the front bonnet if anyone needs. There's a fire in the stove and a flame in the lantern.

Lizzie is drinking cider too. It's Mich's own brew: cloudy, meaty and fearsome strong. Lizzie can feel it beginning to rearrange her insides and she takes smaller sips. After the shock of the fall, the sleepless nights and the deep chill, the alcohol has free rein, and the last bit of Lizzie's consciousness is hanging on by its metaphorical fingertips; the now-slurring voice in her head is warning her not to drink any more. Soon the slurring voice will fall asleep, and Lizzie will be adrift while

Sarah Maud and Mich talk lazily about poetry, and brewing, and sheep.

Sarah Maud has come where she has always found help. Earnest and eternally hopeful, John has gone over the ridge to other friends outside the valley, kind-hearted fringe-dwellers like himself. They're moving around the area, with black Jesse and other dogs leading, looking in sheds and streets and barns, unlocked cars and open caves. The homely people of the valleys are disturbed to see these gentle, weaponless hunters; respectable people are always distrustful of strangers, and more so now that their imaginations have been given the blessing of the vicar's sermon.

It begins to rain. The converted bus that is the London escapees' home is holding the north wind at bay. Once Lizzie would have loved the adventure of this place, but now she feels sad and cold. John hasn't returned. A whole day has been wasted, for an early twilight has arrived. She attempts to stand up. She loses her balance, for the second time. London John is not there to catch her, and she closes her eyes against impending pain. Here, a quarter of a mile above her home, Lizzie falls.

-oOo-

Under the same vast clouds, miles to the north Jenner needs to find food. It's dark. The rain has blurred the streetlights and fractured their glow so that she can't see her feet in front of her for the miasma of bright raindrops and shiny pavement. She has tried to get Smalldog to stay in the hardware store with her blanket and the precious book she has tucked away there, but he is following her, dashing in and out of doorways and across the mouths of alleys, a pale disconnected shadow passing along behind her. She can't find her way, and as she steps across a gutter in the footpath, one knee buckles; Jenner's instinctive attempt to right herself sends the other leg skidding to the side. Someone calls out, but they are too far away, and she closes her eyes.

Here, over the mountain, Jenner falls.

When she looks up, Jenner is the focus of a small crowd. Around the streetlamp the misting rain falls as if from a yellow rose of light, but the child can't see whether the shadowy faces are looking kindly at her or not. She is wet through; her clothes stick to her shivering skin, and a pool of water freezes her backside and trickles into one shoe. Her dark hair looks like paint on her scalp.

'She's not from round here.' The observation is repeated round the circle of concerned heads; no, she is not.

'Are the gypsies around? Are you a gypsy, then, bach?' No, she shakes her head, and the speaker is chided for their silliness: the travelling folk aren't due for another month. Someone wants to call the police, but the police sergeant is there already, and he doesn't want the responsibility of a child in the cells.

'Take her to the Carmelites,' he suggests, 'they'll be the ones.' Everyone knows that's just the sergeant pretending to be a bystander, because he doesn't want the responsibility, or the paperwork. But it's a good suggestion, for she is shivering beyond any ability to speak. Once it's re-established by consensus that Jenner is indeed not from round here, she is lifted into a car, and driven to the convent's side door.

In the street, a small posy of leaves and flowers has fallen from Jenner's pocket and been stepped on by the people crowding round her. As Jenner leaves in the police car, and people disperse, a woman steps forward from the edge of the crowd and picks up the posy, shakes it into some order, and considers the plants it contains. The woman puts in in her raincoat pocket, turns and walks quickly into the night. It must be the rain, for it's impossible to tell her age, or height, or the colour of her hair and eyes and skin. She is certainly wearing a raincoat. She is certainly walking towards the old hardware store. Whistling softly, she has now acquired a small pale shadow that follows her, dashing in and out of doorways and across the mouths of alleys.

At the convent, an amount of negotiation is carried on while Jenner leans against the door post; she hears '... not from round ...' as she slides to the floor unnoticed. Eventually she is taken inside and warmed, and fed. A bed is prepared. Jenner is startled by the strange decoration she's noticed: tiny gaunt men have been nailed to crossed strips of wood and put to hang in every room. She's seen farmers string up dead crows to warn off the living crows from their crops. Since she has only seen women in this house, is the tiny man meant to warn away the men: don't come here or we'll starve you, nail you?

But there are no men in her house either, and yet no household gods or nailed mannikins. She is now shivering hot, and too tired to think any more about it. Worry about getting home, about Smalldog, and about Sarah Maud, spin her into darkness.

-oOo-

Lizzie is fretful and awake. Her back and shoulder ache where she hit the furniture in John's bus. Her dignity aches where she was helped down the hill in the gloomy rain by John and his friends, come back to report sightings of Jenner a day ago in Ponty, but nothing since. They don't mention that rumours of a tiger at Ty Merched are going round the pubs. They don't mention that wilder stories of Jenner seen riding the mountain ponies, with a small dog in her lap, are heard on street corners.

Sarah Maud is in bed too, withdrawn and febrile; Mich is sitting by her, crooning a folk lullaby in her west country accent, and wondering how she can help. Mich has been a rare find in Sarah Maud's life: tall and capable, with a sharp mind and a quick tongue for most humans but with a patience that made Sarah Maud feel —without any protest— that she was one of Mich's rescue animals. They had bonded within a few days of the hippies arriving in the valley, when Sarah Maud wandered into their camp, needing to talk about art and music and the old night sky. Mich for her part found Sarah Maud such a generous relief from the villagers' entrenched suspicion of newcomers, she is ready to invest time and understanding in her damaged, gentle friend. 'There's no need to feel alone,' she once said, and Sarah Maud knows she meant it. Mich is noticing a change in Sarah Maud: darkness round her usually misty eyes; tightness round her usually soft mouth.

Lizzie can hear John and Myfanwy talking in the kitchen in guarded voices. What are they talking about, the fussy widow and the hippie? Lizzie feels left out of her own life, tonight. Her house is full of strangers, but only two of them don't live there.

-oOo-

Unbeknown to Lizzie and all inside Ty Merched, the garden is also occupied. Two strangers—one, more strange than anyone suspects—pass by the long side fence. Had Lizzie's ears been sharper, she would have heard a conversation suggesting they're here to see the fey folk, in the midnight shade of the ruined back road. There's a stumble in the dark, a puzzled call. A scuffle; a cracking beyond hearing. A falling. Later, just silence and ghosts.

# Chapter 6

# Dydd Mercher
# (Mercury's Day)

It's the most peculiar garden to find a dead body in. Not that you ever see a garden that is normal for dead bodies. Not that you ever find a body that isn't dead.

But this garden is planted with waist-high posts along a winding path and on each post a tiny object: miniature statues made of wire, broken crockery, wood and bones and beads. Large figures strut the retaining stone wall or cower under bushes. Some are probably meant to be birds or people but most look like, well, other things, but with heads. *Weird*.

So thinks the rookie police officer as he ambles behind his chief, his boss, his ... inventing slang is a useful deflection from the actual voice in his head: don't be sick, don't be sick, don't be sick. This is about to be PC Jones's first dead body.

The DS keeps stopping to look at the posts and their objects. Jones feels his guts clench in dread, then relax as each stop is found to be harmless; clench, relax, clench, relax. By the time they come to the blackberry thicket at the far end of the path he's exhausted, and barely acknowledges the sight of a tipped-over pair of rain-soaked shoes just visible in the brambles and long grass, netted by a bit of spider web. Yesterday's snow has been washed from the bank by overnight rain, and everything is dark with moisture.

Then he notices the same thing that had startled Jeremiah Jenkins away from his pre-dawn search for tigers at Ty Merched: the glimpse of a sock, the form of an ankle, the presumption of a foot inside each shoe. Finding himself unable to be sick thanks to his rigorous self-hypnosis, PC Jones faints.

Detective Sergeant Watcyns detachedly watches the damp grass soaking his new recruit's uniform. He wonders how long until someone offers him a cup of tea. Torn between nabbing the glory of an actual crime, and the disruption any work might cause his normal routine, Watcyns is settling easily into his accustomed bad temper at this early hour.

The body is eventually uncovered from its swaddling of brambles, but the site is ruined; a nightmare of mangled evidence with so many pieces of fabric, blood and skin attached to those binding thorns it is impossible to attribute the rags of flesh and hair to either the body, persons unknown, or to the police team itself. The ground has been trampled into a quagmire, for yards around. And it is raining again.

Above on the bank, a fist-sized hollow where a stone has been dislodged is filling with rainwater the way the socket of a pulled tooth fills with blood. Down at the store, Jem Jenkins has every shopper's attention. Every gaping mouth is swallowing his words with relish, every functioning ear is waggling in the breeze of his story.

Mercury has returned to the valley; a god of many things, including, today, being responsible for getting the dead to where they need to be.

The women of Ty Merched are unaware of the early-morning presence of PC Jones and his wet uniform on the grass of Sarah Maud's garden, of DS Watcyns's need for tea, or of old Jem hightailing it over their own stone wall on his running way to the shop, even though it'll make him late to work– for gossip is gossip, and this is gossip of the highest grade.

Sarah Maud is abed. She expects to feel bad after every visit to the old bus, despite the pleasure of Mich's conversation and the ideas they spin over the emptying flagons. But today the darkness is even closer—darker than yesterday—and Sarah Maud is shivering uncontrollably. Recently she's felt more unravelled, more ... past... and unable to hold herself in place. Her mind is cruelly clear, and dagger-like images are coming unwanted and intolerable behind her eyes: night shadows like quicksand over her face, and tinkling carnival sounds fitting their rhythm to the pain that crushed her flat; hot breaths of power, hotter breaths of shame, and a curse regretted as soon as spoken into the emptied air above her.

She presses her hands hard down her belly, to push her sullied skin away, slough off the mired flesh, get rid of herself, to let out the blackness pooling in her blood. Her body is burning with sadness, and she cannot rub or scrub hard enough to stop it. Sarah Maud reaches for something sharp. Her grief is unbearable and must be let out in silence, drawn off, drained away. But there is nothing sharp within reach. Sarah Maud uses her teeth to open the skin of her arm, let the sadness out.

And she hasn't remembered about Jenner yet.

Lizzie is abed. She must be dead today if it didn't happen last night. She aches everywhere and mostly in her head. Her belly feels watery, the dregs of the cider gurgling round the bends and loops of her old guts, pooling in her bladder and loosening her bowels; but, so far, she's resisted the urge to move. Maybe if she moves there'll be an accident, a spillage, and Lizzie cannot face the thought. *Ooohh William, bugger this!* She can feel William smile, through the clouds in her head: *now, now; language, cariad.* She draws her mouth tight shut, grips her arms around her stomach.

Lizzie's satisfaction in being tough, her determination in proving herself worthy to her mother and grandmother with an unconscious, contained elegance that brought farmers to pencil their names in her dance card every hunt ball, long after William had died; Lizzie's confidence at the stock sales for half a century and more, wearing her husband's moleskins and shirt; Lizzie's ease through her physical body, quick childbirth, easy menopause and no arthritic aches and rheumatic pains—no need for reading glasses, no problems with hearing —Lizzie's stamina through ten decades of valley winters and mountain summers; all these things have been lost in genetic translation from Lizzie's bird-like body forever on the brink of regained youth, to Myfanwy's mediocre bulk, forever on no brink at all. Myfanwy is as tough as Lizzie, but she wears it like a sweat-stained harness; Lizzie has aged with grace, like the ruby necklace.

But this morning when Myfanwy put her head round the door to check on Lizzie, she could see a difference in the old woman. A lamp that has burned almost all the oil in its reservoir, Lizzie is going dim.

Now, Myfanwy is making excessive noise in the kitchen. The fire is blazing, and the boiler is roaring, for she needs to be scrubbing and washing and banging the silence out of the place. She had talked late with John last night, spilling out her fears for Jenner and her blame of old Lizzie with a freedom that is foreign to her, while the dirty dishes wallowed in grey water and the night drew long. No one else would care what she thought; John's uncritical attention has loosened her tongue and Myfanwy has said more than she meant to, to a stranger. Now she's cross, rueful. Once more she feels the need to re-establish her influence somewhere, but her domination over the kitchen is the only satisfaction she has within reach today. She doesn't want to recall that once she might have used Jenner as a target in such a mood. She bangs the pans louder.

*Not unkind, I was never unkind*, thinks Myfanwy.

*That all depends on what you mean by 'unkind'*, think the ghosts.

She has been out at first light to see to the hens and the sheep. Now, it's the noise of the geese that alerts her, something is up. Next, a polite pounding on the side door.

A large policeman of some authority politely barges his way into the hallway. Over his shoulder Myfanwy can see a green-faced policeman with a few dead leaves stuck to his soaked uniform. She thinks of Jenner, but her fear of bad news saves her from immediately speaking the name out loud. Clearly the centre of the large one's focus is the kettle he can glimpse on the stove behind Myfanwy.

DS Watcyns is a polite man, so bobs his head once to the woman, to her flowery cross-over apron and capable arms, to the apparent fact that she's some sort of kitchen person.

'DS Watcyns. This,' he moves a shoulder slightly to indicate behind him, 'is Constable Jones.' Watcyns lifts his ID badge about an inch out of his breast pocket, drops it back. 'Tea, two sugars, thanks. Where is your husband, is it? I wants a word.' PC Jones had tried to brief the DS on their way up from the Ponty station, but the prospect of a murder was too exciting; Watcyns had not been listening.

'Well now, he's up by chapel' Myfanwy looks at the mud running off the constable's trousers and pooling on her clean flagstones. 'But you won't find him much to talk to. Can I help?' she looks up at the sergeant. The earlier thoughts of how she used to treat Jenner have made her defensive, no matter that she longs to have the child safe home again.

'I usually speaks to the man of the house; I'll wait. Cup of tea would be great; two sugars, a bit of cake if you have it.' He looks carefully at the kitchen chairs, for DS Watcyns is a large and unfit man and the chairs look both appealingly comfortable and dangerously fragile.

'You'll be waiting a while. There's not been a man here for, oh, decades. Not in the house here, no.' Myfanwy tops up the kettle and puts it on the hot part of the stove, having decided she can sweeten bad news by serving this oaf as he clearly expects. Myfanwy has heard a bit about the new ideas of women, and liberation; about not being 'sub servants' to men, but, since she was rarely in the company of men, it was an idea she was puzzled by, had missed out on. The only woman she connects with her need for liberation is Lizzie.

She reaches down the cake tin from the pantry, lifts out the last two inches of a *bara brith* from the party and places it on the bread board in the middle of the table, then makes a fresh pot of tea. She sets out two cups and saucers, is just getting her own from the draining board.

'One cup will do me' says DS Watcyns. Myfanwy looks at the constable. The constable looks at Myfanwy. She pours two cups, then her own, sets out the milk jug and sugar bowl and teaspoons. As Myfanwy turns to get the bread knife, DS Watcyns puts the whole piece of bara on his saucer, puts his cup on the tablecloth, slops a puddle of tea. Myfanwy in the presence of the DS draws close to Lizzie in the presence of the vicar.

DS Watcyns drinks noisily. 'No man?' He looks around. Polished dressers and china in matched sets, tidy array of cans and jars and packets, a bright fire and dry windows; no smell of damp or manure or silage. Not at all like the usual hill-farms he visits. 'How ever do you manage?'

'We gets by.' She leaves it at that. 'Should I get my mother then? What is it you want?'

'Your mother? God, woman, isn't she in the ground as well? How old is your mother and still standing?' DS Watcyns spits out a laugh, a currant crumb spilling from his mouth and bouncing down his uniform onto the tablecloth. Myfanwy thinks about burning her bra; right here, right now. If only she'd got into the habit of wearing one.

'I'll tell her you're here. What did you say your name was?' Myfanwy has learned something from Lizzie, that's certain.

-oOo-

Over the hills, in the Llandovery convent, Jenner has been left to sleep while the nuns worry about her thinness, her fainting, her pallor. Last night they had washed the clothes she'd been wearing, and they're drying on a line in the boiler room. A novice keeps an eye peeped through the cubicle door to where Jenner sleeps. Mother Superior is looking through the charity bins for warmer clothes to fit a thin girl. Jenner is feverish and silent and is kept in bed all day. She resists, then she sleeps. Twice she wakes for food, followed by more sleep. The novice, at the change of shift, says it's like they could almost see through the child while she slept, so pale she was on the pale pillow. The next shift, they think the girl is running with wild horses in a fever dream.

The Llandovery police sergeant calls at the convent front door later in the day; he felt the need for a walk and thinks he'd like an update. No, she hasn't spoken yet. No, she's not from round here. The sergeant goes back to his desk, satisfied with his astute decision of the night before.

Smalldog is sitting by a small fire in a tiny kitchen a few miles distant from Llandovery and the policeman's desk. He's lost his sense of direction, has lost Jenner, and lies flat and dejected, resting his muzzle on one front paw. A woman of uncertain age, height and colouring comes in from her yard: 'Have you finished your breakfast, little dog? Here then.' She takes a crumpled posy out of her raincoat pocket, tucks it into a soft twist of fabric she's tied round his neck. Smalldog feels a bit better, looks up a moment. But drops his head onto a front leg again, for he's only a little bit better.

She settles down beside Smalldog on the hearth rug, makes the posy sit more comfortably against the back of his neck, strokes his head. 'I knows,' she says, 'I knows.' She takes a battered old book, wrapped in a scrap of oilcloth, out of her pocket, settles the loose pages—of English words in a child's script—into place, resumes her reading. Over their heads, a white and green Welsh tapestry blanket is drying on a rack.

-oOo-

Myfanwy, in her own place, leaves DS Watcyns staring at her pantry shelves in bemusement, while from the shelves the ghosts stare back at DS Watcyns equally unsure of what they're looking at but dying of curiosity.

The house is paused; Myfanwy's slippered feet make no sound as she passes all the enmeshed clutter of the ancient hallway and taps on Lizzie's door. But before Lizzie can draw breath to reply, the stillness snaps apart. From the next room Sarah Maud is making an inarticulate wail, so much in the minor key it seems to be sinking into Sarah Maud, not coming from her.

Myfanwy in the doorway is now staring perplexed at the window. Lizzie hasn't had time to register what is going on, as sitting up upon Myfanwy's entrance has precipitated an emergency. Her body overrides all else, forces her out past Myfanwy and into the bathroom, where she just manages to shut the door before she is sat on the toilet, passing a great purging shit of cider. She hears Sarah Maud and Myfanwy trying to talk and cry at the same time.

Myfanwy is banging at the bathroom door, then gone again and in the kitchen: talking at someone. Lizzie doesn't know who else is out there and she's afraid she cannot move. *Please,* she begs the void, *am I dead yet?*

No, she is not dead. But someone is. And Sarah Maud is sobbing at the bathroom door.

'I'm sorry, I'm sorry,' says Sarah Maud. Lizzie doesn't know what she's sorry for, or who she's sorry to, but the words are said with a rare conviction. Lizzie shakes herself together and opens the door. Bent over in the doorway, Sarah Maud has twisted two sides of her nightdress hem around her wrists, holding them pressed against her chest so she is naked from the ribs downwards; blood is soaking the fabric, and smears of more blood are drying on her arms. But that is not why she's sorry, not what she's crying about. Sarah Maud says she has seen the dead go past her window. Lizzie opens her arms, and Sarah Maud falls into her shaking embrace.

A man is standing open-mouthed in the kitchen doorway. He's chewing on a lump of cake and looking at Sarah Maud's naked backside before he sees Lizzie regarding him coldly around Sarah Maud's shoulder.

'Who,' she asks with crisp pronunciation, '*y ffwc,* are you?' He retreats backwards into the kitchen as Lizzie draws Sarah Maud into the bathroom and shuts the door.

When she has seen Sarah Maud washed and bandaged and quiet in bed, Lizzie goes into the kitchen.

Watcyns has been making notes on his little notepad, with his pencil. They don't say anything of relevance to anything but Watcyns's own amour-propre. PC Jones has been steaming gently by the fire and Myfanwy has been standing guard, shifting between the stove and sink, uncertain what line to steer and waiting to see where Lizzie takes things. Myfanwy has seen what made Sarah Maud cry: a shrouded body on a stretcher, carried past the windows. Was the body a small one? She can't remember, but the question drowns out all other thought.

'Is there tea for the girl?' Lizzie addresses Myfanwy and ignores the men. For Lizzie has not seen the stretcher. There is tea, and Myfanwy takes a cup into Sarah Maud, and a secret piece of bara in her apron pocket. Lizzie in her nightgown and ruby necklace considers the strangers.

'Are you the...?' Watcyns is unsure what the word might be, leaves all the options hanging mid-air.

'Mrs Coombe,' Lizzie manages more propriety than a queen.

'DS Watcyns, PC Jones,' Watcyns, repeating his earlier gestures, indicates the other officer, nudges his badge in his pocket.

Lizzie focuses on the pocket. After a pause, DS Watcyns takes the badge out.

'Hmmm' Lizzie clearly speculating that the badge might be chocolate inside a foil covering. 'And what can we do for you, Mr...?'

'DS Watcyns. Mrs... A body has been found on your land. Mrs Coombe.'

Myfanwy at the door 'A body in Sarah Maud's garden, Mam!' and locks eyes with Lizzie. The women draw together, the rest of the world is invisible for this moment.

'Who is it?' Lizzie holds her shoulders rigid, eyes closed.

'We don't yet know, Mrs Coombe. Is anyone missing from this household?'

No reply for a heartbeat, then:

'Any man missing, Mrs Coombe? Maybe a farm hand?' PC Jones feels the need to clarify.

Lizzie and Myfanwy resume breathing. They hold each other a moment, hands on upper arms, then Myfanwy turns back up the hall to soothe Sarah Maud.

'Man? No, no man that I know of' Lizzie notices her legs are failing her again, sits quickly by the table and reaches for the teapot. PC Jones steps across, hands her the pot and even looks for a clean cup on the dresser. The ghosts are beginning to like PC Jones.

DS Watcyns is continuing to dislike his tyro. That the body was a man was something he'd wanted to keep in reserve for a while. One naked beauty, as mad as a hatter, and two ancient witches, one as sharp as nails; there is something unsettling about these women and this house. What with the body, and the garden of figurines, it's adding up to an unusual morning for DS Watcyns. He never does like unusual mornings. He decides to regain control of the interrogation, by—

'Was there a wallet, maybe a driving licence?' Lizzie gets in first.

By the way Watcyns shifts his haunches on the chair PC Jones recognises that Watcyns will shout at him for the next few days, at least. 'Perhaps more tea for the DS?' he suggests to Myfanwy as she returns to stand guard over the stove. She reminds him of his aunt.

Myfanwy is willing to make fresh tea. And the colour is coming back into Lizzie's cheeks.

'We can't release that sort of information to the public,' says DS Watcyns. He has not looked for a wallet, or a driving licence. Someone else can touch the body; someone else can look for a wallet. He looks with interest at the cake tin, but there is no more bara forthcoming. DS Watcyns gurgles his tea down, heaves himself off the chair and kicks his boot into PC Jones's ankle before PC Jones can get out of the way.

All day there is traffic through the yard, in stops and starts. Now that DS Watcyns has gone back to Ponty, Myfanwy makes hot Welsh cakes for PC Jones and the other officers sorting through the wet grass for anything that might explain who the man was and why he was there. Myfanwy begins to enjoy the attention, and the distraction, but: *where is Jenner?*

Sarah Maud is fretting, as memory returns: *where is Jenner?* The sheep need tending, but there are strangers in her garden;

she starts to rub again at the bandages under her long jumper sleeves. Lizzie is keeping close to Sarah Maud, seeing the younger woman's distress; *Ah, William bach, where is Jenner?*

The geese are hissing nervously in the pond, the hens are off the lay, broody on their nests; the ghosts are shivering on the roofs as they watch the living and dead come and go. *Where is Jenner,* they all ask.

Mercury, god of communications, god of trickery: there's a slippery combination. The neighbours begin to suggest thing. To each other, at first. The vicar hears whispers as he leans against the inside of his bolted front door; some of them are from outside his skull. No-one would have said the vicar was an evil man, but he is becoming one.

For the first time in years, fragile and tired, Sarah Maud does not go to the pub. For the first time in years Reverend Morgan does go to the pub. He is acquiring the look of a man taken to walking the village at night; his boots are damp and uncleaned. He nods to all but sits alone at the bar. He holds his brandy and lovage cordial close in his curled arms. He mutters as if he's praying to himself; in a way, he is. The words he speaks are unholy, though they lilt and scroll along the polished bar like incense. He speaks about blood at midnight, about the foreboding and the forbidden, bent shapes in the forests; he speaks about these things and Jenner is in every story, every sentence. No-one is looking at Reverend Morgan. Everyone is listening.

After closing, Gwyn the Publican makes a call to a number he knows by heart, speaks low and softly.

'Hello, Mai bach, can I speak to your father...? ... ah, now, Watcyns? Rhiwfawr Gwyn it is. Listen man, here's the thing...' Gwyn the Pub hopes thereby to pay off a very old debt that the DS has been quite meticulous in maintaining.

# Chapter 7

# Dydd Iau
# (Jove's Day)

A young woman police officer has been ordered to stand guard in the lane by Ty Merched; her breath comes in sharp as ice, goes out soft as clouds. PWC Davies has two pairs of socks on and envies the men's regulation woollen trousers. Her gloved hands are tucked up the sleeves of her coat. The weather has turned back to the winter she'd thought had gone.

There's a rustling in the hedge on her left. Nothing is visible, but she shifts a foot, gets a better balance in the frozen mud. The hedge on her left rustles again, harder. But WPC Davies grew up here: she looks to her right.

One urchin, on the brink of running out, retreats in a skittering of twigs and last year's leaves. The hedge on her right rustles, loudly, a bit further along. To her left there is a ducking down and she sees a small shoulder in a home-knitted scraps-coloured jumper poking from the hedge; a small, booted foot slips out into view and is as hastily withdrawn.

'Now then, twins. Get back home before I tells your mam. I see you there.' Silence. 'Go on with you. Now!' Davies stamps her regulation shoes on the stony lane, one after the other.

The hedges on both sides rustle in a receding wave along the lane for a couple dozen yards, then two small boys break cover and run the rest of the way to the crossroad, where an adult hand pushes out from a gate, pulls the nearest one by the hole-freckled sleeve; both boys disappear into the field.

For another hour WPC Davies watches the road, stamps her chilly feet, wants a tea and regrets not bringing the thermos flask; thinks of her sweetheart in Ponty and what she'll wear next Saturday night, thinks of where he'll place his warm hands, where he'll have trouble with the buttons and hooks of her dress, where he'll put his hot wet mouth...

The hedge on her left rustles again. And that on the right. Small faces are peering through, two here, three there, a handful further up the track; and now bigger faces join them with staring eyes and tight mouths, grubby fruit on an unlikely tree, pushing the little ones aside, bulging out of the concealing foliage and overhanging the lane. If the devil could cast his net along the lane, what a harvest of the idle.

'Get off with you all! No entry to the crime scene!' says WPC Davies. She longs for reinforcements. She longs for a toilet break. But the schedule was written by a man; it's assumed she can piss in a hedge. And if she can't, well, serves her right for not being a man.

The watchers in the hedge don't move. For along the lane here comes the newspaper photographer from Ponty. Behind him, it might be that all the reverend's parishioners, and some that haven't seen the inside of a church for years, are shuffling, in visible conflict between curiosity and caution.

'Press pass.' says the newspaper photographer.

'I'm sorry, sir. Not today. Crime scene' says Davies. 'Call into the station, ask for DS Watcyns.'

'Hey, I'd like to hear your version though! A lovely girl like you, bet you're real smart! What can you tell me about the ...'

'Call into the station, sir. Ask for DS Watcyns.'

'Yeah, but the boss'll do me if I don't get a photo. C'mon girlie, it'll be OK.'

'Station. DS Watcyns.'

'What's wrong with you, want to get me into trouble do you? Bit of a cow, are you?'

'Station.' Too quietly said. WPC Davies takes a surreptitious, deeper breath, stares ahead, feels the blood flush her chilled face. 'Please ask at the police station for DS Watcyns!' she tries again. Everyone is watching her, from the lane and over the hedges. She has her orders. Trouble is, the watchers just don't care.

'Bitch' says the photographer and pushes past. His kit bag hits her in the ribs. The crowd hesitate, take a step forward, avoid making eye contact. WPC Davies takes out her whistle, blows hard and long, an alarum echoing across the space between the valley walls. Even the photographer stops in his stride a moment.

But no-one comes. WPC Davies bites the inside of her cheek as from lane and hedges people swarm past her towards the farm gate.

'No! The crime scene will be wrecked...!' But WPC Davies is outnumbered.

Inside the house, barriers had been thrown up yesterday: windows clothed in thick curtains and tacked-up blankets against the grim activity outside, doors and gates locked behind the departing police. In the shadowy rooms, Lizzie is counting her dead. She's closer to the ghosts than to her living family. Faces slide over the curtains: old cousins that did well by her mam, uncles whose prickly chins and grey cheeks she had to kiss as they loomed like giants in greasy waistcoats, a farm hand slimy from his drowned grave in the old well, a farm girl she doesn't know with a smoke-coloured baby in a bundle she doesn't remember; her boys, her mam, her William... her William. Even as she is buoyed by the certainty that Jenner is not among the grey visitors, the feather of her hope shifts uncomfortably under the weight of her years. Lizzie is counting her dead and she cries that she is not with them. She is deaf to the noises of the morning.

Which are rising to turmoil, out by the gate.

Llundain John had come down the night before, bringing a few friends with him from out of the woods. From his high perch on the west valley wall, he and Mich saw the activity around Ty Merched yesterday and gathered their contacts. This alone would have been enough to draw alarm and outrage from the valley community. Hippies in the barn? Set the dogs, call the sheriff, ring the church bells! Has no-one read the newspaper stories of what these monsters do: undermining society, living wild, buying no beer?! But John and his comrades had come to work the barn shifts, for the sheep and their gravid urgency make no allowance for dead bodies, or grief, or fat policemen. Sarah Maud needed help and John is here. He had brought a few old farming books, because he really has no experience of sheep; more, usefully, he had brought his more experienced friends from outside the valley. The neighbours had looked on and done nothing, said nothing, thought everything; mainly, thought with disappointment that the sheep are cared for, and the family has avoided both distress and disapproval, that the neighbours will not be able to condemn them... in this regard at least.

'*Bugger!*' think the neighbours.

John has heard the police whistle. Up on the ridge, so has Mich; she comes running down to stand by his side. When the photographer from Ponty reaches the gate, he finds it defended. John and two friends—colleagues of the night watch, with eyes gritty from lack of sleep and hands rusty with birthing blood—lean against the wooden gate and hold it closed. Their appearance is so alarming that doubt enters the leg muscles of the would-be gawkers. Like flying pickets, more of John's friends gather, filtering out of the sheds and down from the field to slip out the farm gate and stand astride the lane, just as more people are trailing along the lane to swell the numbers of the curious, outside Ty Merched. For the first time ever, the longhairs are supporting the—absent— police. They're doing it for Sarah Maud. But also, this: some hostile yokels deserve payback.

'Press pass. Want your faces across the front page?' says the photographer with practiced aggression. John does not answer. The photographer lifts his camera, adjusts the focus, triggers the shutter. And is pulled sideways by the strap round his neck, as a huge arm reaches across the gate, grabs the camera and disappears it within the press of hippies. This is not their first protest.

'Hey, he stole my camera!' says the photographer.

'What camera?' asks John. Someone laughs quick and short. A thick walking stick appears, raps twice on the gate. Someone presses into the hedge from the lane. But the hedge is old and thick and holds firm.

'What do you want here?' asks Mich.

'Fuck off, Londoners!' It sounds like Gwyn the publican, way back in the crowd, raising mutters of agreement.

'From Cardiff I am,' calls one of the longhairs.

'Fucking worse then!' and laughter from the mob in the lane.

'What do you think you're doing here? This is private property. Go home.' John, loudly, reviving his past life's teaching voice. But these are not the scrawny-necked, aimless boys of his housing-estate school career.

'Get out of the way, toe-rag! We wants to see the body what the witch has killed!' The mob move and sway towards the gate again, mutterings turning to growlings.

'What the fuck are you on about? The body's down in Swansea morgue!' John and Mich exchange glances.

'Liars! They're lying to protect the witch!' The photographer, quick to spot an opportunity for a story, moves well to the side of the restless mob. And what had started as idle curiosity is now roiling with something fey and ancient, tribal fury rising out of the old stones of the road like a race memory of sacred, sanctioned acts that ended in blood and the cleansing of strangeness from the community.

'What the hell are you talking about?' Mich calls the question, but she thinks she knows the answer, for Sarah Maud has been worried about someone. Someone was named, pointed out, on Sunday, in church; someone must have sinned. Someone who has sinned has got to be punished. Who needs a reason if a god has spoken—even if it is a foreign—English—god? And better, here is a reason, laid out ready and dead in the long grass.

The longhairs fall into defence mode, tactics learned from London squats, peace protests, anti-nuclear marches. A barricade of hurdles, branches, timber and handcarts is magicked out the five-bar gate and now blocks the lane beside the front gate, backed up by solid human muscle and a sense of justice. The crowd of locals, underemployed and idle, or boys dodging out of school, drawn up the lane by the novelty of a murder in their own little valley, outnumber the defenders several times over, but are outflanked in both intellect and experience. Although any mob has the advantage of rabid unpredictability.

'Where's the witch? Bring her out!' a few local lads start chanting, grinning at the novelty. The ghosts of Ty Merched come out onto the rooftop to stare and listen, for they are afraid of witches. One pale young man in the crowd sees them, shakes his head in disbelief.

The pale young man shouts louder, 'Bring out the witch, bring out the witch!' and the cry is taken up by the rest. Sticks and boots crack against the wooden gate, the hedges, the corner of the house itself.

The hippie guard hold their ground; they have been tested under fire in the streets of Paris just a year back, and a rabble of farm hands and schoolboys is undaunting. Although they are mystified by the scene. This mob has nothing to gain from a fight; as far as the defenders can imagine, the valueless aggression makes no sense. They have missed the cues.

The aggressors might not be able to articulate why, for it's about the bones of the place—the ancient landholdings scratching along side by side for a millennium; the inhabitants bumping elbows and stubbing toes against each other for generations across the thin soil—and now they feel the liberty, the permission, snatched from thin air and the vicar's say-so, to push back. To shove into the rumoured wealth of these old moneybags as hard as you shove into the hunger of a hard winter or a tight market. To beat the successful ones down for a change, even while you're being beaten down yourself. When you have nothing, you may as well gamble the lot.

The mob becomes ragged, breaks into slumps of bodies stoning the walls with ineffectual rage, and wrestling the fenceposts to and fro. There's an attempt to jump clear over the barricade that fails, another that almost succeeds.

Inside the house, the women huddle in Myfanwy's room above the kitchen. Lizzie has not visited this room since Myfanwy the widow returned to her childhood home, and she's already annoyed by the effort of scaling the constricted stair for the first time in near forty years. Momentarily forgetting the events outside, Lizzie has looked around with startled distaste at the gaudy wallpaper, the scented cushions and chintz frills, and sniffed her accustomed contempt, even as she was fearful for their safety. Myfanwy for her part feels her precious privacy has been breached; so many nights staring at the roof and whispering bitterly over the cast of each night's tarot: her heart, her mother, her wayward crazy daughter, the strangeling Jenner. Sarah Maud has clung to Myfanwy's skirts as they clambered up; now she's tucked in bed. Lizzie sits by the pillow, with one hand awkwardly on Sarah Maud's shoulder.

'What can you see?' Lizzie asks. 'Can you see anything at all? Lift it more! I want to know what's going on. But how dare they!' —and, more puzzled, inturning the inflection— 'How dare they...'

Myfanwy is crouched on her haunches, leans over her broad thighs to lift a corner of the curtain and squint out through the tiniest gap in the already small window under the eaves. 'I don't want them to see us. Leave it be so.' She has only a thin wedge-shaped view of the barricade and the backs of the defenders.

'Is that Dai Jones? And the twins. I can hear the twins! What are they saying, what do they want?'

'Hush, hush, I can't figure out what they're saying over all your mithering! Yes, it's half the riffraff of the valley and some from over Rhiwfawr. Glyn the Pub! And the Newspaper who was here just last week... Oh!' A clod of pitched mud has hit the wall just below the window and Myfanwy, startled, topples backwards, her arms pinwheeling as she grasps the air for balance.

Sarah Maud flinches under the layers of quilts 'What do they want, Mamgu; do they want the sheep? The lambs?'

'Hush now, dwt'

'I'm sorry, Mamgu... sorry.' Sarah Maud is living through some other fear, she huddles in another Ty Merched, cowers in a story of her own.

'Now, now; Llundain John is here. We'll be a'right. Hush now' Lizzie pats the bed again, self-consciously. Myfanwy glances at the gesture jealously.

Even to Lizzie's habitual suspicions of her estranged neighbours this makes no sense, this shouting urge to cause harm, to break and enter and... do what? Where is the vicar? The duplicitous vicar should be here with his flapping hands to control the crowd, keep the peace his god seems so fond of. And where is Jenner? *Make her safe. Please, keep her away.* Lizzie isn't sure to whom she's praying.

Outside the noise grows. Seeing that throwing stones at a stone wall isn't making much of an impact, some in the mob turn their frustrated attention to the defenders, and one huge stone is hefted to shoulder height, hurled. It arcs lumbering through the air towards Mich and time slows...

-oOo-

Jenner has woken into a warm room as bright as the inside of a kingcup. She can remember slipping in the dark street, and looking up into gilded threads of rain, and a tiny man nailed to wood, and little more; she stays still, and waits to see where in heaven or under it she is. The bed is delicious, she wriggles and flops her head against the soft pillow experimentally, kicks her feet a little, and watches the blankets lift and float back down. She does ache all over, and the room swims when she turns her head, and now she misses the cupboard of simples and remedies back home; she closes her hot eyelids and knows just where she should reach for the necessary jars and packets, were she home again. Jenner wants to go now; but when she starts to sit up, she falls back onto the pillow again.

The door is slightly ajar, and Jenner can hear rustling of cloth, whispering. A moment later a tap on the wood, and the novice brings a tray into the room, followed by Mother Superior.

'Stay easy, child; you've a fever.' Mother Superior pulls a chair from the corner to the bedside, and the novice places the tray on it. There's a glass of warm milk, and toast with butter and jam. Both women draw back a little, smiling hopefully.

Jenner smiles back, looks at the milk and toast. She isn't sure if she's hungry yet, for her first thought is to run. Not away from these nice-smelling women; but just out in the sunlight. Jenner feels the shadows on her skin like too-tight clothing. Only, when she goes to swing her legs out of the bed, she falls feebly still.

'You have a fever,' repeats Mother Superior, 'I don't think you're better yet. More rest, I think.'

Jenner takes up the warm milk, for she's used to assessing what adults want. Only:

'Where's Smalldog?' she asks. She cannot mention the book; she believes the book is lost now, and she can't think about how that feels. 'My little dog?'

'Ah. I don't know about any dog, child; there was no dog with you when they brought you here.' Mother Superior has many questions herself but feels it wise not to press them now; surely there's no rush. 'Eat up and rest some more. Novice Jane here will read to you if you like.' And that is the end of everyone's questions for now.

But Jane only has bible stories to read, and Jenner falls asleep almost as soon as she's licked the last dab of jam from her fingers. In her dreams, she meets a woman; as is the nature of dreams, Jenner can't say exactly what the woman looks like. From the deep pockets of her raincoat, the woman draws things to show Jenner: Smalldog in a necklace of flowers, a horse the colour of storms, a bird that sings of sailing ships, red dragons in an unfamiliar night, fire and kindness, and golden cattle, a lake of swords, a high path ...

'Oh!' Jenner wakes again. The sun has shifted a long way round the sky, but the room is still quite light. There is a plate with a cheese sandwich covered by a napkin, and a glass of water, on the chair by her bed. She looks at it for a long time. 'Hello?' she calls in a small voice.

After a moment Jane puts her head round the door. 'Hello?' she smiles.

'My dog?' Jenner, taking her cues from these strangely kind adults, mimics a smile in response.

'No, no dog has been seen, my dear.'

At Jenner's falling smile, Sister Jane wonders aloud if there's anything she could get for Jenner? Or could she show Jenner the bathroom?... Yes, there is something she could get for Jenner. And the toilet, of course. Jane even finds a toothbrush.

So, when Mother Superior passes in the evening, Jenner is frowning with concentration among the bedding and pillows, and muttering as she works to fill a notebook with her clumsy script, her precise drawings.

'What is she doing?' the mother asks Jane.

'She's remembering,' says Jane. 'It seems important.'

-oOo-

On the flanks of the Gwrhyd Valley the siege continues, but no police have returned to the murder scene, nor checked on WPC Jones, nor questioned her when, dishevelled, she returned to the station. For DS Watcyns has lost interest after all; finding the next steps of even a murder are so dull as to require paperwork, he hasn't bothered taking any next steps.

The curious mob of a few dozen locals has drawn in the left-behinds of a changing society as word spread down the valley; the dreary, timid, shattered and unloved have swarmed up the lane to muddle about in this battalion of Luddites and seek some tangible validation by throwing valley mud at the ancient farmhouse.

The huge stone has fallen short, into the outer side of the barricade, flinging timber back onto the mob itself and causing a row within the ranks. One man is hit by a heavy picket and grabs it to turn on the hulking brute who threw the stone. A few start yelling that 'us workers are always our own worst enemy' and are themselves the target of others' inchoate anger, or desire to just carry on with the troublemaking: against anyone... it doesn't matter anymore...

As the day draws on, the focus shifts and slides and shifts again; Jenner, the dead man, and all of them are adrift in an eddy of time that stretches out of reach. Grabbing for the imagined safety net of status quo, instead they press their palms against an entrapping web that bends under their feet and rises to smother their faces; they dangle and twist in space, entangled in unsettling progress. A war would be preferable to the new order of things; you knew where you were with a war. Throwing, pushing, being one of a crowd, fighting something: feels better, traditional; easy. It's peace that's difficult.

John, Mich, and the rest of the longhairs have moved their stance over the hours from defenders to gatekeepers to watchers. The mob, leaderless and misdirected, is turning in on itself, thrashing and swirling about the lane as strangers fight locals, neighbours end—or start—personal vendettas in a mess of punching and shouting, frightened of losing their footing in this unfamiliar world. If shouting for the pillorying of witches will make them feel safer, then here they are, shouting for the pillorying of a witch.

But for all the throwing and shoving and yelling, no witch appears.

The dozen or so longhairs stand down; some tend the sheep, or return to their own work and homes, some bring tea and buttered bread to the lately besieging crowd. In the hard valley, no-one has firm stone beneath their feet. The angry have no focus. The curious have no satisfaction. The tribe has no headman. A sit-in: not the tear-gassed rage of Ohio University or the bloodied streets of Northern Ireland, just Myfanwy's Welsh cakes and a brew of tea, the bandaging of bruised knuckles and silent acknowledgement of this unfamiliar place they occupy. Something has flexed here: the red dragon sleeping underhill has yawned awake, causing the lane to flinch under the mob's boots like a pulled blanket.

Disquieted to see their fear confirmed in each other's faces by the slanting afternoon light, the farmers and schoolboys and layabouts fall slowly silent, sip their tea, nod to the long-hairs as they leave the drained cups on a stone, walk away a few yards to piss in the bushes, then shuffle down the lane. One stops to press a few stones back into place in the bank, a smidgen of repair.

Those of the valley itself shuffle off home. Others make it as far as the pub or the smokes shop, or hang round the Ponty garage, for there's an unsettlement in them now. And the unsettlement spreads like smoke haze, thick and thin, up and down; from Varteg to Panteg and Y Allt, there's a dissatis-faction in boots and a scritch down spines... the very chalk in the schoolteacher's hand niggles as it crosses the blackboard; the workers' tools, the roadmenders' shovels, are all deserving of blame.

Shuffle. Niggle. Scritch, scritch, scritch.

-oOo-

Each valley home too is in turmoil; wives are talking. To each other, of course; who else?

They know where their men are and guess pretty closely what they're about. The women have their minds turned to-wards the events of yesterday too, and not just because WPC Davies's mother has called into Protheroe's. But since she's there...

'No name then; fancy... How could it be we never seen him come past?' Querulous Younger Miss P puts great store by names and has indeed bestowed them on all her favourite household items; Elder Miss P had to learn that 'Cindy' meant the broom and 'Polly' was the kettle, and 'Mary Rose'... well, Mary Rose was a private matter.

'*Ie*, no name or necktie, as my old mam'd have said' says Mrs Barry and everyone nods sagely; it's true, she would have.

'Well,' Mrs Davies feels she has the authority to dispense information. 'He was well dressed, and young; a shame, such a tidy young man. Maybe only thirty, at tops. But yes, no papers. Nor name on his watch.'

'And where is he now? The body I mean. I suppose the rest of him's in heaven, isn't it?' Miss Protheroe is keen to keep the chat going; sales of sugar and Parisian essence have been steady all morning, as her customers look to justify lingering in the shop.

'Mmmm. In Heaven, isn't it?' several murmur together. There's a rustling of hair nets and curlers as they draw together over this consideration.

'Well, to be hoped, poor man.' From Elder Miss P.

'Ohhh,' again the chorus. The headscarves and handbags droop in concern and doubt. Someone buys a packet of baking powder.

'But what if he's not seen off, like?' Miss Protheroe has an idea. Unusually well-nourished as a child by her shopkeeper parents, Maris Protheroe has been prone to ideas her whole life; she is a spinster as a natural consequence of having ideas, but a contented one. 'What if they never do, and he's just buried like? Or the crematorium! What if he's just in Morriston crem and no-one to see him off, like? There's worse than lying in the Ty Merched brambles, even on a cold night. We could do it though, right?'

Mrs Dai Davies, not to be outdone by her sister-in-law, sees a chance to join in: 'Whatever do you mean, Maris? He's nought to do with us.'

'I mean... I mean, we could do a seeing off for the poor man. We could send him off proper like; you know... have a song or two, and a bit of afternoon tea. I mean, he came all this way from... somewhere... to die by here, he might have expected us to do the seeing off, like.'

'I doubt he expected to die here. Did he?' All faces follow Maris's eyes and turn to Mrs Davies, Mother Of The WPC. 'Did he? Was it, you know, do they think... did he commit, you know... sewage pipe?'

The thought is too awful. Mrs Dai Davies buys a packet of hair dye in her distraction.

-oOo-

In the close room above the Ty Merched kitchen, the women have long ago collapsed into silence, unable to leave the room; they've never shared such a space and such an experience, and they have no idea how to manoeuvre within this bubble without breaking it.

Myfanwy wonders who is keeping the kitchen fire going. Lizzie wonders where is the authority she once assumed was hers? Sarah Maud wonders who it is that's getting closer.

# Chapter 8

# Dydd Gwener the second

Jenner is not able to get out of bed. The nuns say she must stay until she recovers, but the longer she stays in this shady room the less she can move. Her skin is as pale as frost, and almost as cold. She shivers in her sleep, blown by the first gusts of some approaching storm. The usual care and medicines are ineffectual, and the nuns wring their hands and draw their veiled heads together and count off their prayer beads. The mother superior prefers to consult the doctor.

'I can find nothing wrong with her. And yet, I can see there's everything wrong with her.' The doctor tucks the head of her stethoscope in the neck of her dress, warms it on a matronly breast, then listens to the girl's breathing again. 'Nothing. Everything.' The doctor mentally counts off her prayer beads. 'Keep an eye.' she advises, as she drives away. The nuns keep a rota of eyes on Jenner, but she continues to fade.

At mid-morning a bunch of flowers is found by Jenner's bedside. No-one knows where it came from, which could have been unsettling in this closed community. But the air is sweet with the smell of blossom, and eglantine buds have lit Jenner's cheeks with their flush of pink. Her head is turned towards the posy. Forget-me-nots reach out to trace her eyelids with blue veins, and her brow relaxes. She smiles in her sleep. Her shivering stops, a breezy meadow falling still in sunlight. Novice Jane thinks she sees a woman in a raincoat walking out the drive but when Mother Superior asks for a description, it seems the novice cannot recall the woman's height, or colouring, or even her age.

'There was a small dog in one of her raincoat pockets.' offers Jane. Mother Superior notes in her book that Jane could do with more sleep.

Before even the lunchtime cawl is begun to get hot on the stove, the sergeant arrives. And he is positive Jenner is not from round here.

'I've had a report.' He hopes to tantalize the nuns, but they are unimpressed; they've long ago dealt with bigger news. 'We've found where she's from. There's been a murder. Murder!' His emphatic breath reaching clear across the big desk and into the mother superior's sharp face is not helping anyone.

'Well, this child hasn't been murdered,' points out Mother Superior, almost tenderly; she is trying to manage her unchristian annoyance.

'No, not her; not her the body. Her the murderer! There's an APB came over the radio, from Pontardawe. We're to look out for a child.' The sergeant reads from his notebook. 'Any girl not from round ... hereabouts.' he finishes, by way of variety.

Mother Superior looks at the uniform before her. Her childhood bible stories, of the baby Jesus and the persecution of infants, wake from slumber in her mind; she sees Herod sitting across from her desk, hears the tramp of soldiers' leather sandals along the bluestone streets of Llandovery, smells the blood of the Innocents on the damp spring air. 'The child has left...' she is out of practice at lying. 'The child has left us. Almost. She's ... dying...' She simultaneously knows this is not true, and fears it is. Or, if not true a moment ago, will be true now that she's spoken the word. 'And you haven't given me evidence of anything.' Now she sees she has undermined her first statement; what evidence could raise the girl from death? Surely nothing within this philistine's say-so, or there is no God.

'Dying? Well, I don't care.' The Llandovery sergeant has a lot to prove to his superiors and especially to DS Watcyns to whom he owes a massive favour, according to DS Watcyns. The Llandovery sergeant's inner vision is filled with the image of DS Watcyns. 'There's an order for her arrest.' He swoops a folded paper from his inner pocket and lays it on the mother's desk. The world sinks with the weight of it. 'I have brought the car, and backup.'

Back-up. For a child. Against nuns. *Forgive me, Lord, but this man is lower than the worms' bellies.* Mother Superior asks for tea to be brought, and commences to read the warrant slowly. Then it is time for midday prayers. The sergeant must wait.

Mother Superior is surprised at herself. Not at her obstruction, for she lived her childhood under the constant threat of Irish bailiffs. Not at her imperturbability, for she has dealt with devious sinners all her life. But at the groundless folly, the deep-felt hope, the act of faith, that whoever left the flowers will come back and fetch Jenner off. That, if she leaves the window open somehow Jenner's paper-pale body will float away. That somehow, if she can stall this man long enough, Jenner will find a place of safety.

At one o'clock, three policemen enter the small room where Jenner sleeps. They fill the space: six-feet tall clods of earth in hobnail boots, ceiling-high oafs in navy twill. Stooping over the bed like all the nightmares ever drawn, all three attempt to pick up the unconscious girl. After much fumbling and shuffling about, one of the three wraps the blanket around Jenner and carries her out in his arms. Glancing down to check she hasn't slipped weightlessly to the floor like a length of white silk, he trips on the carpet but instinctively rolls his upper body sideways against the wall, keeping the child steady. He might have been carrying the crown of Wales. Or a tray of beers on a Friday night.

He'll never carry a tray of beers again without thinking of this. He will resign his job within the month.

Behind him down the wide convent hallway comes an indoor parade. The sergeant jangles the car keys with metallic authority. The other officer, a clumsy farmer's son, tries to hide the mud on his boots, and not step too hard on the threadbare carpets. The nuns, led by Mother Superior, have mouths shut tight, eyes alert to every moment.

Jenner is laid across the back seat of the police car. Jane pushes her arm in the door before it closes, slips the posy of flowers from her sleeve and tucks it under Jenner's blanket. The car drives away, no sirens are sounding. The farmer's son stays by the convent gate, guarded, guarding. The nuns stay on the driveway for as long as it takes to say a rosary while, indoors, the kitchen fire dies down, unattended; the cawl thickens and goes cold again on the stove. Jenner's notebook has fallen behind the bed and been forgotten.

The car turns south out of the town. The Pontardawe road follows the valley floor for a while, through smaller and smaller villages, low with moss; skirting the legend-towns of Myddfai and Bethlehem, it turns south-east past the ancient earthworks and hill forts of this embattled country. The broken crown of Carreg Cennen's castellated ruins peers darkly first in the front windows, then on their left, then in the rear window, as the car follows the road that writhes across the floodplain before bunching itself like a leaping pony and springing up the north escarpment of the Black Mountain, past the limestone quarry—once murderous and now a place of picnics and wildflower hunts—and over the high blwch, chill and windswept under a vast sky, to where the cotton-grass bends over the peat bogs and the face of God frowns in the windscreen at the officers in their pranked blue and white car while through the rear window the sunlight taps on Jenner's passive body. As the valleys spread away to the horizon in all directions, the peaked giants, Pen Y Fan, Corn Ddu and Fan Fawr, show their cold shoulders, turn their icy heads away into the clouds in disgust. Beyond sight of the officers, the peaty waters of Llyn Y Fan Fach turn black, a whirlpool sucks all light down, shreds the surface; a brace of German tourists is startled from their ambling walk into a run, and they hurry to Llandeusant for loud company and a pint by the fire of the Red Lion.

Ammanford and the mines' black scars can be glimpsed through creases in the folded hills as the car winds down the cliff-hugging road while, a thousand feet below the passenger's door, ponies clomp and stumble over granite sand and peat bog to race to the cattle grid. As the car rolls past, the ponies look carefully in the back seat at the still sleeping girl; they snort hot breath on the window glass, they paw the ground anxiously. They get a berating from the nearby sheep, who swear they would never have left her alone in the first place.

'All well and good,' the ponies breathe, 'but she didn't ask you, now did she?'

The car slips down into Brynamman, and swings left down Arthur's valley to follow the canal into Pontardawe. DS Watcyns is waiting for them.

He has sent no more officers to study the site of the murder, or to keep the mob away. He has sought and followed no leads. He has no interest in any gangs, scritchy with discontent, now moving across the landscape even as the weather turns threatening. He has spent the day blocking up the holes in what he calls 'evidence'. He has no interest in evidence, only in arrests; the easier the better. And there's little easier than getting a phone call in the night, from a publican, after the pubs have closed. There is a witness: a witness of unquestionable probity.

The police station is located, unusually, well off the high street and close to the trouble spots of a hundred years ago, now abandoned ground and quiet streets. DS Watcyns likes it so, out of the common paths. As the Llandovery car arrives Jenner is stirring awake, revived by the sun's warmth on her face, and she walks the few steps from the street into the charge desk, wrapped in the convent's white wool blanket and clutching the posy of wilting wildflowers. Were the bricks and walls to fall away, the police station to disintegrate and the teacups and pencils fly upwards, the streets and foundries and mines to be unmade, to rise as dust into the sky and sink as grit into the river, the town to return—past night flashes of bombs, mine blasts and campfire, past snow and bluebells and apples and snow again under sun and scudding cloud, past returning troops, blacklegs, huddled refugees, chilled invaders —to the forest and field and sacred stones, leaving only Jenner standing in the same homespun white wool and with the same hedgerow posy as time spooled away down a thousand, fifteen hundred, two thousand years she would ever still be recognised for what she is right now: a child-bride of misfortune, a virgin sacrifice to the knives of rumour.

As she sags against the high desk, the child disappears from the view of the admitting officer behind it. 'Where is she?' he asks.

'Where am I?' she asks. But no one bothers to answer. Jenner is put in a police cell. The sun falls into afternoon. Shadows spread.

-oOo-

A sudden storm has blown down from the mountains, and rain is squalling off fields and stones and pavements all across the southern valleys, when PC Jones makes his way into the Ty Merched yard and kitchen doorway. He holds his hands before him; he holds his discomfort up like a shield, or a warning sign: *rough surface ahead*... 'Mrs Coombe?' he calls into the kitchen but sees only a few strangers, startling women with long hair and rainbow clothing. Although a bright fire and a smell of baking feels reassuring.

One of them steps forward to the doorway; it is Mich. 'What is it?'

'Mrs Coombe inside, is she? I need to speak with her.'

'Wait.' Mich nudges the door slightly closed. She turns and ascends in a way that would be alarming to anyone unfamiliar with the sudden stairs of these old houses. The two other women watch him ambivalently from their places by the sink, the pantry door. John can be seen passing the windows as he dodges the rain; Jones feels surrounded. He fills in time by breathing, coughing, breathing again.

Myfanwy appears down the stairs, clumping and frightened-angry; settles into herself when she sees who it is. 'Mr Jones, is it? Have you come to sort out those rioters? Never have I ever seen such a thing and no-one to order it away.'

'Has there been some trouble here? I didn't know. No. No, I've come to say we have, apparently, I mean we have your...' Jones is unsure of the relationships within the house, gropes for the words. 'We have a child. We've found the child that...'

'Jenner? Jenner? You've found her, ah...' Myfanwy looks to-wards the door as if the policeman might have left Jenner wait-ing out on the step like a parcel from the shop. Lizzie hurries from the hallway; she half-heard a name.

'Jenner? Where is the child, is she alright?' Lizzie demands.

'I have to tell you she is in custody. She has been charged with the murder of person unknown. You are to, one of you is allowed to bring a change of clothes and identify the... pris-oner. As she has no... driver's licence or identifying papers.'

Jones finishes in a fog of words. Sarah Maud has followed Lizzie, roused by hearing Myfanwy shout Jenner's name, and the old kitchen is suddenly claustrophobic. The women shuffle towards each other at this appalling news, then apart as Sarah Maud flinches away, beats her fists weakly against her forehead, gasps for air. She pushes past the policeman and outside; disappears into the late afternoon rain. Mich and her friends go after. The room is hollowed out, but the tension remains.

Lizzie hears herself insisting that she go with Jones. But it is Myfanwy who loads a satchel with clothes and shoes, only to empty the lot—on Jones's insistence—into a bundle of paper and string in case the satchel contains jail-breakers' tools; Myfanwy who clambers into the back seat of the squad car and rolls along the lane and down into the cauldron of Pontardawe. She looks for but doesn't see Sarah Maud anywhere.

But Myfanwy and the squad car are seen by the Perry women, home from the shop. The Younger Miss P calls out in astonishment from her advantageous seat in the window overlooking the lane:

'Oh! Oh! Now they've arrested Myfanwy Ty Merched!'

'Never!' says the Elder P, from the blind spot by the stove.

'No, but they have! I just saw her go by, and in the squad car. So!'

Elder P just looks at Younger P.

'Ah no, of course you're right. She'd never be that interesting...' Younger P sighs and returns to her magazine. Elder P comes over and kisses her forehead, strokes her fair hair.

'Tell me again.' says Elder P, 'What was that idea you had for us, about the memorial? Du; let's make it lovely.' They settle into the window seat, wriggling together to get comfy. Soon they'll need to put the light on and draw the curtains; so they won't see Myfanwy returning home, her face frozen, her hands trembling in her lap.

-oOo-

A nervous woman walks out from the Pontardawe bus station, as the departing bus continues its winding climb up the valley; blonde, thin, maybe 24 or 26 years of age, she carries herself like she's not used to being looked at but is trying to learn. A dress and jacket home-made but copied from a stylish magazine, a green velvet scarf, gloves and a smart green beret. Under the glove on her left hand, a new gold ring. On her arm, a handbag of no particular style. In the handbag, her new husband's wallet sits shyly against her purse, a hotel key, and a mid-priced lipstick. She looks into every shop, and at every man's face, and she doesn't find what she's looking for. Distracted and lost, the young woman makes her way to the end of the high street, where it dwindles into a lane near the pub by the bridge. A group of children spill out of a hedge to block her path. The dozen or so boys are around eight or ten years of age, gaunt and manic-eyed; their leader is a tall girl, thick legs and strong neck but weak in the head; maybe fifteen years old, she can't write her own name but that's not important; she is fearsome in schoolyard battles. Indeed, conflict is the only thing she enters the schoolyard for.

'I likes your scarf, Miss.' It's almost a challenge.

'Oh, yes, thanks. It's a present. From my fian—... from my husband.' The woman must catch her breath. 'Can you help me please? Are you local to here?'

'Ydw. Yass. You're not, but.' Another challenge: don't try to trick me, foreigner!

'No, we're here, well, Swansea, on our honeymoon. But, I've lost, umm, I've lost my way.' She considers the grubby knees and hard knuckles of these children. 'We were to meet yesterday here in Ponter, Pontay... but I got held up at my stupid cousins' and I was late and he'd left his wallet but he wasn't...

'—she is aware she's talking too fast— 'Can you direct me to the police station, please? I don't know this place, Ponter-whatsit'

The children, if that's the right word for them, look silently at her handbag. Except the large girl, whose eye is still caught in the green velvet scarf.

'If you could show me the way to the police station, I'll give you...' the woman opens her bag, leaves her fingers dangling uncertainly at the clasp of her purse inside.

'Sure' says the large girl. 'Follow me, I'll shows ya' and she leads the way, around the pub and under the bridge. Towards the waste ground up-river. A week later, when the woman revives in Morriston Hospital, she won't be able to write her own name either; she has lost her memory, along with her wedding ring and the sight from one eye. A handbag of no particular style is quietly filling with river weed as it jiggles under a snag in the neglected canal; it contains an empty purse, a mid-price lipstick, a hotel key, and a man's wallet with his driving licence but no cash. The green velvet scarf is snug round a large girl's thick neck.

-oOo-

Sarah Maud is in the pub. She has again had too much rum and black and not enough soup and bread. Her bandages are coming loose under her sleeves, her eyes roll low from side to side; she cannot hold her head up easily. Llundain John is asleep from his long days in her barn and tonight he will not get her home. Gwyn is smiling to himself, and the men hugging the bar are studying the darts schedules, the announcement of last Christmas's charabanc tour, the erratically lettered plastic price board; no-one wants to think about recent events; well, not out loud, anyway. Later Sarah Maud will fall asleep in the lane for a while, until the cold dawn wakes her, an urchin under a hedge.

# Chapter 9

# Dydd Sadwyn the second

By the shop, women in their second-best hats are queuing for the early bus to Swansea; they are as talkative as ever, but today the conversations are all spiralling round the same topic. For Mrs Barry is calling on the vicar—du, but she's had a lot of social mileage from that daytrip to Abergavenny.

To all appearances, Reverend Morgan is ruminating over a well-thumbed bible as he prepares tomorrow's sermon, the light of God gilding the pages in this sunny corner of the vicarage garden; even so he wears light gloves and a long coat against the morning chill. Certainly, Zipporah Barry thinks the Reverend is deep in thought as she pushes open the gate. 'Reverend! Such a morning!' she calls as she steps carefully on the damp slate flags of the path. She has her best shoes on; and a well-flowered hat that almost matches.

In fact, Reverend Morgan has acquired a fear of the dark and its new tenebrous inhabitants, and had sat awake all night hearing, listening, shivering; the shadows of his drear, celibate bedroom were full of urgent whispers and shifting pressures that hurt his ears, dragged at his belly and challenged his balance. Now he's sleeping in the welcome safety of this patch of sunlight and nods his head unconsciously.

'And how do we find you this morning? Such a day, wasn't I just saying to Mr Barry! The women of the valley, now; they've asked me to come and speak to you. Not my way to put myself forward I'm sure you know it, but they did insist...' Mrs Barry settles onto the bench opposite the reverend's deck chair, but her habitual coyness in the presence of the bachelor cleric has precluded her from noticing he is in fact still asleep, and her long-winded simpering has only helped to keep him so, '... and far be it from me to deny my help be it ever so little that poor I can offer, especially in such a good cause as in this case...'

The vicar sleeps on.

'... so we would like to use the church hall. Tomorrow. After service.' As a regular donor to the funds appeal, Mrs Barry sees no reason for the customary '*os gwelwch yn dda*' and the lack of such a cue as 'please' —in either Welsh or English—fails to alert the dozing man that something was being expected of him. 'You will be there? To add some gravitas, isn't it?'

The vicar mumbles.

'Pardon, Reverend? I said you will be there? We'll see you tomorrow?' Zipporah's voice rises in volume, she peers uncertainly at the vicar's face for the first time. There's a smell of heavy spirits hanging round the vicar; something about being unusually close to him makes her grimace a little and draw back. 'Reverend Morgan? Twdr Morgan? I said, Twdr, you will be there tomorrow?

The reverend snorts awake, the dream-dust of his childhood's recurring nightmare muffling his ears. 'Yes, yes!' he blinks as the face of Mrs Barry swims into focus while the bloated ghost of his rampant father, bullying brother, recede. 'Hu-hem! Yes, Mrs Barry. Tomorrow; of course.'

'And we'll need the keys today, please. Do you have them here?'

'Keys, Mrs Barry? Chapel will be unlocked before service, as always.' He struggles to sit upright in the canvas deck chair, and his bible slips from his lap to the grass, falling opening at a red silk bookmark.

'No, Reverend; for the hall. Not the chapel, no; the hall. To rehearse, isn't it.' This is harder than she had expected. Mrs Barry starts over. 'The women of the valley, now; they've asked me to come and speak to you...' but falters as she focuses on some startling doodles in the margins of his bible. Blushing, she clutches her handbag tighter and carries on. The vicar snaps the book shut. He is still not listening, not really.

The hall key is found under a pair of muddy leather gloves in the scullery, and Mrs Barry hurries on her way. As soon as the door swings closed behind her, the reverend scrubs out the rowdy marginalia of his bible with a piece of stale bread, glancing up once to notice, through the window, that the sun has been clouded over again.

He returns to sleep, indoors by the electric fire. He dreams his nightmare again, only this time it is Twdr who holds the whip.


-oOo-


By the Ty Merched yard, the lane is empty of movement. Scattered clods of earth lie where they were thrown against the fences and walls; some hang suspended in the hedge-row branches, more are flattened under boot prints. The bank they were torn from is as dishevelled as a rugby pitch turned side-on. Cigarette butts, a rag of someone's shirt cuff, and the WPC's whistle—clogged with mud— are visible among the kicked-about litter covering the road. The hippies, in the communal spirit of their kind, have tidied away the stones and rubbish and barricade, reset the fenceposts as best they can, and left the air thick with bitter-sweet smoke.

In the barn Sarah Maud is wobbling through her duties with the sheep. Sarah Maud is running on automatic, an abandoned engine rolling down a shallow slope. A casual observer might think she has forgotten her child.

Lizzie is trying to help, but the skill has slipped from her fingers these past days; what she knows is losing its connection to how she moves, and she is surprised to find, again and again, that she's sitting on a bail of straw, her mind a dark blank, when the last thing she remembers is going to help Sarah Maud with this or that small task. The stillness is soothing after the strife of yesterday and the expectation of more police intrusion at some point. Lizzie is surprised—angered— at how little investigation is being done; though she is growing in rage and frustration at any mention of DS Watcyns and his actions, following the report Myfanwy has brought back from Ponty, surely there must be some more activity to be endured; some proof to be hunted down that will exonerate Jenner, find where the real guilt lies?

The quietness is framed by the occasional bleating of a new lamb, the shuffling of a sheep in the hurdles, or Sarah Maud clattering a bucket in the feed bin. Lizzie takes a ragged breath. She stares out the doors to where a robin is nest-building in the ivy: surely that's a good sign. She breathes deeply to release the tightness from her chest, and sees some silvereyes flitting by the chicken coop...

Has she dozed? The sun is veiled by thickening cloud, and the air is turning chill, even while the quiet remains deep and unruffled.

'Sarah Maud? Do you need any help? I might get us a brew of tea if you're alright for a minute...' Lizzie speaks over her shoulder, while still watching the pair of silvereyes with tired contentment. The birds peck away at the mud, where bread-crumbs are plentiful after the closing moments—the awkward sharing of tea and cake—of the day before. How like the valley it is, to end a row with tea. And cake. She smiles for the first time in days, watching the birds tussle over a raisin and waiting to see who wins. It is the one with the largest white rim round its eyes that carries off the prize. Their small chirrupings fade, leaving silence. 'Sarah Maud? Where are you at, dwt?'

Her eyes still adjusting from the yet-bright sky, Lizzie can't make out the shapes when she turns to peer into the gloom of the barn, but she can tell there is nothing moving.

Myfanwy is alerted by Lizzie yelling and comes sour and disapproving to the kitchen door. Myfanwy is all finished with shouting, forever if possible. Her sleep was shredded by worry for Jenner and what she'd seen in the Ponty police cell. In her dreams she searched through rushes and *rhos*, tore her hands looking for a key, a sign, a door; she ran uphill with grey hounds behind a grey king; she cried for her failures until the pillowcase stuck to her plain sad cheek.

'What is it?' she calls, but Lizzie isn't visible. Myfanwy goes to the barn door where Lizzie is bent over the shape of Sarah Maud prone in the straw. Sees Lizzie cwtching Sarah Maud in a nestling embrace and whispering to soothe. Myfanwy opens her mouth and the wrong words come.

'Why did you always hate me? Always. You were never this kind to me.'

'What?'

'Why did you hate me?'

'I never hated you, bach. I just didn't want you.' Lizzie doesn't look up. 'Can you fetch some help here? Don't just stand gawping, woman, your daughter is hurt.'

But Myfanwy was a daughter herself, before ever she was a mother. She turns and goes back inside the house. Lizzie closes her eyes. Accidental truth has undermined her. She whispers 'Shhhh now, it'll be alright,' and she cannot be certain who she's hoping to comfort.

Mich finds them there, Lizzie stiff and numb with cold and crouching, Sarah Maud's dress dark with muck and water from the barn floor. Sarah Maud is put in a warming bath by the sisterly Mich, while in the kitchen Lizzie and Myfanwy cannot hold each other's eye.

Soon, 'We're low on tea' says Myfanwy and reaches for her hat and coat.

'Myfanwy—' Lizzie starts. But the door is shut on her before she has figured out what to say. She gets up to stretch her knees again, lays a hand on an unopened packet of tea that sits on the pantry shelf. The outer door opens again, and Lizzie is caught in the pantry doorway.

'Shut up!' Myfanwy comes abruptly back into the kitchen. 'Shut up.' Her face is inches from Lizzie's. They can see the old skin of each other, smell the soap and talc, feel Lizzie's heat, Myfanwy's chill. 'Just... just shut up. Nothing you can say. Shut up.' And Myfanwy is gone again.

Myfanwy walks the lane like she's stepping on expired obligations.

The shop is crowded, for the bus from Swansea has not long disgorged its final passengers with their baskets and string bags. The women are clustered in close little groups that break apart and reform anew in flurries of words and gestures. Myfanwy enters and there is sudden, sharp silence. All eyes are turned away. She stalls in the doorway.

'Maris,' she nods to the proprietress. There's a murmur of agreement through the crowd, for that is Maris's name, yes. Myfanwy knows these people, sees she is out of the loop, intruding on something. 'Oh, I wanted some tea but now I think about it...'

'You had half a pound from me just last week.' says Maris, careful to keep everyone on side. 'Isn't it?' she nudges.

'Du. What am I thinking? I'll call another time... *Bore da...*' Myfanwy can barely get the farewell out, so hasty is her retreat.

The shop bell dings in the silence behind her. But once out-side, under the slanting afternoon light and the high chill air and the vast architecture of the clouds, Myfanwy stands by the crossroad a long while. Not wanted at home, not welcome in the shop, she reviews why life is so small and mean and besmirched, ticks the points off on her fingers until she has it settled in her mind where the fault lies. It's not with her.

Behind her, the shop is quiet. It is unspoken but agreed: their plan excludes the family at Ty Merched. The women wait till Myfanwy has moved off before any leave for their own homes. Some few link arms and head towards the chapel hall, heads together and singing quietly, occasionally breaking into dispute over pitch or lyrics. Over the western ridge a low cloud bank has rolled in over the hilltops and now spills down into the afternoon shadow at the bottom of the valley; a dragon's breath before sunset, draining away to Ponty. Out of sight, someone's laugh on the cooling air; someone's sigh.

-oOo-

Down in the Pontardawe police station, there is muttering. Free of the DS's caustic weekday presence and vicious, suspicious eyes, the weekend shift is fidgeting about the tearoom, the locker room, the corridors. The officers are anxious about the welfare of the strange child in the cells; they're unhappy about the lack of progress of the investigation and the invisibility of the reasons for her arrest. There isn't any evidence. There isn't even a name. Just a man on a tray in a fridge in Swansea. But they also feel powerless to stand against DS Watcyns. He has the longest tenure of any in the force, and threads run from his stubby fingertips through the entire South Wales Constab-ulary with a pervasiveness that would surprise even the most senior. He's a gross idle bastard, but a cunning one.

PC Jones is suffering yet another weekend shift, punishment for some unknown slight to the DS; or maybe not, maybe just that Watcyns is a small-minded poisonous toad who likes to test his powers, 'Working Time Directives' be hanged. PC Jones hasn't had a day off in three weeks. But today, it feels a good thing, so at least he knows how the child is being treated.

Jenner will not eat or drink anything. The morning sun had woken her a bit and she had roused to ask again where she was, and to take some porridge and milk with wide-eyed distress at the strange men all watching her through cell bars; but now the room is in shadow and she has curled under the blanket, crushing the tatty posy into her crossed arms. Jones is unable to answer her question about a dog, nor was it mentioned in the Llandovery officer's report.

Jones goes looking for the post-mortem report; it hasn't arrived. He checks the paperwork; no post-mortem has been scheduled. The duty officer is watching him but gives no clue as to allegiances. Jones looks in the folder for the site examination documents. They seem to have had tea spilt on them. He holds the illegible page up to the duty officer, who shrugs noncommittedly before returning to his newspaper. This is not the first time Jones has checked through his DS's paperwork and found it wanting; but in a murder case, he had hoped for more rigour; there was no rigour at all. A pencilled note, 'Witnessed it!!!' in heavy capitals and underlined three times, seems insufficient.

Jones considers phoning WPC Davies and asking her advice... he glances up as the first rays of sunset reflect off the eastern valley walls and shed a dark gold, formed more of shadow than light, through the station windows, to the cell doors.

'Hello?'

Jones hears the girl's repeated call, goes to the door and looks through the bars.

'Yes? What is it?'

'Hello.' A few dapples of reflected light shine on Jenner's foot as it hangs over the edge of the cot; improbably, she smiles. 'Can I have some paper and a pencil, please?'

-oOo-

Sarah Maud sits cross-legged in her birds' nest of a bed, with a tea tray nestled between her knees. She lifts a spoon, she opens her mouth, but forgets to connect the two. The spoon hangs mid-air in her hand, trembles, then sinks back down to the plate. She hasn't seen Jenner for days and she had meant to be such a good mother. She can remember that: she had meant to be a good mother; but she is failing to remember what that was going to look like: something about touch and song and... looking each other in the eye, yes; recognition. Care, in heart. Strength, in... Words form in her head. She looks for a pencil and paper to get them out, but as she reaches towards her bedside table, the tray tips off her lap and the boiled egg in its willow pattern cup rolls down and onto the floor, trailing a tail of yellow yolk like an incoming comet in the shadows; thin strips of toast spill onto the quilt and leave a buttery stain overlaying older buttery stains. Sarah Maud slides back into somnolence as she watches the drizzle of yolk turn opaque, solidify, and crack into a dozen tiny lengths. When she next wakes from a doze, the house is silent.

The house is too silent. Sarah Maud has been feeling more frightened of late, frightened of being alone; she's aware that the old fears have snuck back into her head. She gets up and puts trousers and shirt over her nightdress, and steps carefully out into the yard. There's a bruise on her hip, and she limps to protect that leg. Her bare feet flinch in the gravelly mud, and she remembers there's a pair of Lizzie's old galoshes in the shed, so Sarah Maud heads there before slipping out the yard gate and into the lane, where there is just enough light to walk by. The waxing moon is overhead.

Myfanwy in her room, and Lizzie in hers, do not hear Sarah Maud leave. Mich standing outside her stationary bus on the hill does not see Sarah Maud leave, although her empathy to Sarah Maud's fractured affection usually keeps her attuned to the slightly older woman's movements. But Mich is looking across the darkening valley to where unusual activity has the church hall at its centre. And she can hear scraps of music on the air, from one place and another. John comes out with two mugs of tea.

'What do you make of this?' She smiles as she takes the proffered mug.

'What?... Oh... Ooohh.'

They lean against each other's arm, look down and around at the lights in house doorways, the people moving along the tracks or clustering in the lanes, the drifts of music and song.

'*Ach!* In all my years. Well, I never.'

'Ha! I dunno what accent you think you sound like, but it's not Welsh!' Mich laughs aloud and turns out of the descending cold and into the bus for a smoke by the stove. John glances at the sky for a moment then follows her, ducking under the doorway. He doesn't notice the stars are pooling and reforming into constellations older than those European newcomers; that the stars are dancing across dark space.

When he next steps outside, the stars are all returned to their charted places, moving through the set pieces of a vast choreography as galaxies roll and suns dwindle. Below, he sees Reverend Morgan is at the crossroads again, moving past the streetlight's reach.

-oOo-

It is late; very late for a troubled woman who's had nothing more than a few cups of tea all day. Sarah Maud sits staring glass-eyed at her sockless, galoshered feet, limp and shivering by the pub's blazing pot belly stove. Gwyn has ticked up several drinks that never existed, and Sarah Maud feels she should go home if only she had that much volition, while her second rum and black' waits untouched on the table beside her.

The door opens. The usual quorum of drinkers is already at the bar; even so, they look at each other just to make sure it's not one of themselves, as you do.

''Evening, vicar.' Gwyn covers his surprise—two visits in a month! —by lifting a wine glass down from the rack and polishing its dusty foot. 'White, isn't it? On the house, vicar.' And, in a lowered voice, 'But not this house,' he winks as Reverend Morgan slips his wallet away unopened. Gwyn adds a tick to Sarah Maud's perfidious tab.

'Uncommon activity in the valley tonight!' suggests the vicar. The Quorum look at each other again, uncertainly. This pub-visiting vicar is an unsettling development.

'Ydu. Happen.' Jem mutters.

'It's the women, isn't it?' Mr Barry looks even deeper into his pint glass with the jaded eye of a habitually drowning man. 'My Zipporah's been up to summat with the women.' He paused a beat. 'All of 'em. Allus up to summat'. He returns to peers into the depths of beer-bubbled memory; his happy bachelor days lie wrecked at the bottom of every pint. No matter how much he drinks, they stay drowned, and he cannot retrieve them.

'Hmmm. She came to speak to me.' Thus, the reverend confirms Zipporah's long-winded account to her husband, earlier in the day. 'Now, what was it she was saying?...'

'The memorial, it'd have been, surely?' prompts Gwyn.

Reverend Morgan's eyes narrow under anxious brows. 'What memorial, remind me?'

'To the dead man by Ty Merched. They wants to send him off to heaven right.' Jem feels an element of ownership. For years to come, to his grandchildren's giggling confusion, Jem Jenkins will still talk about 'the day I found me body in Ty Merched.'

Morgan smells danger; feels something crawl up his spine and squeeze his ribs in fear, and stronger: in anger. This is not the way it will go: outside his control. This attention, no; attention on the body is wrong.

The reverend is just drawing a deep breath and is just about to object, just about to say that it cannot, must not happen. For aren't the dead his responsibility? Surely the dead are his dead; they belong to the church. The reverend is just rising from the stool to draw a breath and open his mouth to object, as their moral lodestone and guiding star...

... when Sarah Maud also rises, unsteadily, from her bench by the fire.

'Dewi?' she falters. She sways towards, then away from, the vicar. Her face is unreadable, her voice a croak. 'Dewi?' Her arm stretches towards him then recoils as if her fingers touched on something hot, or sacred, or foul. She stops in the middle of the room, bent at the waist to lean both towards, and aside from, Reverend Twdr Morgan. 'Dewi? Oh Dewi, I'm sorry, sorry. Where you been, my love?'

'I don't know what you're talking about, woman,' says Reverend Morgan, ripe with ire. For he and Sarah Maud have never met; she's never been to church since she was an infant—too restless, too noisy for Myfanwy to endure—and he's got no idea who this shabby drunk is. Only... when she repeats that name, he flinches ever so slightly, flushes red-cheeked then goes as waxen as one of his votive candles. The name flicks a whip in the back of his mind. Off-balance, he shifts to strike a more deliberately nonchalant pose but his foot slips awkwardly off the bar stool rung and he jerks upright. 'I said I don't know any Dewi.'

*Well, there's two lies in one breath,* think the pub ghosts, called away from their game of cribbage in the cellar by the crackling of tension in the bar. Pub ghosts have the longest memories.

Gwyn is polishing a glass. The other drinkers have stopped reading the charabanc tour notice one more time and are, as one, staring slack-jawed at Sarah Maud.

'Dewi, love. I waited I did, but you never came back. Why's you hurt me so, Dewi? When I said no, not there, not in the mud.' Sarah Maud talks slowly, carefully, but there is no other noise and even the fire has stopped muttering. 'Why did you do that when I loved you? Dewi, but I had our baby, didn't I? You didn't come back. Dewi? And. And I means to be a good mother, Dewi. I do. I loves her.' She shakes her head a little, as if to clear some dust from it. 'Only, well, she... she reminds me that you hurt me so. I wanted to be married, and yes, I will marry you, like you said we would, Dewi. But *nage*, cariad, not like that. In the mud, and then you gone. Not that...' Sarah Maud is gripping the bar with whitened knuckles. Edging closer to the vicar but still holding the bar.

The glass Gwyn is polishing cracks in his hands. Some of the Quorum breathe again.

'I'm not Dewi, that's not me, my name.' says Twdr Morgan. 'I don't know you, woman, I don't know who you are, and I have never seen you before this moment.' He backs towards the door, one arm raised before him with the hand palm out, fending off Sarah Maud, obstructing the things she's saying. '... Prince of the heavenly armies, defend me...' Muttering, he gestures to ward her off, glances at Gwyn and around the bar, then is gone.

Sarah Maud is marooned at the bar.

Gwyn hands her a drink unasked for; but before he marks the slate, someone in the Quorum clears their throat. Gwyn wipes one stroke off the slate. Another cough at the bar, louder. Gwyn wipes the slate clean, with a grunt and a nod. He had never reckoned on his customers watching. But of course they were always watching.

Sarah Maud coughs on the brandy; she holds the bar with her right hand, she shuffles her left foot, she cries soundlessly. There is a long—a very long—quiet moment.

'Well now,' says Mr Barry carefully, looking at the counter before him, 'that's one old question raised and answered in the same night.'

'But, he's not called Dewi.' Dai Jones, a relative newcomer now married into the valley, is only five years before the bar of the Rhiwfawr Arms.

Gwyn and Jem sneak a look at Sarah Maud, then at each other. 'David?' says Jem softly, and several nod in agreement: David, indeed; David. They know that David Morgan called himself Dewi... when he chose to.

'I never knew there was a David...' Voices are barely above the whisper of the fire.

'Dead, he is. Trouble. He was always into trouble, that one. Drove his father crazy though they were the spit of each other for temper and tamping. Some years back, it'd be... Oh, some years back, he lived by here...' Gwyn slides away from his calculations of years. 'Dewi, eh? Ydu, there's a bugger of a question and an answer in one night.'

They look again at Sarah Maud, lost in grief and hugging the empty glass to herself; she's as thin as a bad dream these days, and yet was a time, so beautiful no-one thought they might have dared to touch her...

The older men are slowly filtering through the memory cards in their beery brains, backwards from when Sarah Maud 'went awry' with the fatherless baby, back to the happier young woman, the girl they'd known; back when everyone was younger. Why didn't someone... at the time... was it all condemnation, wasn't there one friendly... well, but ... Du du du.

Gwyn checks the mantle clock. It's nearly 'time', and if John isn't here already, then he's not coming. 'Tell you what, Sarah Maud, how about Dai here walks you home? Would you do that now, Dai Jones?' Gwyn reaches over to pull the empty glass from Sarah Maud's locked hands.

'I'll come too,' offers Mr Barry, and soon all the Quorum is out the door, shuffling into their coats as they go, lighting cigarettes two off a match, and encircling Sarah Maud like a herd of old sheepdogs bumbling about the single sheep in their midst. She hasn't said another word since the vicar left, and remains silent, as the group is drawn down the lane by the thread of Jem Jenkin's torch light.

There are no lights on at Ty Merched. Jem knocks on the kitchen door, hears footsteps from the room above skittering about a moment in the dark, then coming down the stairs; lights come on. Jem slips behind the other men, as it just occurs to him that he might not be well received after all.

Myfanwy in a pink chenille dressing gown and her grey corduroy slippers is backlit by the kitchen light. 'For the gods' sake! Sarah Maud? I thought you were in—' Myfanwy moves sideways and the light streams out over Sarah Maud and the rotund forms of the nearest few chaperones. Myfanwy knows enough to see that everything is not right; these men would never come this far down the lane, and certainly not at this time of night without it being at the very least a war... 'Sarah Maud? What's happened. What is it?' She is unable to stop talking even after the men nod to her and turn away into the night, mumbling good night.

The outside door is closed and locked. Leaving Myfanwy to dither alone, Sarah Maud goes into her room, falls into bed. Later, when she wakes to go to the toilet, she finds the spilt egg and toast with her bare feet and is startled into tears, and hunger.

Alone in the pub, Gwyn is reviewing some recent conversations he's had with the vicar. Jenner has been much talked about by Morgan, and with sanctified venom; now the publican is reassessing everything he's heard, and said, and done. He locks the pub up carefully as ever but stays a while longer at a seat by the fire as it cools. Then climbing to the bedroom above, he starts talking to his sleeping wife, for he must share with someone. She wakes, ready to harangue, but this night she listens, and she doesn't say a word.

-oOo-

Twdr Morgan is pacing the pathless heights beyond Rhiwfawr. In the darkening moonset, under cliff and over stream, he navigates by the muttering in his ears, the chill fear in his backbone. His head, never strong when left to itself, is twisting in the push and pull of long-smothered conflicts: public family and unsafe family, duty and desire, loyalty and cowardice; vanity and the devils of his soul; vanity and fear and vanity. Before such a flagellation of the spirit, God flees in self-preservation.

With an audible snap, Morgan lets his mind go; this liberation is so much better, for now he can see the gates of glory.

# Chapter 10

# Dydd Sul the second

The tiny chapel is crowded this Sunday morning; every seat taken, every pew crammed, best-dressed shoulders rubbing against best-dressed. Any spaces along the side and back walls are rapidly filling up; feet are stepped on and hats are bumped awry. Someone drops a glove, and it stays dropped. The room is hot with the press of bodies.

Yet when Myfanwy enters, space is found around her, and she walks to her accustomed place with increasing dignity and discomfort, feeling everything is wrong but having no clue as to why. She has come alone; odd but not unusually so. Myfanwy would never dare miss a Sunday, for what would people think of her then?

Lizzie—whose chapel attendance had once sprung from a sense of high position in the valley— has announced she'd rather not see the vicar this side of Hell, and now waits to be helped into the squad car by PC Jones, before setting off to Ponty. And Sarah Maud, once too bright for the sombre chapel, then too clouded, is still in her room, pacing the littered floor and talking to herself, with the door locked hard.

Myfanwy sits in a small island of open space, a few inches of smooth oak pew either side of her. Since the mood at the shop two days ago, she has felt contaminated, but doesn't know by what. She can guess, but today she is wrong. She has never been so out of place in the only place she knows.

The men have all given over their seats to their straight-mouthed, Sunday-frocked women and line themselves thickly along the walls; the short nave holds the congregation as dark flowers nested in a black dish. The noise is steady, a low droning of distant warplanes, or the static when a radio dial has slipped off the station; a white noise of speculation so dreadful it goes beyond gossip. Myfanwy hears nothing clearly. When the congregation in front of her shifts, Myfanwy glimpses that Mrs Barry—the vicar's most loyal supporter— also has a cordon sanitaire around her, a few rows away. In the congregation, tongues move faster than a nest of grass snakes.

Myfanwy grows beyond discomforted, but she can't find the courage to retreat. She had thought she should be here, in defiance of the situation with Jenner, in defiance of the shame and rumour; show herself to say 'I'm here and it's right I am, a god-fearing valley woman.' Now, oh god, she thinks she was wrong to come. *They're talking about... And I can't answer to it. I can't.*

Red-eyed and crumpled, Reverend Morgan enters from the vestry to a crescendo of murmurs that collapses into inward-breathing anticipation as he begins an approximation of the usual rites, avoids all eye contact. He looks ill, thinks Myfanwy, before she's startled by the movement around her. All the women lean back and cross their arms, narrow their eyes; while all the men lean forward, and cross their arms, and narrow their eyes. The silence is total; there are no children here today. *This isn't about me!*

The reverend goes through the first stages of the service, and no-one moves, neither sits nor stands when they should; when the antiphon is reached, the silence remains unbroken. Reverend Morgan repeats his lines; the congregation does not answer. The very air is muffled, as if damp velvet was draped over every ear and mouth. No prayer books need to be opened, no throats need to be cleared, for no hymns will be sung here today.

The vicar tries again: 'Dearly beloved brethren...'

They do not identify.

'Dear brothers and sisters...'

They are not his siblings in Christ.

'Let us...'

'Tell us the truth now, Twdr.' Mrs Barry, ever the natural leader, and considering the moral fence a comfy place to sit for the best view. 'Truth, mind!'

'I'm sorry, Zipporah? We are all here for the Truth of God ...'

The chapel shivers with a righteous anger not a little tempered by the relish of pinning a hypocrite down...

'She means about Dewi,' chorus several voices along the back.

'...You old charlatan.' finishes one of them, solo.

'I ... My name isn't Dewi...'

'No. Maybe not. But you know who's was.' Mr Barry has stepped forward into the aisle, from his place in the back line. Dai Spuds, a teetotaller and lately come to the news, stands beside him, frowning so intensely that his eyes and neck have virtually disappeared with indignation.

'No.' Reverend Morgan. Shifting his stance off the red altar carpet in a twinge of guilt at bearing false witness while actually standing by the altar, he perforce gets close to the foremost chapel elders in the front pews. Torn between the theoretical wrath of his god and the living coldness he feels radiating from the front pews, he slips back onto the carpet again.

'What was it David was doing here anyway, back in '58, '59? He had no business here.' challenges Dai Spuds. 'Ach, I remember him then, a bad boyo.' Several heads nod in unison.

'No.' repeats the vicar. He shuffles his feet forward, off the carpet; 'He wasn't. He didn't...' A diminutive elder in the front row stands up, his gold fob chain across his fusty waistcoat winking with authority, and the vicar slides back onto the red carpet for the second time. It's painful to watch. His face is contorting as the muscles of his mouth and jaw are battling each other for control: to open his mouth and speak against these accusations, or clench tight against the rant rising up inside him. The final battle for the vicar's sanity has started; and frankly, it's a bit one-sided.

'He was! And he did!' Mr Barry's affirmation is met with grunts of agreement from the other men. Some of them had known David. Yea verily, some of them were as well, and some of them had done, right alongside the errant David, once. But now...

'And he certainly had no business with that Ty Merched lass, or any woman of these valleys!' Barry finishes, glaring at the vicar, 'For we know he was married already. Wasn't he?' The small chapel building seems to pulse; its walls, built from the very stones of the timeless valley, expand and contract: breath, heartbeat.

A roaring comes to Myfanwy's ears. The vicar might be talking; the vicar might indeed be lying, or defending himself, or singing backwards in Russian, for all Myfanwy can tell now. Sound waves beat on her eardrums and do not register. Light reflects off the vicar's sweating forehead but doesn't reach into her eyes. Inside her clothes, the temperature has become arctic. She remembers a man called Dewi. She remembers a sharp man called Dewi who called at Ty Merched only once, but who she often saw leaning by the lamp at the crossroad to the Ty Merched lane. Until suddenly she never saw him again. And the months and years of Sarah Maud's rising strangeness fall into a rough pattern. Just as, Myfanwy now sees with crystal clarity, the pale skin, the black hair and green eyes of Dewi fall into place beside the face of Jenner with her ivory skin and raven hair and emerald eyes. Myfanwy wants to move but nothing physical is working. She wants to shout but has no breath. She wants to cut and stab and hammer at something, anything. She holds her prayerbook until the spine cracks. It isn't about her, until suddenly it most horribly is.

The noise is growing around her, there is no escape.

But it's the vicar who's shouting.

'... how dare you question my authority in this place!' He's on the top step of the dais, clinging to the altar, shielding himself with the sanctuary of the building, the sanctity of his office, the status of his family. But he has overdrawn his assumptions, for all his fine clothes and his resonant voice. He knows this now. 'That dreadful child, that... bastard witch!... is no part of my family. Daughter of a whore! Child of Satan!... she must be staked ... burnt...'

The congregation, that has for the past few minutes been shouting accusation at the vicar with all the affront of a proper, God-fearing community that sees it has been conned, falls into disbelieving silence.

'Whitened sepulchres! The lot of you. Just dead man's bones... I, He, would bring a flaming sword down amongst you. How dare you?' The vicar wipes his chin on a sleeve. He sways out from the dais towards the elders, one hand clinging to the old altar and the other waving over the congregation, as if he held a scimitar to sever their heads clean off their necks, slice, slice, slice ...

'I'll get her, I'll get her and her... and her fucking ignorance of my authority...' Twdr Morgan takes one final swipe across the room, swings back and scrambles up onto the altar, kicking over the vases of flowers, the accoutrements of worship '... she, they, daughter and mother, sorceress and bewitcher! Witches, all witches. They shall be cast down! For these things they did are detestable... stealing the seed... the Lord will cast them out and all you are accursed that stand with them! He will divide you, and destroy you, and you will burn!' He scrambles up onto the altar, backs up against the wall and holds his arms straight out, his forefingers stabbing at the astonished faces before him. 'For I have snared her, and she will be punished. I will be avenged for the traps of filth and witchery. And I will be held on high. And you! you… you…Stinking sinners. All burn! I will bring the holy fires down on you all! I will…'

… the altar, decades ago given over to woodworm and dry rot, collapses. He falls, cracks his skull against the floor. The old velvet curtains slide stiffly to the ground and drape the insensible figure of Gwrhyd Chapel's vicar, prostrate among the splinters, his throat rattling as he gasps at the musty air. His spine twitches, his eyes roll in independent directions, before shuddering shut.

There's a long moment of silence as the dust settles. Someone coughs. The dour chapel elders stand as one and file out, heads together in twos and threes as they plan an immediate succession. 'Not another of the Morgans, I think' one of them can be heard to suggest.

'Du, Du; look at the old bugger. I always thought he …' Younger Miss P falters into silence under Elder Miss P's cautionary glance.

'Stealing seed, my arse. It's clear the brother raped Sarah Maud.' says Mr Barry. 'Get the women out, would you.' He looks to the fellow members of the Quorum, but the women are already flowing out the door in as much of a rush as narrow space and Sunday clothes will allow. As soon as they reach the open air, the women's voices rise into a flood that can be heard receding across the road.

Dai Spuds cautiously approaches the detritus-sprinkled vicar, who is mumbling unconsciously in the litter of the altar. 'What'll we do with him? He's as mad as a two-bob watch, for my money.'

The men hold a brief conference, but when they come to lift him, thinking to tie him in a curtain and call the mental hospital, Twdr Morgan thrashes in their grasp, flings himself at the wall with a crash, kicks out and breaks free. Stumbling over a hanging shred of his cassock, the vicar runs headlong out the chapel door with blood streaming down his forehead; the men hurrying down the aisle to grab him feel him slip through their fingers. The leading few of the Quorum spill out the door in time to see him take the same path as Jenner that other day, flighting over the crest of the ridge to disappear down into the woods. It's clear that beneath the cassock he is bollock naked.

Dai Spuds shakes his head. The men look at their boots a while. There's a small snort of breath, quickly stifled. They nudge each other out the door and leave without speaking... for they each hold a hand to their face, and their shoulders shake and quake. They step into the sunlight and down the gravel path left vacant by the women; by the time the group reaches the gate they are gasping for breath and crying with muffled laughter.

By the time they reach the pub for the most essential lunchtime pint they've ever known, they will be ashamed of laughing at such madness, and drink themselves sober.

But to be fair, and all crimes aside, it was bloody funny.

Behind in the chapel, Myfanwy is still in her seat. A few flakes of altar wood have drifted along and settled on her left shoe. Slowly she bends to brush them off, but her hand is shaking beyond control.


-oOo-


Jenner in the Ponty police cell is writing in an exercise book that the duty officer found for her, with a small pencil stub that's all the regulations will allow. She leans into the corner, and the book wobbles on her knees, for there's no chair or table. The air moves through her lungs like mud. She wheezes, she mutters to herself, she dozes and wakes with a shiver. She grunts as the pencil breaks. The duty officer brings a new one into her cell as he removes the uneaten breakfast.

'You need to drink something. At least that.' He nudges the water glass closer to her, worried by her pallor, her damp hair stuck to her forehead, her laboured breathing.

Jenner doesn't hear his voice.

Off- and on-duty officers, passers-by, a couple of drunks from the other cells, all come and peer in the door, and linger.

'Oh dwt, look at the size of you in this place...' Lizzie has bought the quilt from Jenner's bed, and a change of clothes. She now wonders why she hasn't brought some flowers, or a bit of Myfanwy's bara brith.

'Hen Nain.' Jenner smiles in greeting, beaming right into Lizzie's eyes. Her eyes are huge, hot and dry in her shrinking face. She looks at the quilt as if it came from a fairy story, pats a loosening thread into place, and shuffles the quilt round her shoulders. '*Diolch*, Hen Nain...' she turns back to the exercise book and resumes writing.

Lizzie recognises the words on the page. And the drawings, as Jenner works on. Recipes, instructions, details of plants and their seasons of usefulness, seasons of danger; pencilled on the scruffy pages. Jenner is rebuilding the Ty Merched *Materia Medica* from memory.

'I lost my book, Hen Nain...' says Jenner, after a minute.

'Ah, never mind, cariad; we'll find it again.' Lizzie for no sane reason feels this to be true.

'Yes, but there should be two anyway.' Without explanation, Jenner continues to write, mutter, wheeze. Lizzie can feel the heat of the child's fever coming through her clothes as they sit side by side. She looks at the group of watchers at the door.

'Maybe a bit of fresh air, do you think?' she gestures with a wave. And the officers move back. One opens a window to the chill sunny day.

'I can give you half an hour,' Jones says as he hands Lizzie a cup of police station tea.

'She needs a doctor!'

This was also suggested when Jenner had arrived at the station. But Watcyns—seeing, for the first time, the strange waif he's arrested for the murder of an adult—had dug his heels in: no special treatment. The case was making him uncomfortable. DS Watcyns didn't like feeling uncomfortable.

So no doctor is to be provided. Lizzie sits in the cell and watches Jenner write until the time is up, then kisses the girl's feverish forehead and gets driven home by Jones.

Into a disturbed landscape.

Fanning out from the chapel in both directions, the road is dotted with little clusters of women, speaking and stunned by turns; they move off the road to let the car through. The faces that peer in at her suggest a story so muddled Lizzie has no way to read it. And fair enough: this is gossip beyond ordinary imagining, and simple valley folk haven't had time to decide whether it's pity or curiosity or a sense of twisted justice that's running through their minds and showing on their faces, or maybe all three at once. Some cannot hide their awkward uncertainty, managing to appear both honest and alarming.

Jones winds a window down as he draws near the Misses Perry and slows to a stop. 'Is something happened? What's to do?'

'Oh, Officer,' Elder Miss P leaps into the vacuum with the first thing in her head, thinking to take control of the conversation before Younger Miss P can say something awkward to the passenger she's spotted in the back seat. 'Do you know now, we're moving the memorial into the week. You can still come?' But she remembers that the Ty Merched women were not in on the discussion about a memorial. 'Anyway, there it is. Say hello to Jenner for us, Mrs Coombe?' she starts on a cheerful note, before collapsing to silence at the end of this road-crash of a conversation. Younger Miss P is having just the best morning; this is all going in her private journal, word for word. Elder Miss P hurries them both off the road into the heather.

The few women still on the road are now alert to the presence of the squad car and have also begun to cut across the rhos, awkward in their Sunday frocks and best shoes. Jones is frowning as he drops Lizzie at the house gate, with a comment that he'll see what can be done about a lift tomorrow, although he's conscious that Watcyns's presence at the station will make such consideration very difficult to deliver. Before he returns to Ponty, however, he turns left at the crossroad, parks up at the Rhiwfawr Arms, orders a raspberry soda at the bar. And there he will learn something about the vicar, and something about the memorial, and a lot about David Morgan and Sarah Maud, and Jenner.

So it is that the four daughters of Ty Merched inhabit separate worlds; in different orbits under different stars they each spiral alone. In the interstellar dark, they cannot see each other.

-oOo-

The Ty Merched kitchen is not the 'beating heart' of the house. Nothing so inadequate. The kitchen of Ty Merched *is* the house. The walls so thick you could conceal a woman lengthwise and neither her head nor feet would stick out. The hearthstone so old that swords as well as ploughshares had been whetted on it betimes. Niches for storage that, with a couple of hammer blows, became arrow slits and embrasures. The rest of the building—rooms, storage, passages and lofts— has sprouted from the frame of the kitchen in outgrowths that came and went with the generations. The kitchen, with its solid flagstone floor and near-perpetual fire, is the only certainty that Lizzie has, or expects will endure. Even that has changed since she first looked upon the candlelit world of her childhood; she sees each layer of change as a faded gauze behind the electric light, radio, refrigerator. She sees the shadows of her ancestors move across the room: liquid under the light of other nighttime fires, dust motes in the beams of other sunlit mornings.

As she heard the squad car struggle through a cramped U-turn then recede up the lane, Lizzie had raddled the fire into life. Now she fills the kettle, which stays in her hand a while before landing on the stove. She hangs her coat, leans against it on the hook a moment as the ache of her flexing arms recedes, then stands in the inner doorway; she looks up the hall and sees the worn-smooth floor, the sideboards and pictures and umbrella-stand, the baskets stacked on boxes, the cupboards and closets undisturbed for most of her long lifetime. Minor details have changed; old Elizabeth's cane has been relegated to the barn and hangs with William's sheep crook, while the wolf's head walking stick now dominates the hallstand hodge-podge. The indents of different pram handles overlapping in the plaster, the hieroglyphs of boot marks big and small over generations...

The door to Sarah Maud's room is closed, and stillness covers everything like dust. An anonymous portrait holds a curling unframed photograph tucked into its frame; in the photo her sons' young faces are clear, but their uniforms are out of focus, and fine detail has disappeared from half the print where the summers have washed over it these fifty-two years past. The kettle boils as Lizzie continues to stand in the doorway; she too is unfocused, losing detail, fading. She can hear the hot stove clicking, the clock ticking, a tree branch tapping...

Myfanwy comes home from chapel, and without acknowledging Lizzie, knocks on Sarah Maud's door and disappears into Sarah Maud's room.

-oOo-

When PC Jones returns to Pontardawe police station, Jenner is the small centre of a growing crowd. A curious dislocation from their daily routine has drawn the families of the officers on shift, to 'just call in' and then to linger. The open window has attracted a few coal tits and nuthatches to the sill. Soon the cell is alive with larger birds: jays and ravens; one small chicken has taken perch on the end of the bed. A neighbourhood dog stands almost on guard by Jenner, two more hold watch over the cell door. Cats, well... cats are everywhere. But they don't bother the birds and are in their turn tolerated by the dogs. A bullfinch flutters in, lands on the quilt by Jenner's side, offers a twig of feverfew in flower, then other bits of the greenwood are brought in by birds, cats, a mouse. Jenner nods a thank you, nibbles the herbs, sips from the cup of water the jailor has given her, continues to write and draw and mutter under her breath. Her words are almost solely old Welsh now, no-one can understand what she's saying... but they stay, they watch. The oldest amongst the crowd begin to recognise the work she's recreating, understand what she's doing; they remember hearing such words and seeing such a book as they lay feverish in childhood sickbeds, the doctor consulting the wise woman...

When Jones looks in the cell, over the shoulders of the others, Jenner glances once in his direction and nods, before returning to her task; she fills one notebook, asks for a new one.

An old woman, having done with watching, makes her way out of the station, and up to the western hills, walking an ancient path to the ring of standing stones at Carn Llechart, where she sits for a time. Later, others follow her up the hill, clear the litter and leave flowers on the stones. They agree that it seems a nice day for a walk.

DS Watcyns is taking the air on his front porch, high on the eastern hill. The last of the Sunday roast is drying to leather in the oven. His wife lies a-shambles on the kitchen floor, but he doesn't call an ambulance.

Much flaunted as a delicate child in her youth, Mrs Watcyns's only fragility in middle-age is a tendency to fart in such prodigious volume that the sudden drop of abdominal pressure causes her to faint, which she has just done. So DS Watcyns is taking in the fresh air on his front porch. He sees the steady rambling and ambling of locals around the police station but thinks nothing of it. He feels the ground soften beneath him but puts it down to indigestion.

So hard is he concentrating on not feeling the ground shift, that he doesn't really hear any rustling in the shrubbery. It's almost dusk before he's aware that he has a visitor, in a torn cassock, hiding in his tool shed.

It's Morgan's muttering of curses that gives the vicar away.

'The hell you doing here?' Watcyns peers harder into the gloom of the shed. 'Jeezus H Christ, man; the hell happened to you?'

'A temporary set-back.' Morgan isn't interested in explaining himself. 'The child is evil.'

'Well, yes, man; all kids are evil; nasty piglets every one o' them. But what...?'

'She's a witch.'

'Right. Is that... is that still against the law, though? I'm not sure. You say you witnessed the actual crime, right?'

'I did. I saw exactly who did it. She's behind it all. All the...'

'Can you come in and make a statement, I need that.'

'Certainly. Word of God I can. I was there and I saw it all. She's to be stopped and locked and barred.' The vicar shivers; something in his manner is unsettling. And Watcyns hates to be unsettled.

'What... Out of interest, man, what were you doing at Ty Merched around midnight, then?'

'I? I was on God's business, it's none of yours... Throw the book, Watcyns! Lock her and stop her and chain her up. Lesson to them all.' He gulps, his throat is congested. 'The child is a witch.'

'Riiiight. As I said, I don't think that's a ... '

It's Watcyns's locking of the shed door that keeps the vicar in. He returns to slide the last of the Sunday roast through the gap under the shed door, 'The missus, you understand...' he apologises. 'Sleep well, Vicar.'

A question that Watcyns is yet to ask himself: can we still call that rabid creature 'vicar'? Watcyns has made his reputation as a detective by not asking questions he doesn't know the answer to already, and now is not the time to start. But he's getting really annoyed by all the uncomfortable feelings lately. Ever since Gwyn phoned him to repeat Morgan's words, things have been getting messy, and messy is always uncomfortable. He wonders about calling at the Rhiwfawr Arms, fails to come to a decision. DS Watcyns casts round in his mind for someone to blame.

# Chapter 11

# Dydd Mon the second

Lizzie rises at dawn. She feeds the hens, gathers eggs. She sees to the few remaining sheep in the barn and checks each of their leggy babies. Two are dead and she covers them in sacking, hoping John will return soon; she has come to rely on the kindness of hippies. If it weren't for the cool and damp, she'd be unsure if she was dead herself: the air is still, and light gleams directionless from the opaque sky, the pallid earth. The quietness feels ambivalent, as if heaven and hell were the one single place, as if up and down were fantasies of convenience, as if contradictions and similarities were one and the same. Lizzie can feel a strangeness though her fingers are stiff and numb. She can taste the silence, smell that something has disappeared and hears that something else is waiting to happen. She sees a weight of absence.

Change is come to the valley, invited or not. Change is kicking its heels at the cross-roads, sniffing round the streetlamp, poking the nests in the hedgerows and dislodging the slates from the roofs... you might think it's a change to something new. You might be wrong.

When Lizzie returns to the kitchen, there is still no-one else about. She climbs the awkward stairs to see Myfanwy's chintzy bed hasn't been slept in. She walks down the hall and puts her ear to Sarah Maud's door. Lizzie wonders if she can hear two people breathing. Opening the door softly, she sees Myfanwy cradling Sarah Maud amongst the nest of quilts. There is a smell of rum and forgiveness. Lizzie hovers round the bed, leaning in on one side and the other, laying her hand in the small gaps beside the women's bent and spooning legs, by their heads on the pillows. She feels insubstantial and in-complete; she wants there to be room for her but has arrived at this bedside, this want, too late.

She sees back past the sleeping women to child Sarah Maud, and further again to infant Myfanwy: exuberant and curious children toddling round the old rooms, as familiar as Lizzie's own childhood. She sees herself so frequently irritated by their innocent presence; herself too impatient; too busy looking out at what she couldn't have. Lizzie wants what she can't have now—those times; some time—back.

The boiling kettle breaks the vacuum of noise. She is filling the teapot when Myfanwy is drawn into the kitchen by thirst... and the need to share a burden.

'What's going on?' The habitual brusqueness has fallen from Lizzie's speech. 'What's with Sarah Maud?'

'David Morgan. You knew David Morgan.'

'A good while ago. What of him?' and as she brings the long-forgotten man to mind, Lizzie sees something familiar.

'Why didn't we care, Mam? What the ... bloody hell.' Swearing comes hard to Myfanwy. 'Why didn't we... we should have talked. Never bloody talked, just condemned, and watched her fall apart, and didn't ... talk...'

But here is Myfanwy, and here is Lizzie. Facing each other over a kitchen table. And a gulf of decades. 'Not talking' was the way of them both. The way Sarah Maud grew up. Sarah

Maud's trauma is Myfanwy's guilt is Lizzie's failing. *We never bloody talked.* Lizzie thinks to step towards an appeasement with Myfanwy if she can. But this is not their day. Myfanwy is in shreds, but this is Sarah Maud's time.

Myfanwy tells—in broken, incomplete phrases—of the man with the black hair, and the awfulness and the humiliation. And the abandonment ... and yet... and yet after it all, the fact of Jenner's existence makes it somehow, almost, unbearably alright.

The day is shattered, nonetheless, and they stare at the pieces of it. Until there's a knock at the door.

Mrs Davies it is, bringing her cousin who's driven up from Ponty surprisingly early; Mrs Davies has brought an apple cake still warm from her oven, and asks after Sarah Maud: is she... well, is she... alright now? The visitors linger in the kitchen, whispering a while.

Myfanwy is washing the tea things when there's another knock at the door. Jem's wife and daughters, the Jenkins women.

'Brought a Bakewell tart and a tiny pot of royal jelly. For Sarah Maud,' says Mrs J. No, they won't stay. But they do hover a moment in the space around the cwtch doorway. The kitchen fills with a slight discomfort. A knock at the door and the Jenkinses are sliding inside Jenner's room now, making room for Maris the Shop with a packet of lavender soaps. And then the foreign woman who lives beyond the pub, with the name no-one remembers; she's brought a pot of pinks, new buds on grey wiry stems smelling of cinnamon in the warmth of the women-cluttered room. She lingers a while, rests a hand on the coats by the door...

It's late lunchtime before the stream of visitors quietens to a trickle. Women barely remembered or total strangers to Ty Merched, along with more regular acquaintances, have called, hovered a while, left gifts of food and flowers, dainty handkerchiefs and packets of pins. Trinkets and jams and freshly baked cakes rise like a harvest offering on the big table. But still, no car and no PC Jones. Lizzie retreats to Sarah Maud's bedside. Sarah Maud hasn't moved for a very long time; she sleeps peacefully now, and deeply as if she were a sick child whose fever has finally broken.

Myfanwy stays in the kitchen. She hasn't forgotten Lizzie's words of the day before, and all the events of this morning make it harder to forgive anything. Yet, overriding even all this, as the house falls quiet again she feels something is out of place; there's a prickling behind her eyes, a tickling at the back of her neck.

Myfanwy was once in the habit of casting the tarot, and she was good at it; only it wasn't the churchmen who persuaded her to pack the cards away. It was the constant readings of her own bad fortune that got her down. Her share of the family's erratically distributed second sight, was an instinct for things beyond the known; an insight beyond the veils of the community that was stronger than a radio signal, more reliable that the newspaper. And now something is twitching her skin. She can't sit until she finds the source of this itch. *Where are you, you beggar...* Something's amiss.

Myfanwy locks the gates and visits the hens, and they all talk at once to tell her their news. The roof ghosts are peering in at the windows, listening to the house ghosts. They are comparing notes on what they know, what they saw, from whom do they wish to scare the bejeezus. And a newcomer on the roof ridge; speechless, and much more dead that they'll ever be. He makes the older ghosts nervous.

Myfanwy prowls. In corduroy slippers and faded apron, she is beating the bounds of Ty Merched. Is it here? Or here? She rifles through the straw in the nesting boxes; upturns the buckets in the barn; runs her fingers through the sheep's greasy fleeces, through the grain in the feed bins. She plucks the geese from their grass mounds, looks in their evil eyes and down their hissing throats. She paces Sarah Maud's garden in the warming spring and counts the statues for supernumerary limbs. Lifts the shy heads of the fiddle ferns and makes them look her in the eye; rings the bluebells, listening for a flat note, a cracked note, an out-of-pitch foreign note.

Back inside Myfanwy paces, and growls through the pantry and its winking jars and cans, through Lizzie's tissue paper-crackling bedroom, through the front room dusty and doubtful; past the old faces fusty and fretful, flat on the walls. Myfanwy prowls the cupboards, the cloths, the carpets and the clocks. Lizzie dream-hears her and stays cautiously asleep on the bed, curling round Sarah Maud and the old grey cat all asleep.

Myfanwy prowls on, and examines the windows and their views, the doors and their creaks, the taps and their drips. Until she comes to the cwtch door, and there she stops. In Jenner's room, small, folded papers, pencilled requests for help of all kinds, peep and flutter from the bedding, the shoes, the schoolbag.

Myfanwy lays her hand where Mrs Davies did. She stands on the rag rug where the Jenkins girls clustered. She runs her eyes where the recent guests looked. And Myfanwy has found the source of her anxiety: the blank spaces where a pencil, a sock, a stub of bedside candle, a pebble, have been lifted into pockets and taken away. Tokens, souvenirs. The idea of owning a relic is older than Christianity. Did the neighbours really think Jenner has imbued her books or clothing with healing qualities, as if she was  radioactive? ...*Really?*...

'The beggars!' she mutters. 'The beggars; they're after having a piece of Jenner, poor child. A touch of where she's touched; a bit of her bits and bobs.' And Myfanwy can only guess why. And she's right. For of course Myfanwy shares in the other-worldly genes that, from ancestors under time, through old

Lizzie and herself and Sarah Maud, have culminated in Jenner; and for the first time Myfanwy is listening to herself properly. And her bones tell her something is dawdling at the phone box, kicking a pebble down the lane, rattling a stick in the fence wires. She goes out to the lane. Still no sign of PC Jones and his promised lift to the station. But she does see, along the lines of trees and across the folds of hills, along the paths from Panteg and Rhiwfawr, even up the Gwrhyd Road from Ponty, the land is flickering and shifting as if seen through wrinkled green glass.

'No!' Myfanwy calls to the empty lane, the fields and hollows beyond. 'No! You will not make any shrine in my house. You will not! She's a child, not a bloody... magician. And she's not bloody dead.' She spits on the stones of the old lane.

Something has brought change; something is putting snow down Myfanwy's back. Something is lighting the tinder in Myfanwy's breast. Myfanwy is being unbound from the decades of her self-swaddling anxiety. The village women's gestures of solidarity and the ending of concealment, the bringing of light into dark places, have played a significant part in her unsmothering, strengthening her heart as they bled out the toxin of rancor and judgement and secrecy. The Old Ones held mothers more significant than fathers; in the Gwrhyd Valley, there's an Old One walking, somewhere.

'... She's not dead!' Myfanwy is quieter now. But no less defiant.

-oOo-

Where has PC Jones been all day? In fact, he's been at Ty Merched: after Lizzie's morning shuffle; before Myfanwy's afternoon prowling. But his day starts at the police station as usual.

When he checks in, he sees Jenner is sipping a cup of tea, again surrounded by small animals and the bits of flowers and leaves they have brought her. She's small in the bundle of quilt and blanket. There are now three exercise books on the floor by her feet. There are no regulations covering the presence of animals in cells, even if the largest of the dogs does growl at him, so Jones returns to his desk and opens the file on the Ty Merched body. After his call to the morgue, he pockets the illegible crime scene report.

A woman in a raincoat, with deep pockets and a small dog, is waiting at the police station entrance when Jones lets the front door swing closed behind him. He nearly knocks her over.

'Ty Merched?' she enquires without preamble. 'I'm to accompany you.'

'Really? Did CID send you?'

'I've been assigned, yes.' She nudges the small dog back into a pocket; in the manner of small dogs everywhere, this one seems very keen to get inside the police station. 'We'll take your car, OK? I'll show you the way.'

'I know the way,' Jones is fumbling with the keys, distracted by a nagging thought he can't quite put his finger on but anxious to leave before Watcyns arrives; late though he habitually is, at some point the DS is certain to show up.

They turn right as usual, then the woman— 'You can call me Blodeuwedd'—points to a side road he's not noticed before: 'Take this turning.'

'Why?'

'It'll bring us up at the far end of the farm; we don't need to trouble the household quite yet.' This seems such a sensible, considerate suggestion that Jones settles down as he drives. The road follows the far western flank of the valley, rising along the line of the once-busy rail and passing ivy-shrouded brick-lined embankments, small grass-filled sidings, a haunted land of extinct industry. But the road itself is in surprisingly good order; considering he'd never seen it before, the solid black bitumen looks almost...

'Here,' Blodeuwedd points to a patch of gravel, 'pull in here.' A slight footpath leads down from the left bank and across the road to a mossy wooden style over the fence on their right, and into the neglected end of Sarah Maud's garden; the same path that Jem Jenkins had taken just a week back, hunting for tigers.

She leaves the dog in the car; 'to keep the site clean' she explains. In the manner of small dogs everywhere, it certainly seems very keen to get into the garden. Jones doesn't really expect to find anything, after the rain, the snow, the trampling of feet and the passage of a week. Certainly, any individual footprints are obliterated. The many shreds of fabric on the thorns and twigs could have belonged to anyone, and a predominance of navy-blue twill suggests that most belonged to the local constabulary. Some belonged to Jones himself, a week ago.

'How was the body found?' asks Blodeuwedd, crouching down and squinting into the tunnels of arching brambles. Dai Jones indicates with his arms outstretched this way and that, tries to describe the watery images he remembers despite his bout of rookie nausea.

'How do you think the victim could have gotten so deep into this?' Blodeuwedd rests a finger on the topmost thorn of the highest tendrils 'How bad would your hands be cut, working here...Or maybe gloves...' she murmured to herself; so quietly that Jones almost thinks it's his own thoughts he's following. 'Gloves. And strength; maybe just one sudden burst of strength would do it. If the killer were a tall man. But a dead body, that'd take some manoeuvring. Your prisoner?'

'Sorry?' says Jones, for he is distracted again.

'Your prisoner. The suspect you've arrested. Do they have scratched hands or arms? Are they tall, and very strong?'

But Jones has something quite different on his mind as he stares at the crime scene: 'Who sent you? CID didn't know I was coming here today ... nobody knew. I didn't even know myself until I ...' he turns to press for an answer, to find that Blodeuwedd has gone. Dai Jones turns back to consider the site of the murder, and it's blazingly obvious the child couldn't have done what they saw. How did Watcyns convince them all to think otherwise? Jones is mystified.

He opens the car door and the small dog leaps past and away into the garden. There is no catching it, so he doesn't try.

Driving back to Pontardawe, he's not at all surprised to see, in his rear-vision mirror, the road disappearing into the undergrowth behind him as he descends. Now only ivy covers the gravel ditches and ridges of the forgotten trail, the fresh blacktop vanishing immediately the rear wheels roll from it. But it doesn't matter, for Jones has learnt all the place can tell him now.

When he returns to the station, there's a small crowd milling around the doors, a couple of officers in uniform mingling with the dozen or so onlookers in confused shuffling.

'What's to do?' asks Jones, from his car window.

PC Williams bends down, close to the car. 'It's the DS. He's locked us out...he's worse than usual.'

'The girl? Who's looking out for the girl?'

'Watcyns it must be; he's the only one in there.'

'But...'

'I know! Well, no, I don't know. Actually, I don't have a fucking clue! He came in late, tamping at all the crowd inside, threw everyone out. The 'Drunk and Disorderly' in Number 3, everyone. Us! It's just her and him. He's pushed a desk to the doors now. My keys are in there, I'll have to walk home isn't it' Williams looks at the slowly dispersing crowd, 'Oh, maybe I should stay, try to talk sense to him?'

'Nah, hop in, I'll give you a lift. Maybe can you phone Swansea when you get in, get some advice—' they look at each other '—cover your back. You've got a phone in the house, yes? Tell me more while I drive; what did he say, exactly...' Jones starts the engine.

Twenty minutes later PC Jones returns and rolls his car, engine off, into the back corner of the station car park. From the boot he takes a tarpaulin, a sleeping bag, and a satchel; he creeps quietly round the walls until he's beneath the now-closed window to Jenner's cell. Squatting on his bag and leaning against the wall, he settles down with a paperback and a thermos of tea. He coughs quietly, and says his own name, twice, in a voice so quiet it's hard to be sure if he really made any noise or was it just the wind in the bushes trying out some consonants for a change.

After a short while, the window squeaks open and three exercise books full of Jenner's pencilwork are pushed through the bars to fall beside him; the window closes again. Jones puts the books carefully in the bottom of his bag under a tattered copy of the Police Manual and begins to arrange his camp before it gets dark. He glances up to the high shadowed hills of the western horizon. Somewhere behind that blackness, the girl's family wait.


-oOo-


Myfanwy is in the yard, closing the hens up for the night. When she turns back to the door, there's a small dog, sitting on the threshold and regarding her knowingly; his head cocked to one side, his tongue slipped along a huge grin, and a surprised mouse under one front paw.

On the house roof ridge, the ghosts have to shuffle up, for another stranger, and then one more, and yet another, have joined their number: a gathering. They steam with anticipation of something undefined. They overlap, sitting and wriggling partly next to and, partly inside, each other.

'Don't squabble!' Myfanwy tells them, as she locks up for the night.

# Chapter 12

# Dydd Mawrth the second

Mars is back in play. But this day he's finding the older gods are here as well, tramping the field with their red-gold weapons of cunning and blood ties, song and shadow. Underground movements of scale and tail and slippery thoughts, transmutation and reincarnation and new growth long suppressed are nudging the iron-clad warrior into the sidelines; ice and wind are cracking the marble of a warmer land. Heroes with the names of Risk and Doubt, Care and Steadfastness, have returned. And Change, Mistress of Arms, blows the battle horn above the high lakes, the crumpled mountains.

But Mars, defender of field and forest and home, will run yet longer. For he runs with the wolf. And the sun is strong today.

PC Jones has spent the night behind the police station, below Jenner's cell window. He can hear the DS having erratic angry conversations with himself, way off in another part of the building; though the content is largely inaudible, there's clearly a lot of questioning self-reproach going on: '...the fuck was I thinking...?' repeated several times, is all Jones can make out for sure. He once heard the word 'Christ!' followed by a long silence, although he didn't get the impression that Watcyns was praying.

Jenner makes no sound. She's possibly had no care for twenty hours. Though the station was designed to keep people in the cells, it's coincidentally very effective at keeping people out. Jones can't think of any way to get round, literally or figuratively, the locked front door, so he stays beneath the window. He hopes that Swansea has been alerted; he hopes that someone who doesn't know Watcyns was on the duty desk when Williams's call came in. He begins to doubt that Williams made any such call despite the monstrous illegality of the situation; Watcyns's net of control is known to be as pervasive as smog.

It's chill and damp in the waste ground behind the station; he feels crumpled, and in desperate need of a toilet. He struggles up from the tarpaulin-wrapped sleeping bag, stretching and stomping his legs and slapping his arms about himself, until a large grey dog appears through the straggly privet hedge and looks at him with timeless dark eyes.

'You want to guard my things?' he asks. The dog settles down on the tarp. 'Oh! Right. I was kind of joking. Tea for me, then' He hesitates, all the same. The child is all alone in there, with only Watcyns between her and... Jones shies away from all the possibilities. The dog looks up at him, then across the road past the shrubbery. Jones follows the dog's gaze. There's a woman in a raincoat with large pockets, sheltering under an ash tree. Her face is shadowed, but she might be smiling. Jones nods once and walks home with his satchel and empty thermos.

While his breakfast is cooking, he calls WPC Davies. The notebooks are stashed in the spare room, in a carton of old schoolbooks. Then he dials the number for Swansea district commander, but disconnects quickly, consults the phonebook a moment, and dials again.

'You've reached Wrexford Constabulary, what name please?' says a voice down the line.

-oOo-

Sarah Maud has fought herself, through a day and a night. There is nothing left to be masked or buried or denied; the room is heavy with understanding, light with confession. Sarah Maud steps out into the morning and lifts her head to face the sun and screams in song; one long clear note that echoes off the peaks of Myddydd Drum and Yr Allt, scales the Black Mountain, rolls down to the Gower and out into the blue pleats of the silken sea. Then she takes a hammer to her sculptures in her garden.

She beats any sadness from them: the bent heads and the supplicating gestures, the glum and the weary and the covert, and all the gaunt, is hammered and shattered. Most of the figures fall apart; those that survive stand with tiny daggers of light where the assault has fought new metal into view from among the rust.

With every breath, she's missing Jenner; awake now, she's missing the whole of Jenner's short life.

Lizzie has slept fitfully, hearing the murmurs from Sarah Maud's room and feeling removed from her family, separated as if they, or she, were in a box, a glass booth, a cage. The feeling is familiar, but no longer acceptable; all through the night her sleeping hands reached for an opening, a latch, a clasp. This morning, Lizzie closes her eyes to the wedding portrait watching from the far wall, unable to endure her young self's judgement. She hears Sarah Maud go outside. She hears the one long scream of music, washed over by harmonics and echoes. Then Lizzie hears Myfanwy moving around Sarah Maud's room, closing drawers, opening the window. Lizzie can hear the care with which Myfanwy is now fussing about Sarah Maud's things. Lizzie needs to see her daughter. To explain about the glass cage... and why she can't find its door. She slides off the bed, steps into the hall.

'How is Sarah Maud today?' she means to speak with feeling, finds her voice falls into the safe old patterns of coolness, distance, perfunctoriness. 'I... I want to know.'

Myfanwy looks up, her hands full of dirty crockery, dried foliage, a laddered stocking she's just picked up. Lizzie is standing in Sarah Maud's bedroom door, an old shawl thrown over her nightgown and the ruby necklace, her feet are bare on the rugs. She's backlit by an optimistic shaft of sunlight that's somehow broken through her bedroom window; reflecting off pictures and mirrors and bouncing along the hall it catches the back of Lizzie's hair, shines through her nightgown and casts her into silhouette. To Myfanwy, Lizzie looks encased in morning light, an etiolated shadow-bird with shawled wings, cut away from the walls of the ancient house and placed under glass, a preserved specimen. Isolated, not warmed, by the blade of sunlight down her back. Myfanwy can feel the want in Lizzie's heart.

But Myfanwy doesn't care for her mother's want; she never learnt how to.

'I do what I can for her. The cleaning, the washing, that's my world isn't it.' Myfanwy looks down at her mother, the tiny woman from another century. 'I do what I can.'

'We can only do that and no more,' says Lizzie as Myfanwy moves past her and into the scullery. Lizzie had meant to sound... what? Appreciative, connected, familiar? It came out all wrong.

'I'm not enough, is that what you mean? I'm not up to, not good enough?' Myfanwy drops the things into the trough, grips the edges, leans heavily. 'Well, I'm ... I'm bloody sorry for you Mam, I'm all you got left.' The bare honesty. 'My daughter needed me, and now I see it. I see it now, and I need her, and I told her, and she told me. So, there it is. Us. And you?'

The ringing of a hammer, over and over, breaking the red rust and green mould, in Sarah Maud's distant garden, beats in time with the pulse of blood in Lizzie's ears. She should speak. She should say something, anything... no, not anything.

'You can't do it, can you?' says Myfanwy with a hard sigh. 'You know what? I'll make it easy for you, Mam: give up. I'm tired.' She climbs the stairs to her room.

Lizzie's heart is hammering but the barriers stay up. For she has forgotten how tight she's holding on. She's forgotten how equal the strength of her heart's enemy is. *Oh, William, cariad...* But this time there is no comfort to be found; there is no answer. *Bugger this...* there is no gently laughing voice to chide her.

Shaking herself, Lizzie runs water into the sink, to soak the old cups. She can't be still. She raddles the fire, puts on more coal. She needs to fill the silence, echo-locate herself in solid space. Moves through the house, touching walls, chairs; turns back Sarah Maud's bed clothes and shakes out the quilt. In her own room now, she opens the closets and stares into the empty shadows. Then out to the hens, the feed bins, the shed. Then to watch Sarah Maud working in the garden, wrestling with wire and tools, weight and form.

*What's she doing?* Asks a spectral newcomer on the roof.
*Wait...*

To the sheep, where John has turned the last mothers out into the sunshine of the home paddock. The geese. Lizzie drifts from house to sheds to gate; she's following Myfanwy's steps of the day before if only she knew it. On impulse Lizzie walks out into the lane, her wolf's head walking stick on the gravel making the only sound below the crying of a hawk, for Lizzie still has no shoes or stockings. Lizzie is walking the valley in her nightgown. The smoothed pebbles of the lane press into her old feet, and she feels a welcome sense of place, a kinship with the hardness. On and up she tramps until she swings the chapel gate open.

The black granite of Gwenllian's grave is sun-warmed under Lizzie's thin nightgown and bony thighs. She sits, but doesn't at first speak to her dead mother, or any of them; the women layered one against the other in the crowded pale of the chapel grounds, the men's absences leaving space as their mortal remains lie in distant fields or deep under hill and mine, their catafalque names pinned in sunshine and memory, lead or gold letters against stone. *What did you all want?* Lizzie asks the graves. *Did you get it? Was it all, was it enough, the life? Did you love...?*

The sun moves, predictably. The granite gets cool under Lizzie, but she doesn't move, until she becomes aware of someone watching her from the other side of the low stone wall.

'Mr Jenkins.' She nods a formal greeting, rises as smoothly as her now-chilled knees will allow. Notices she's still in her nightgown and closes her eyes a moment.

'Mrs Coombe' Jem taps his hat brim.

'I needed to ask my mother's opinion of something.'

'She were a fine proud 'omman, was old Gwenllian.'

'She was, indeed, Mr Jenkins.' The wolf's head walking stick is retrieved from where it's fallen in the grass.

'How's young Jenner?'

'Good day Mr Jenkins' Lizzie walks decisively through his hasty farewell, and back over the gravel and stones until she gets to her own kitchen again. Her feet are chilled; they burn when she stands on the hearthstone. She clambers into Myfanwy's old slippers left to warm by the fire.

'I was young. I had other plans. You just came too soon.' she calls up the stairs.

Myfanwy is lying on the counterpane, looking at the low ceiling; for the first time in her motherhood she's delighting in

Sarah Maud's ringing focus, her hammering out in the garden. Myfanwy wonders at herself, all those years resenting Sarah Maud's energy and passion because 'what would the neighbours…' and hating the flamboyance of it all, so when the light went out in Sarah Maud's life, Myfanwy wasn't looking. Now she cherishes the noise, even if she still doesn't quite understand.

Myfanwy hears and doesn't hear all that her mother has said. She cares and doesn't care. She wonders what will befall her if she never does the washing up ever again… she wonders how brave she would need to be, and she fears she isn't brave enough to find out.

*Plans?* Myfanwy asks herself. *So? Didn't I too, and didn't I feel* … Myfanwy is not keen on finishing the thought. Anger helps her out.

'Sorry I was an inconvenience,' she calls down, feeling empowered by such irreverence.

'No, not…' but Lizzie is unsure she wants to be in this place, this conversation, now. 'Was I that bad a mother?'

'I dunno, do I? I don't know that I could honestly say what sort of mother you were.' Myfanwy gets up and closes her bedroom door, turns back to her bed again.

Lizzie is alone again. But so is Myfanwy. And Myfanwy is thinking if only she had a hammer that she could beat like Sarah Maud is bashing the misery out on those dreary old statues, maybe she'd feel better; because when Myfanwy had asked, in the night, if she was a bad mother, and Sarah Maud had said she didn't know, couldn't say… and then, maybe if they asked Jenner the same… Myfanwy lies back on the bed again, but the hammering from Sarah Maud's Garden has stopped. Guilt is the bent wire, the rusted nail. Indignation is the hammer swing.

Lizzie looks at the pile of their recent visitors' offerings on the kitchen table. Lacking Myfanwy's second sight and Sarah

Maud's fey intuition, Lizzie's older eyes yet see a different message from the villagers: alms for the wounded women, the weirdish child; an unexpected balm for the isolation of Lizzie's lifespan, outliving so much that she'd known, so many who she'd loved. She was unable to read whether these offering were an atonement for recent hostilities, or a forgetting—not forgiveness, that would be too much—a forgetting, a tolerance of the arrogance Lissie had unthinkingly built round her, of Ty Merched's contrived ostracism at the end of the lane, an acknowledgement that the proudest can be brought low by anguish just as much as the rest of us—sometimes. Lizzie is confused, softened, made hesitant by such gestures.

She puts the pot of pinks in a sunny place outside the back door, pauses to enjoy the flowers' colours against the stone wall. Bending and stretching with all the creaks of age she starts to put things away; food in the pantry, soap in the linen press under the sheets, cake in... Lizzie slumps into a kitchen chair. She needs a cup of tea, but this is like a task from a fairy tale: never-ending. From where she's sitting the gifts form a wall between her and the windows. *I don't want this!*

*...it's not for me...* and then: *what do I want?*

Lizzie gets up from the table with such speed from her well-worn body that the ghosts—who had been leaning into the pile of gifts, poking with their ghosty finger bones and sniffing with their ghosty nose holes—flit backwards to the top of the cupboards, under the chairs, behind the flour bin.

She throws her waxed coat on over the nightgown, clambers into boots, and tramps out to drag open the wide gate. Chickens scatter, Smalldog barks as he runs up from the lane where he's been interviewing rats. Lizzie feels like she's in a scene from an Ealing comedy but is all the more determined for it. Sarah Maud looks up from her work in the garden as Lizzie struggles open a garage door and takes down the tractor key from its hook on the wall inside.

'What you doing, Mamgu?'

'Sarah Maud, bach!... help me here, girl' Lizzie is stepping up into the seat of the orange Nuffield Universal, brushing straw and leaves aside; she waggles a hand at the second still-closed door: 'open that would you, my dear? I'm not sitting here another minute doing nothing.' The key wobbles into the ignition, the engine coughs, coughs, coughs, catches chg-CHG-chg-chg-chg; the garage is filled with blue diesel exhaust.

Sarah Maud laughs. It's a sound not heard this decade past. 'Mamgu? What on earth?..' she laughs again, and jounces on her toes. 'What on Earth?'

'Sarah Maud my dear, you're back! My beautiful girl, look at you today.' Lizzie yells over the noise of the engine, which begins to over-rev.

'Ie, Mamgu, I spat the lying bugger out of my head.' Sarah Maud is shouting too; the unaccustomed noise, the sun after rain, her tired arms, her work of the morning make her feel like being loud. 'Fuck him and all the shame, Mamgu. He don't own me no more. Oh, sorry I said 'fuck' didn' I? Is this for Jenner?' Sarah Maud leans in and depresses the choke; the unloaded engine drops its revs. Smalldog prances round Sarah Maud's jiggling feet.

But Lizzie can see in Sarah Maud that the change has been painful, that she carries scar tissue; the light is back in Sarah Maud's eyes, but so is caution, and care, and loss. Lizzie has fought against loss her entire life, and yet here it is.

'Ydu, dwt. Fuck him, fuck them all. Coming to see her?' Lizzie shouts into the relative quiet as the engine hits its rhythm in a steady purr. Dropping into gear, Lizzie guides the Nuffield towards the lit square of the open garage doors.

'I loves her I does, but I've not been...'

Lizzie hopes and believes there will be time for Sarah Maud and Jenner; she doesn't know if there is time for all of them. But the Nuffield is taking all her concentration.

Sarah Maud plucks Smalldog from under a wheel and leaps onto the back with the dog clasped under one arm, to cling on with her free hand. They chug into the yard, Lizzie wrestling with the huge steering wheel. Diminutive but accustomed in her metal seat, feet stretched to the floor, she peers through the steering wheel's high curve to see her way round the hen-house, then:

'Wait!' Sarah Maud leaps down, with Smalldog under one arm. 'You go on, I'll catch you up.' She holds Smalldog as the huge orange tractor noses its way through the gate, tips dangerously into the turn, then steadies in the middle of the lane and heads away.

By the time Myfanwy has made it to peer out the kitchen door for the source of all the row the yard is empty, but for a blue haze of diesel in the empty barn doorway, a jabber of ghosts on the roofs and the engine noise receding towards the crossroad.

Sarah Maud has leapt up the bank, Smalldog keeping close by her feet; the pair are scampering up the hill to John and Mich, where she arrives breathless and coming to the edge of laughter, where she hugs until she cries for the inability to say and tell and hold all at once, even though they know, have known for a long time, all about the lying bugger that had been in her head. Smalldog and Black Jesse sniff and greet and circle each other, before loping down the hill ahead of the friends, towards that interesting noisy orange thing with the tiny old woman rattling around in the driver's seat, clinging to the steering wheel, tears streaming down her face and catch-ing in the corners of her wolfish grin. Fck-fck-fck-fck calls the Nuffield to the bright open sky, as the engine warms and the wheels pick up speed over the ancient stones: fck-fck-fck-fck-fck.

The pale young man, on his way home from early shift, who's not gone near the Ty Merched lane since the day of the riot, is startled into immobility. Not just by the tractor heading towards him, though it seems to be aiming straight for him. Not just by the tiny old woman driver who seems to be too small to reach the brake, although not too small to have the accelerator flat to the floor and thundering along at 17 miles per hour. But by the lines of spectral figures, hazy blue-grey and swirling as they burst in puffs from the tractor exhaust like swimmers rising from a deep dive, squealing in glee, and waving to him as they float a moment before dissipating in the warm air, or diving back into the engine air intake; the farm ghosts are having a day out. He spins slowly to watch the Nuffield chug past him fck-fck-fck-fck.

'What in hell? Fck-fck? Why not?' The pale young man drops his snap tin in the hedge, and jogs down the lane behind the tractor, being very careful not to breath in any of the exhaust.

The Misses P have been mystified, behind their kitchen window, and soon are out at their neat little picket gate. 'What are you doing, Mrs Ty Merched?' they call, but Lizzie is concentrating hard on the road ahead. Younger Miss P runs along, Elder Miss P follows more slowly. Mich, John and Sarah Maud jump down into the road from the field, the dogs behind them. The school mistress, alerted by the noise, tries to get the children back into their classroom before any of them spot the Nuffield, but it's too late. At a rising 19 m.p.h. the procession ploughs down into Pontardawe, and to the police station.

PC Jones and WPC Davies have been taking it turn and turn about since dawn, knocking on the station door, calling to Watcyns. They've tried reason: Jenner can't be kept without charge for more than 24 hours. They've tried unreason. They've held fresh hot bacon butties by the windows. Mrs Watcyns has been down, cried awfully and hastily been driven home again. They can hear the phone ringing over and over.

A growing crowd of people has been gathering in the car-park for some time; hovering at the edges and with a good view of whatever might happen. The Newspaper is there as well; as usual it's a mystery how they always know when to show up. Someone starts a song, some wag with a satirical sense of Welshness and a gift for the theatrical no doubt, but the crowd take it up with glee and soon the air is thick with multi-layered harmonies fuguing across words of faith, saucepans, candles, hearts, eyes, and someone named Delilah. A festive air, regard-less that no-one could say why they're here nor what they're celebrating. The sky is so blue, there's enough in itself to cele-brate, but today it feels like the beginning of the world.

In the crowd, people with pain, loss and misdirection all hankering to see the wise child; the myths and the half-truths about her have spread like gorse fire in the hopeful morning. For she has cured a man of the black lung; gave him a bunch of leaves to make tea, and he coughed afterwards a huge gris-tly grey and blood-flecked phlegm (which he keeps in a jar of vodka on the mantle) and now is as right as a set square. And the woman with the mucky eyes is seeing clear and direct. The dogs have stopped brawling. The lambs are quick and their mothers full of milk. The apple buds have not dropped. Sure, the child is still strange, but she's no longer suspiciously so: look what she can do, will you!

And the vicar has vanished; this the most interesting... Gwrhyd's Mad Vicar has vanished.

So when Lizzie and her travelling companions come fck-fck-fcking round the corner, they're greeted with a sight as strange as the one they make themselves: celebratory, optimistic, in-explicable.

'I want to see the child!' calls Lizzie.

'I wants my baby girl!' calls Sarah Maud.

'Let them in! Let them in!' call the crowd. There is much stamping and whistling, and dogs from far and wide come and bark at the tractor, and leap at people' legs, and jump at the doors.

Which stay closed.

'Let them in! Let them in!' screams the crowd, a darker edge to their song now; until on someone's lead the chant changes: 'Break in! Break in! Break in!' Lizzie is startled when Jones jumps up on the footplate beside her. He's intending to explain the situation, estimate what's happening inside the station, but she cannot hear him clearly. He slips as he jumps up, grabs the steering wheel to catch his balance, and brings the tractor round to lurch towards the front steps.

Lizzie thinks he's guiding her.

'OK!' She turns full on to the doors and presses the accelerator; the Nuffield lumbers easily up the shallow front steps, bumps a porch post, crunches into the locked doors, which shatter impressively. The chanting stops, the crowd watches immobile as the splinters pivot across the air, dust blooms then starts to settle...

Then a crack winds its way from the doors, climbing slowly up the wall, slowly... slowly... inching to the roof. A creaking. A longer, more painful, creaking.

The side wall collapses, smashes into the ground. Bits of brick and glass flail through the utterly silent air, to crash around the feet of the watchers, ricochet off the tractor. No-one is breathing.

A slow tile slips from the roof: smashes on the path.

Everyone is breathing, loud. 'Get back' shouts a choir master in his big voice. But Jones runs forward, into the building. Sarah Maud is trembling at the doorway, fearless for her child, confounded by the shadowy corridors. Lizzie is crying. John and Mich grab for Smalldog but he widdershins around them and runs inside, and Sarah Maud follows him. The building creaks again.

'... what have I done?' Lizzie is ashen.

'Don't move the tractor, Lizzie!' John leaps up beside her, holds his hand steady on the wheel. The whole world falls silent... but for Jones's voice calling, louder or quieter as he moves through the building.

'There's no-one here!' Dai Jones comes out, half-carrying Sarah Maud with his arms around her waist as she fights to get back inside. 'No, no-one inside! Oi! Get back there, get back!' For the building is creaking and squeaking, and mysterious things are loosening inside, breaking asunder with softly audible pops.

Jones is holding Sarah Maud firmly as she struggles. Davies is pushing the crowd away from the sundered building, the smashed windows, the reversing tractor with Llundain John reaching out towards Lizzie perched tiny and trembling at the wheel, unable to do anything more than follow his instructions and stay upright.

With a whip-crack, the police station folds in on itself. The roof pleats down as if it were pressed by a giant knife across the centre of the ridgeline, and the cream brick oblong sags like undercooked bread. The watchers exhale as one, step back once, twice, three times; some stumble and run further... but not too far. There is a moment's stillness, then down and down and further down the roof sags again. Inverting, if such a thing were architecturally possible. The walls follow along, drawn down as if the land was inhaling the building. A sink-hole opens, and the whole bland edifice slides quietly into the caverns beneath, as gently as a coffin. The dust and grit follow, until nothing is left above ground except a few bits of shattered glass, and those shallow front steps.

The crowd's frozen astonishment is broken by Smalldog leaping out of the cavity, barking and grinning. The other dogs jump and frisk, almost knowingly, but Smalldog goes straight to Lizzie, nips her nightgown once (for yes, she is still *deshabille*, under the waxed jacket), pounces at her feet twice, three times. Barks. Runs off down the road.

'Hey. Why didn't I notice Watcyns's car has gone?' PC Jones asks WPC Davies. For gone it certainly is.

Lizzie is trying to turn the Nuffield around, but the front wheels are caught on the very lip of the sinkhole. She wrestles the gearshift, revs the accelerator again, rocks the vehicle forward and back.

'Lizzie?' says Llundain John carefully and quietly, 'Lizzie, just put the brake on dear, and take my hand... shh, there we go.'

-oOo-

Back before dawn, DS Watcyns has woken the fitfully sleeping Jenner in her cell, thrown the old quilt round her and bundled her into the back seat of his car. The pearly sky promises a beautiful day, and Jenner brightens, her face picking up a touch of rosy blush from the few remaining clouds.

'Where are we going?'

'There's someone I need to talk to. You stay with me.' Watcyns starts up the road to his home. He doesn't look at her but keeps his eyes straight ahead. He is twitchy from lack of sleep, lack of the familiar firm ground of confidence and bullishness.

'Your liver is sick.' A matter of fact.

'Be quiet.' Watcyns drives in his gates, hesitates, reverses out and takes a lane round to the back of the houses. 'Just keep quiet and you won't get hurt.' He winces at the thuggish cliché; at the same time he is irritated that thuggery seems so ineffectual against this inconvenient child.

He crawls the car along the lane and into the back gate of his own shabby yard, onto a piece of gravel hard packed by years of night visitors with deals to make. The cluster of sheds helps with both subterfuge and storage.

Mrs Watcyns is about in the kitchen. Watcyns avoids attracting attention. He locks Jenner in the car. He opens a shed door, looks in, looks back at Jenner, reaches into the shed and grabs.

The Reverend Morgan comes out of the shed, clamped in the unarguable hands of DS Watcyns. The reverend doesn't look at all well, especially to his own inner eye. The world has inverted, and he is not at the venerable place he anticipated. Instead of leading the charge against the devil, instead of burning the witch, he's just spent two days in the dark. He's had to piss in the shed and only had a dry mutton bone to nibble on since the trauma of Saturday evening, an entire incarnation ago. In Twdr's head, he's the victim of persecution unheard of since the first Morgan tried to convert these Brythonic heathens to the Christian way a thousand years ago. But his time of bright glory will come; he's sure of that.

Morgan is shoved hastily into the front passenger seat; Watcyns rounds the car bonnet to get in the driver's seat and twists to look over his shoulder as he reverses slowly out. The vicar looks back as well, and screams when he sees Jenner sitting behind him, wrapped in her quilt; she is smiling placatingly. Jenner is used to appeasing angry adults. She coughs, then smiles again.

'Heathen witch!' he cries and leaps around, hands reaching to grab at her throat. Watcyns is knocked sideways, and the car swings into the fence, breaking a taillight.

'Sit still for fucks' sake!' shouts Watcyns and pushes the vicar back into his seat. Watcyns continues manoeuvring the car but is distracted again; this time by a neighbour and their cross-looking dog, a large black Newfoundland. He grunts and nods ambiguously. The dog and his owner continue to watch the car until it turns a corner and disappears towards the west of town.

Watcyns won't go back to the station. He knows the officers will be on watch; the hammering on the station door, the ringing phone wanting answers he was unable to supply, have driven him to unplanned flight. He's hankering after that bacon buttie now; hot or cold he could murder one. But there's a palpable sense of 'no going back' that's terrifying. He's thinking furiously where to go, for he wants no interruptions while he figures a way out of this mess, ticking the snags off with his fingers against the steering wheel.

He's kept a suspect longer than legal, well nothing unusual in that, that stupid law is made to be broken. He's failed to proceed properly, but then who does, really, when you come down to it (god knows he keeps a file of just such minor infringements on almost everyone in the South Wales Constabulary). Evidence gathering is, well sometimes it's just impossible; and if you can't gather evidence then how can you act on it? He's imprisoned a vicar in his shed... actually, is that one a crime, this one is as mad as a hatter? He's locked staff out of the station for twenty-four hours, or thirty, or thereabouts... but same question: is that a crime, who would know? Kidnapped a suspect... Put them one by one they don't look too bad, to this bad cop.

But taken on the whole (and he's forgotten about abandoning a WPC on her post without backup; 'poor diddums got her skirt rumpled; she owes us a new whistle' is how he remembers it), even Watcyns can see difficulties in covering all this up. Not impossible; just, well, he'll have to pay back some favours. And Watcyns hates paying back favours. But first he needs to know what the hell the vicar is up to.

He should be asking himself why he made the poor life choices he did, why the clash of congenital laziness and an obsessive need for attention made him think being a copper was going to be easy, why he felt that a uniform alone would get him places with minimum effort. He could be considering that, for all his career of conniving and chicanery, the only place his moral turpitude—uniformed, pyjama'd, or naked as nature—has got him is to this crazy entanglement with this clearly unstable informer.

But it's less awkward to ask other people and then fit your excuses to suit. It's always worked for Watcyns in the past. So when the vicar again lunges backwards to grab Jenner, and succeeds in hooking the quilt off her, Watcyns is raw.

'Fucking leave her alone!' He slaps the vicar across the side of the head, pushes him back into the seat, punches him in the throat. 'Fucking sit still, you crazy shit. You got me into this bollocks, you got to figure a way out.' The car jerks across the road, swerves to avoid the far gutter, rocks on its tyres as Watcyns pulls it zigzagging back into line. Watcyns briefly sees a pedestrian's eyes grow wide as the man—still on the footpath —is forced to jump out of the way. 'Fucking longhair deserves it.' Watcyns laughs briefly, a hound's bark of a laugh.

'Burn the witch' says the vicar in a voice of cool certainty.

Watcyns is so startled he again hits the footpath. 'The fuck? I don't need medieval craziness, I need evidence. Proof she's guilty like you said she is.' He negotiates a corner, sees a group of people spilling out of the ice cream factory, and turns a sharp left to avoid their sight, only to see a baker's van parked immediately ahead. Without losing speed, Watcyns yanks the car to the right, and they begin to climb a steep lane. He has no idea where it leads.

'Where are we going?' demands Morgan. This stampede through the back heights of Ponty doesn't feel like his road to the gates of glory; this dented car is not the chariot his heart demanded. Having a sacrificial witch in the back seat accords with his visions, although he would prefer that she were bound with ropes. He feels a roaring triumph is near, within reach; but his head pounds, the voices are too loud, and nothing is within his control. The serpent in his belly is thrashing and writhing. He feels as huge as a god. He feels as sick as a coward.

Jenner feels stronger by the moment; this journey up the valley is bringing her closer to her homelands, she knows where they're going. And she's smiling. In the incomprehensible world of adults, she feels the two men are finally acting as she always suspected they would: just grownups with their masks off. And she seems to know more than she should.

'Bore da, good morning, Uncle,' she offers politely. The vicar again lunges backwards to grab her, again Watcyns jerks the car as he shoves Morgan back into place.

The asphalt lane peters out into gravel, winding upwards between the transparent greens of birch and sycamore leaves in the clear morning light, fiddle-head fern and yellow archangel soft and delicate beside the ubiquitous arching briar and brambles, under the forest canopy. The air is fine, clean and slightly musty as if it's been waiting in the sunshine of a thousand leafy years for just such visitors. In a few hundred yards, the lane widens into a circular space, beyond which only a narrow track leads further upwards through the trees. They are high above the town.

Watcyns parks abruptly. Hauls the girl out of the back seat and grips her by the shoulder; opens the door for Morgan and pauses as he takes in the state of the vicar in the sunlight now pouring down. The Reverend Morgan has a dirty stubbled face, his eyes are wide and rolling, hair awry; the skin of his forearms is crusty with thin lines of dried blood. The shredded cassock drifts in ribbons round his knees, and mucky with grease, rust, mud and—by the smell of it—urine. Spittle has dribbled from his chin and dried onto the crumpled dog-collar. There is a reeking foulness about the man. Watcyns sees the disaster he's fallen into with Morgan. Anyone with nothing left to lose is in a very dangerous place, and surely Watcyns is not alone there; but when he's been playing fast and loose with the criminals and law enforcement officers of the entire region for decades, his 'nothing' goes past zero and quite a long way into the negative.

The two men look at each other in desperate, mutual loathing.

'I got to sort something out. You started this, you gotta fix it...And then I have to...' Watcyns leads the way along the narrow gravel trail, climbing yet higher through the fine spring morning. A flock of bullfinches rushes through the understorey, just out of reach; they flash like half-remembered dreams, only more aggressive. A smaller flock of nuthatches regards the walkers cautiously, hanging upside down over the path and dropping flower buds on Jenner's head. The child giggles softly in response and the birds lift and swirl in tiny bursts of glee. Jenner had walked these paths as soon as she was able to walk so far; she feels safer with each step, she feels close to home.

Her mood couldn't be further from the men, who stumble as if they were approaching a gallows. Both Watcyns and Morgan are caught out when the trail spills into another open space: the crown of the hill, rounded and green beneath the warm blue arch of sky and alive with meadow flowers and insects. The path leads them directly into the hill crest's very middle, a few dozen paces from the tree line, where a great coffin-shaped table of flat stones sits in the middle of a ring of huge leaf-shaped menhirs tilting out into a crown-like array. On the table, a robin is pecking at bugs in the lichen. The place disturbs Watcyns in ways he chooses not to examine. Control has slipped away from him.

'Well?' He returns to the anger that's keeping him going. He has no choice anyway. 'What was your plan, Vicar? Where's that evidence you said you had? Because yesterday I heard it that this kid is your niece and here you are saying she should be burnt alive. So, you know: what the fuck?'

Twdr Morgan isn't speaking. He is cold, and feverish, and spins round and round looking from menhir to menhir; when he loses his balance and throws out a scratched arm to catch himself, his hand brushes the central stones, the cist, and he leaps back as if electrified.

Jenner walks to the east end of the cist, high as her shoulders, and finds a litter of pebbles. She clambers up and sits on the edge, facing the sun and dangling her legs down. Her feet knock some flakes of stone loose; under the weathered surface, the freshcut stone gleams red.

'Yes!' Morgan is transfixed. 'Yes. Here. Here in this shamble of the heathens we will sacrifice this witch. Blood on stone... iron, bone... the glory will be mine...' He falls to muttering.

'The fuck?' Watcyns is seeing clearly now: there is no way out of this. 'The fuck...'

A car is heard, other less-definable noises. Through the trees comes a black hound exuberant from the chase; and, bravely keeping pace despite his small legs, Smalldog breaks through the cover and barks his greeting to his beloved Jenner.

Twdr Morgan backs away from the dogs, snarling incoherently, with his arms held out protectively before him. So, the first thing that PC Jones sees when he enters the meadow is the bright sun picking out the long scabbing scratches and already-healing tears of skin, among the more recent dirt and bruises on the vicar's forearms. Things fall into place with precision in Jones's mind, things he's been mulling over ever since the second visit to the bramble-covered site of the murdered man at Ty Merched. He still runs forward, but the intention has shifted.

'Twdr Morgan, I am arresting you on suspicion of murder. You have the right to remain silent, but...' PC Jones is reaching for handcuffs and pacing towards Morgan cautiously.

'Servant of Caiaphas! You can't touch me... I am above your earth-bound laws and your puny weapons. Only God can judge me! I will be found righteous in His eyes.' Morgan is by this time backing around the cist as if to avoid Jones's approach, but he lunges and grabs Jenner by the throat, with a shout of cunning triumph that finishes in a gurgle of pain as Smalldog hurdles across the stone and sinks his teeth into the vicar's shoulder.

Releasing Jenner, and swatting with both hands at the dog's enthusiastic jaws, Morgan throws himself backwards with a roar, then scrabbling upright he runs down the far side of the hill and into the trees where he can be heard flailing about, before a pause, a thump and a howl of agony suggest that he has found—and surpassed— the small cliff that buttresses the ridge's southern flank.

Later, when Jones and a squad car reach the bottom of the cliff, there will be nothing to be found except a few yellow teeth, still damp with spittle and blood.

Meanwhile Watcyns is motionless with indecision. The vicar? *What the fuck?* He's so off-balance he forgets his own culpability, and thus offers no defence when WPC Davies cuffs him.

'What's the charge?' His voice falls in that narrow place between contempt and dread.

'Don't know yet. We'll think of something.'

# Chapter 13

# Dydd Mercher the
# second

The night has been spent in wakefulness. Jenner at home, couldn't sleep for the sense of being watched. Her family, newly wakened to explicit care, are still feeling their clumsy way around her, and everyone is willingly uncomfortable, uncomfortably good-willed. Watching at the windows, neighbours now come to witness the very breathing of this curious child, after the astonishing tales coming up from Ponty. Certainly, they always said she was special, didn't they? And, well... if they might have sided with the vicar once or twice... well, that was just being polite.

The Old Ones are coming back, if Jenner is here. For her, the Old Ones have eaten a building, flung a newer god's priest off a holy cliff. Special, she is.

Or maybe just the Old Ones were done with the insults of a crazy man as he stood on this land. For the vicar is clearly insane, must have always been insane, had tried to spread insanity amongst them; his new-fangled, imported faith is losing its grip on the native imaginations. The valleys have very long memories. These stones and paths go back before the ministers and missionaries, back even before the Romans and their blood-lusty sacraments. Nudge the curtain of civility aside and who knows what waits beyond.

'Blood will out' they nod knowingly in pubs, and under streetlamps, and beside unseasonal fires in homely hearths where sweet herbs and old-fangled brews are the new order. But whose blood, and what it's bringing out, are discussed differently in almost every moment. The Old Ones might be coming back, but no-one's quite sure how that'll work.

As the morning light strengthens, hearts and minds weaken and slip into dreams across the Gwrhyd Valley and by nine o'clock all eyes are closed, be they in school, shop or field of this world gone wrong. Only Smalldog growls softly, lifts his head and gives a cautious gruff as he sits on guard at the end of Jenner's bed. Something wrong has crept into the valley, is wading up the stream and stumbling over the ridge and padding along that old rail track with the ivy-covered revetments and hidden sidings. But it's slow, and distant, and so feeble; probably just a bad dream, a wayward memory. Smalldog settles down.

By noon, the valley is awake. It seems no-one has a job to go to, a farm to tend, a lesson to teach or learn. A steady line of walkers makes its way to the chapel hall, carrying baskets and chairs and cases of instruments. The memorial the women have thought up—echoing the old rites, the songs of all old valleys—the sending-off of the unknown dead man, will not be delayed again; that it's happening on a bright breezy midweek midday seems both weirdly wrong and very right. Optimistic. Celebratory. Again, of what no-one is sure... still, cakes and tea will be provided, music will be performed. And there's little fault can be found in cakes and tea and music.

But the heat increases, a sticky brightness rising off the distant ocean that brings swarms of small black flies to sting bare skin, catch in the corners of mouths and eyes. A summer oppression is rising that smells like sweat and sea spray.

Llundain John and Mich have been invited. They know this was not for the pleasure of their own presence— 'foreigners' —but so they can pass the invitation on to the women of Ty Merched without anyone—Mrs Barry, for example—being embarrassed.

Lizzie has been in the bath for an age; after the exhaustion and ... novelty... of the previous day, she is going to make a special effort today, more than at her birthday that lifetime ago. Her old vanity is awake. Still humbled by the near loss of her new-found darling Jenner, and knowing the wounds and bruises of the recent past, yet her importunate pride is a temporary balm. *Silly old woman. But I don't care.* She prepares to face the neighbours as a dignified landowner; her old mother would have approved.

Myfanwy has thought no further than her floral frock, a dusting of face powder and sensible shoes; mourning weeds seem inappropriate, and she owns nothing better. Sarah Maud and Jenner make no decisions; they put approximately suitable clothes on roughly the right sections of their bodies and good luck if the shoes match. So, it's an almost mythological tableau that leaves the Ty Merched garden gate and follows the neighbours: minute, aristocratic Lizzie in black despite the heat; solid implacable Myfanwy walking the lane as if she's walking a to-do list; and the elfin whisps that are Sarah Maud in umbrous shawls and Jenner in snatches of sky and wildflower. They walk slow; Jenner rests frequently while Sarah Maud wanders ahead, dawdles back.

Inside the hall, coughs and whispers and tuning up of throats and instruments wave through the air. Someone whispers to a wayward child.

A line of kindergarten children and their teacher move to the front and the scraping chairs and coughing throats fall quiet. Without introduction, the children start to their teacher's beat:

'Happy birthday to you. Happy birthday to you...' they warble with confidence, before stepping less assuredly into Brahms's saccharine lullaby. The lower years' school choir, a selection of scab-kneed and skew-haired lads with cherub voices, shuffle along behind them, and a string of childish songs flow one into another, rough words pour out in exquisite harmony. A retired choirmaster nods appreciatively from the second row.

'What?' whispers Llundain John. 'What is this?' Mich shrugs her shoulders, puts a finger across her smiling lips: who knows; shhhh.

The lower grades are replaced by a mob of teenagers with rugby songs bowdlerised in consideration of the older listeners who mime the rude versions anyway, then a couple of pop songs about love and motor cars. Twins, brother and sister, 16 years old and almost fully-fledged of valley life, step forward for a contemporary ballad; unaccompanied and whispering, the voices reach into any wistfulness in the audience, wake it up, knock it down.

John is open-mouthed. 'It's fabulous, but...?'

Jenner leans over to him: 'Maris had the idea. They're singing up a life for the man. So he can go off as Someone, not as Nobody.' Her look says how obvious this should be to anyone. Although it's not been known these thousand years, to sing up a life for the fallen like this, still: 'Keep up.' someone mutters. 'And shhh...'

The performances succeed each other, instrumentalists and choirs and soloists, patiently and without preamble. Songs of youth and school sweethearts, adventure and care.

A gaunt woman moves forward from the side aisle. 'It had to be you,' she laments, carving a victim's grief from a love song by the transposition into a bruised minor key. There was no reason to assume the dead man was a happy man. Or a good one. All possibilities are covered. A Chopin Impromptu follows; tonic, rest, reprieve...

'Fire?' suggests Mr Protheroe from his seat by the door. He looks across at his daughter Maris, repeats the whisper: 'Fire, think you? I'll just go check'. And he slips through the doors like an afterthought.

Only to return rapidly: 'Fire! Ty Merched way! Fire!' And the hall empties as fast as the clustered chairs will allow. People spill out onto the forecourt of the hall and see, eyelevel across the wide space of the humid valley, a hazy column of opalescent smoke rising straight up from the Ty Merched roofs where they nestle against the hillside in the sunlight.

In the hall, the elder Miss P continues at the piano, lost in concentration.

All the strength drains through Lizzie's shoes as she reaches the threshold of the hall. She wonders how she can take a next step. Then realises she has slipped to the ground. From here, she can't see the rooftops, only that column of faint grey against the blue. Faint, but growing stronger, darker, wider. She feels a terrible undoing; the buttons and laces of her body are slipping apart.

Nothing can be done, no matter how fast the crowd runs across the lanes and fields; no matter that Mr Barry goes straight to the phone box and calls the fire in, knowing the truck will be an age getting here.

John, Mich and Sarah Maud are the first to arrive, running full stretch around the lane with the dogs in the lead. They hear the rustling rise to a crackling that rises to a gasping wall of noise as they get closer. They breathe in gulps and lean, hands on thighs, to watch as the ancient farmhouse springs into terrible new life, utterly self-contained, utterly without connection to seasons or inhabitants or purposes.

The front of the house seems barely troubled as the slower crowd arrives; maybe there is smoke without fire, this once. In the front room a curtain is waving in an internal breeze, the polished furniture glints a shifting gold, and some of Lizzie's birthday cards flop sideways as if nothing more were amiss than a door left open on a sunny afternoon. But at the side, the windows hold a fantasy of thick white and yellow plasma, as glass shatters and the heat pulses out. Here and there a silhouette of some familiar object—washstand, bedpost, lamp—appears briefly through the smoke before vanishing into light.

The ghosts are flying high, holding onto each other's smoke-filled hands and screwing shut their clouded eyes. By the yard the geese have fled under the five-bar gate. The hens can be heard in rising distress in the smouldering straw. John leaps to pull the coop door open before being driven back; the poultry escape into the garden or catch fire as they run. The barn doors are charring, the sheds likewise; old paint blisters. Moss is steaming and crisping on the roofs.

The lavender hedge bursts suddenly into hot blue flowers of flame.

The bathroom is alight. The corridor, the rugs and the sideboards and the tall oak clock. The dust below the clock. The old rugs. A photograph of two young lads curls and falls to nothingness above the space where, for hundreds of years, a floor had rested. Bumps and scratches in the plaster are baked, blackened, ablated.

The flames roll along the ceilings, slink up the rafters, rifle through the shards and pieces of past lives. Here and there, roof slates crack, slide apart, explode.

Under the panting of the fire, no other sound is heard. There is not enough oxygen for speech. Black flies are swarming away from the garden, turning to cinder mid-flight in the horrible heat to fall as smuts on people's clothes and in their hair. Ivy heats to flash point, breaking out randomly into flame in the hedge.

The women of Ty Merched are at the front of the crowd; as others move back from the heat they stand close, at the deathbed of a loved one. Then Smalldog springs up, leaves his fretting by Jenner's side, to bark and snarl and lunge into the hedge by the garden gate, into the deep drift of leaf mould. A lumpen shape can be seen, scrabbling backwards and away to the corner of fence and wall; as Jenner pulls Smalldog out to safety the figure throws out an arm to grab at her ankles.

Striding towards the disturbance, Lizzie swings her reversed walking stick like a golf club. The wolf's head connects with the jaw of Twdr Morgan with a sickening crack. The force of it sends him through the grass and into the lane. He is now near naked, a dirty, bruised, cut creature curling protectively round broken ribs and hugging the remnants of cassock around himself. But his face is a caricature, qua-human features stretching around a gaping, blood-dribbled grin as he looks slantwise up at Lizzie. The mark of the wolf's head is rising as a dark bruise among the cuts and mud of his cheek as he lies on the gravel. She lifts the walking stick again and brings it down hard; aiming for that hideous grin she instead connects with his shoulder and ear as he flops away out of reach. Lizzie steps forward a pace. Again, she raises the walking stick and again she brings it down hard, this time with a reverberating crack on his arm. The arm falls oddly, the walking stick breaks in two.

'You... You! Bastard!' she screams, and goes to kick his writhing body, but feels John's arms around her, pulling her back, rescuing her a second time from something terrible.

The farmhouse shifts, over the hallway the roof collapses in on itself, and a rush of sparks fly up, pale in the sunlight. The vicar giggles brokenly as he struggles to get up; the smashed arm hangs loose, and his jaw looks very wrong. Hunched over, he cuddles himself. He cannot run any more.

'Burn.' He coughs. 'Burn the witth and her whore mother.' He lisps through swollen tongue and broken teeth. 'I will be avenged by the cleanthing fireth of the Lord. I will be raithed up and all thinners...' he coughs again, a glob of blood and sputum slides down his chin, 'all you thinners will thuffer in the furnath of my retributhion...' He falls on his side, gasps in pain, then resumes giggling, prone on the gravel.

'Burn!' He spits with sharp clarity, staring up at Lizzie from his one still-functioning eye.

Lizzie struggles in John's grip, reaching to kick the creature on the ground, but she cannot get free and John lifts her from the road, carries her carefully backwards to a safe distance, to stand by Myfanwy in the crowd. The thing that was Twdr Morgan is struggling to its feet, starts to shuffle away along the lane.

'No!' screams Lizzie

'Let it go for Christ' sake,' John tightens his grip. 'Look at the state of him, he's not going far.'

Myfanwy is watching her home discard all coverings, drop the veils of hedge and wall and curtain, reveal the secret cavities and forgotten places and blessed bones of her whole world as it dies, naked before the eyes of all the people she knows. She's never travelled further than a few hours' walk could encompass, tethered always to family and duty and hearth. Since her broken love, her aims never reached higher than these cwtching ridges of limestone, her thoughts never went beyond meals and washing and living in Lizzie's unloving shade. Her desire to be free of the cage has only ever grown to the same shape as the cage itself. There will be no rebuild, no reincarnation. She will not live, cannot live, anywhere else.

'Here. Here is me.' Under these blackening eaves, around this blasted hearth, is the breadth and depth of Myfanwy.

Myfanwy reaches to kiss Jenner on the forehead then presses the child around, to shield Jenner's face in Sarah Maud's clothing; holds Sarah Maud by the shoulder for one hard squeeze: *I see you. I love you. But here is me.* She locks eyes with Lizzie; a momentary, final nod ofrecognition, regret, is passed between them. Though Lizzie reaches out a hand to her, it pauses in the space between them under Myfanwy's hard look. *I'll make it easy for you...*

'John' s right. Let it go.' Lizzie is barely audible above the effort of breathing.

'That's not what this family does, is it?' Myfanwy steps faster than she has ever moved before; the panting house is calling her. She grabs the vicar by the neck, hauls him over her shoulder. He screams, and the wolf's head bruise on his face opens its jaws and howls in derisive harmony. His hair is alight even before they vanish through the bright, bright kitchen door.

Then, just the breathing of the fire and the waves of heat in the bright sunlight, the gauze of smoke and the silence of the valley people. The fire continues, quietly, introvertedly, barely visible in the daylight.

A whisper in the stunned crowd: '...the fuck is wrong with that family?'

-oOo-

It is over, to all intents and purposes. The crowd has gone. Jenner is nestled with Sarah Maud, on a seat of cushions in John's bus. Wreathes of smoke hang in the clear high space over the valley. Snakes of smoke slide through the trees and over the walls in low shadow. Pillows of smoke hold the distraught ghosts in their soft embrace. Lizzie in a corner lifts her head to look at the child and mother, then folds in on herself again. She repeats this action several times over the coming hours, but she neither eats nor drinks; she says nothing, cries not a tear. Eventually the bus falls dark in time with the sky and fields and woods, a healing darkness where the bodies of the occupants are felt rather than seen, offering closeness and comfort and removing the requirements to appear as this or that, as whole or broken, as alive or... uncertain. The three of Ty Merched sleep in the undemanding dark. Smalldog sits on guard in the doorway.

John and Mich stand outside on the hill, cradling mugs of tea and whisky to their chests and watching down below them the small glows of the farmhouse pyre fall, flare, fall again, until just a few scattered lines of dull red remain in the blackness.

Away across the valley, in the village hall, a piano can be heard, though there too everything is in darkness. Elder Miss P begins to step her fingers through Satie's *Gymnopédie Number 1*. John knows it will be as *soto* in the hall as here on the hilltop, a gift for Myfanwy across the rare acoustics of these echoing hills.

Soon, John sleeps under the smoky sky, on a rough blanket with his dear Mich.

Elder Miss P moves thoughtfully through some impromptu variations before closing piano and hall, and taking the path home to bed and her beloved Young Miss P. As she walks, she wonders if, in the morning, she might tell the neighbours that they are not really sisters. She'll talk with Young Miss P over breakfast.

# Chapter 14

# Dydd Iau the seconds

A heat-scaled tin can, a landing pod burns down the sky into the ocean, parachutes open. Three moon-dusted men are jubilantly shaken about inside it, three in the furnace. A man has walked on the moon and made his way home through fire.

Ash angels fall down the winds; their feathers scatter and catch in the wires and hedgerows, skitter down even to the wet sand of a crescent bay. There is no return for Ty Merched.

In Swansea lock-up, DS Watcyns is beginning his second day of remand, pending trial. If there's no more abuse from his fellow inmates than on his first day, then he could consider himself the luckiest bad cop in the Welsh prison system. But some of the inmates, some of the guards, have known him a long time. He is not the luckiest bad cop in the Welsh prison system.

White soot has bloomed across the Gwrhyd hillside in agonal exhalation as the last uprights collapsed. There is something of flowers about the site. These dusty petals were *things*, yesterday: chair, photograph, glove; jug, cradle, cake tin; poem, quilt, stocking; hen, bowl, spoon. Person good, person bad;

person sad, person mad. The old oak timbers burned with such intensity nothing is identifiable, nothing is distinct inside the shell of blackened ashlars. From low orbit it looks like a giant dandelion head: she loved me, she loved me not, she loved me.

The space that was Ty Merched wears its funeral wreath of ash quietly in the early morning sun. A couple of firemen arrive and poke about the sheds for a bit, until they notice they're not alone. The Quorum had staked a guard on the site; in shifts, perched by the hedge with thermos and snap tin and a pack of cards.

'Ta-ra' they smile with teeth bared at the departing firemen. Other sightseers and fossickers arrive: local kids and unknown travellers, a fox with a taste for roast fowl. Only the fox is allowed entrance.

The Misses P are in their window seat, fingers interlaced, watching the passers-by. They see Mrs Barry walking the lane partway, then returning home, only to pause at her gate and turn to walk the lane partway, then home again where she turns back to the lane before finally sitting down on the bank above Ty Merched; they see Mr Barry settle beside her a while before leading her home. The Misses P see people sitting on graves up in the churchyard, looking out towards the gap that was Ty Merched. They see the valley adjusting to events.

The Misses P hear, over the ridge, the hammering of a hand-lettered sign on the wall of the Rhiwfawr Arms: for sale.

Lizzie is floating in a thick cloud of bedding, in the back of a bus and high on a hill. She rubs her fingers over the rough blanket until they are red and raw. She looks at the roof, but only sees flames; she sees Myfanwy walking into the fire. Myfanwy walks into the fire and Myfanwy walks into the fire and Myfanwy walks into the fire. The fire burns and burns and burns, there are a hundred years to burn up; comfort and plenty are in the fire, worn hopes and forgotten days are burning. Myfanwy walks into the fire and Lizzie understands and does not understand the act; Lizzie knows and does not know her daughter now; Lizzie could stop her own breath easier than stop Myfanwy walk and walk. Lizzie hears Sarah Maud moving quietly out of the bus, as Myfanwy walks into the fire. *Why?*

*Why not?* Myfanwy speaks over her shoulder as she walks into the fire; the vicar lifts his head from within her grasp, grins in agreement: *why not, you old witch?*

Sarah Maud has wrapped a blanket over yesterday's clothes and taken a path away from the bus. She sits on a slab of weathered limestone, a fallen bronze-age wall now buried in the grass, and hugs her knees in her crossed arms. She's watching the birds over the valley. But she doesn't see birds. She sees Myfanwy walk into the fire. She sees Dewi, flickering unfocused, overexposed. She sees her notebooks in the fire, and she reaches out a hand to brush along their stained and crushed spines as the turgid words come to bright life for the first and only time. She sees Myfanwy walk into the fire. Sarah Maud toddles along the old hall of Ty Merched; she hears but doesn't understand Myfanwy's rancour at returning home a dependent; she climbs a tree to wave at the ghosts in the loft window. She packs her schoolbag, turns up the wireless to puzzle over the war news and the victory news alongside her mother, dances to a new beat, works the sheep, meets a man at the gate, cries in the dark, clutches her belly, peers into the eyes of a baby. Sarah Maud hears Myfanwy's opinions: pretty, naughty, too slow, too quick; feels Myfanwy brush her hair and chide her for wanting beauty, wanting to make beauty. Feels Myfanwy struggle: 'puzzled' became 'angry' when door was locked, when baby came, when darkness...

Sarah Maud sees Myfanwy walk into the kitchen, sees My-fanwy walk into the garden, walk into the bedroom and reach down into the new crib with crying eyes, walk into the fire and walk into the fire. Tracking concentric orbits all their lives, My-fanwy had been by turns close then distant then close again, to finally bloom like a comet, blazing hot and close as she left Sarah Maud for the last time.

Sarah Maud walks in her mind around the walls of Ty Merched where the stones, now laid bare of plaster and lichen, wear new cloth of mourning soot; Sarah Maud makes her selection. She feels the weight of granite, of hammer and chisel, in her thoughts, as she watches Myfanwy walk into the fire and into the fire and into.

Jenner sleeps on. In her dreams she ticks off the apologies one by one. Noisy: *sorry Mamgu*; wild: *sorry Mamgu*; grubby, *sorry Mamgu*; slow to learn, absent from chapel and school, filling the house with bits of things from the woods and streams and hills: *sorry Mamgu, sorry Mamgu, sorry Mamgu.* Existing, breathing: *sorry Mamgu, I didn't mean to.* Messing the clean apron with an uninvited hug: *not sorry Mamgu, and I do it again, don't I?*

It was impossible to think of Myfanwy without Ty Merched; it's long been impossible to think of Ty Merched without Myfanwy. Myfanwy has simply become absolutely, finally, at home. Jenner takes a mug of tea to her mother but fails to find her; she leaves it on a stone by the bus and slips down the slope with Smalldog, to study the remains of her home.

Standing now on the bus steps, from her high vantage point Lizzie can't see the cupping hands of safety and familiarity she once imagined cradled her home. The land is dragging down, a waste chute of limestone shovelling the habitations, crowding them together as if to pitch them all into the bay along the path of the glaciers, the mammoths and giant forests; the bronze weapons, the ancient pride and the modern hubris that drags godhead down to a clean floor, a tidy cupboard. She sees a land that will discard this short-lived civilisation, shake off the scabby life that crusts its vast flanks.

Lizzie is timid without the wolf's head walking stick now, timid about where to go, or why. So, Sarah Maud has no trouble catching up, skittering down the slope to shuffle beside Lizzie in silent companionship as they make their way along the lane.

Clumps of idle neighbours move aside for the women, and they join Jenner at the most obvious viewing point in the lane, where the hedge is broken; a spray of dried blood is being erased by the footfalls of the curious.

But there is only so long a person can stand and do nothing at the gate of their destroyed home. Salvage can wait; with no place to take things, anything that isn't ash may as well stay where it is. The silence frays, melts, gives way to mumbles, speculation, children pointing and asking loud questions. The neighbour women, practical, nod amongst themselves about spare items to be offered: a change of clothes, a bowl of cawl.

A couple of hill farmers, old gaffers, prod at the nearest bits of soot with their sticks, quietly congratulating themselves for still being alive to see such an amazement as the fall of Ty Merched—old as the very bones of these living hills—even if not the end of the now mythically long-lived Lizzie. PC Jones arrives.

'This is a murder scene,' he reminds them. Is it? Who said that? The crowd thins like fog in sunshine, and he feels, without any reason, that there might be difficulties. But Lizzie in yesterday's clothes wrapped over with a blanket from the bus, Sarah Maud and Jenner too, are the immediate concern.

'Is there someone I can call? Do you have insurance, need to speak to … Family?' Jones can only think what he'd need himself. Mainly, whisky and his mother's embrace. 'A cup of tea?'

'Breakfast. Let's get you some breakfast, and a warm coat,' WPC Davies has arrived, off-duty.

'No. I...' Lizzie leans on the charred gate post where once Smalldog dropped a wormy turd. But there's nothing to be won by resisting. She lets herself be taken down to Ponty: the clothing store where Lizzie has had an account since 1937, the pub they have never entered. The family jiggle and rub against each other, rustle around the unfamiliar table, looking and not looking for the something missing. They cannot arrange themselves comfortably, there's an imbalance they can't settle. Their hair smells of smoke, their eyes are dry and red, blinking and flickering to catch the thing just out of sight, the person who should be standing there but isn't.

Lizzie's agent arrives unbidden—the news has spread like, well, like wildfire—and they talk briefly, privately, a moment of near normality. He is a reliable man.

'There is a cottage,' Lizzie tells the company round the table. 'We have a cottage that's vacant.' And the careful wealth of the Coombe family finds purpose; that long-predicted 'rainy day' has arrived. The cottage, owned since before Lizzie was born, is lovely. Sitting high above even Panteg and Yr Allt to catch the first rays of sun, further up the next valley, a line of well-lit rooms lead through to a level, grassy space by the river where it rushes over stones, bright, noisy and fragrant with the special smell of brisk rivers. The agent had been letting it for holidays, but his wife is even now phoning London, cancelling bookings, negotiating alternatives. There are beds and bedding, furniture enough, a handful of books. A bus stop nearby. Charity is not required.

No ghosts that they know. No old stove needing to be tended like a skittish pony, no sloping-roofed bathroom, or attic of old apples, or cupboard of coats and hats bent to the exact curve of their owners' bodies.

The retained old woman who has had care of the place since she was a schoolgirl has been in and dusted. A bunch of hedgerow and garden flowers in a yellow vase fills the centre of the dining table. The agent unloads the brief shopping they have done; the retained old woman returns, this time with a mutton pie and a dish of potatoes hot from her oven. Lizzie, who hasn't been here since old Elizabeth's death and the reviewing of the estates, is aware of her own age, her grimy skin and dusty hair, against the freshness, the normality, the kindness these employees show.

Only, it would have been Myfanwy who would have thanked the old woman, in the right valley manner. But Myfanwy walked into the fire. There's a clumsy moment, until Jenner takes the old woman's hand, asks her name. Blodeudd it is, a common enough name round here, but:

'They said you'd come by,' says old Blodeudd and peers deep into Jenner's eyes, holds Jenner's hand to her papery breast. 'Before I died, they said; you'd come by.'

PC Jones must speak to them, about imprisonment, kidnapping, rescue, about the fire and Jenner and Myfanwy and Morgan. But PC Jones must wait. There is a new packet of rose geranium soap in the bathroom.

Mrs Davies takes the news to the shop. There is, she tells, a cottage in Ynyswen. There is, she can confirm, an account at the clothes store in Ponty. There is much to consider. Maris is laying in fresh stocks of biscuits and black ribbon.

'Well now, they won't want our help!' Several women are in agreement, not just on that but on the difficulty of hitting the right tone between affront and relief. Someone remembers the cottage, a tale she'd heard from someone else.

'No, that's another place. This one's by the river.'

How many houses does the Coomb family own? A few women fall silent about their landlord... then, no, for this is too big a story and they chime in their part.

'Millionaire then, is she?' and the discussion heats up, swings round in changing moods from admiration, envy, a little laughter and daydreaming, from woman to woman, until:

'Myfanwy, you'd never guess by her ways now, that the family was worth all that...' and the voices fall again with the muted respect that a well-managed household should always earn, even if affection was lacking. That's the thing, see, about the valleys. You can dislike, distrust, even ignore or condemn, but that doesn't mean you don't feel close. Like a coat you sometimes like and sometimes don't. Valley life, village life, it's like that: shared, known, understood. Half the fun is changing sides.

'Did she really...?' asks one incredulously, breathily.

'Ie' several confirm in hushed voices.

'Why, do you think?'

Although 'why' is understood by many, the question must be asked. That's what community does: the healing by talking; the resettling of the village hierarchy, the pecking order, following a change in the participants; the airing of thoughts in the safe space, between shelves of canned fruit and shoelaces, onions and saddle soap. The setting in place, the writing of the story for the next generation, is starting here, today. Myfanwy walked into her kitchen and the dust has yet to settle.

The words come round and round the shop; like a choir these life-old friends and neighbours know the timbre and pitch of each other's thoughts; when to take the solo lead and when to provide the continuo, the antiphon, and the chorus.

'Is there anything left to..?'

'Nage, nothing that we could see.'

'Ah, remember that beautiful sideboard, gone it is.'

'Och yes, and the dinner plate, we used to have it as a treat for Myfanwy's birthday teas when we were but farthings and her Da made us all laugh so...'

'She were a fine cook. Hopeless at lambing time but pastry to die for.' A few chuckles that the solid woman had such soft hands and cool fingers.

'I wonder, did anyone get her recipe for brandy cake. Ahh what a loss that cookbook is.'

'The rooster they had there, I think I saw it up the lane. Sent the boys to fetch it... don't suppose they'll miss him now.' A long pause and the scale of the disaster is visited anew, each thinking how they themselves would cope at such a time, on what chair they could set themselves down after such a total loss.

'You'd remember they had this old harebell jug from Ynysmeudwy potteries; pretty thing. My mam tried to steal it once...'

'She was in love, you know. Before the old man, aye.' And voices huddle round some well-polished old stories. Though all the participants are now dead, still delicacy doesn't hurt.

Elder Miss P has been examining the small selection of stockings for much longer than it warranted. 'Young Miss P, and me. I... we... she's not my... can I just say that, if anything should happen to me, she...'

Maris looks up. 'Oh, of course dear. We know. Beautiful playing you did yesterday. Just beautiful.'

Mrs John Davies rounds her mouth, 'Oh my god was it only yesterday? My god, like a lifetime ago, it feels... Yes, dear, no need to announce. Oh, but have you seen Sarah Maud? Oh goodness, it's like someone's turned the lights on again after all these years...'

'And Jenner. Oh, Jenner. How funny we never...'

And the talk swirls round and round again. Just like it does in the pub. The bank. The hairdresser's and the barber's. A house so old can't just leave, and no-one needing to talk it through many times over.

Memories are dredged, dragged with grappling hooks, for the reasons behind that curse of one hundred years or more; no-one remembers accurately.

'Didn't someone die the day she were born? What was that all about then?'

'Ydu, her da and a half-brother. So Mam said. Du, but Lizzie Ty Merched's had a time of it, all things considered. I suppose, a life this long, can't all be roses now, can it?' and the talk skips over the facts of happenstance and tracks the memoried paths of gossip again. The ruby necklace is mentioned. A mumbling old cousin's apocrypha is discounted as being a different curse over by a different valley.

A story so long and deep and wide that no amount of chat will cover the spread of it. Words turn and turn about the valley. But one thing is certain, a tacit agreement is unspoken; Morgan will not be mourned, he will not be counted, and he will not be mentioned ever again.

-oOo-

PC Jones sets up a table and chairs, notebooks, teacups and an urn, in the meeting room upstairs at the Rhiwfawr Arms. The walls are lined with oilcloth portraits of worthies long gone; familiar noses and hairlines on jaundiced or florid faces, garnished with bat droppings and pockmarked by darts and the thumbtacked, tattered streamers of a forgotten jubilee. Under their painted gaze, he has evidence to gather, crimes to address, laws to uphold.

PC Williams stares into the varnished yellow eyes of a dead Williams predecessor and scratches his left buttock. He has given Jones a list of the most likely people; Jones has given it back and Williams has been out all morning rounding up whoever he could find.

'Mrs Barry, Mr Barry, thanks for coming. Um, together isn't necessary.' Jones indicates the single chair on that side of the table. Barry seats his wife and with a proprietorial air discloses a second chair under the window drapes.

'Shall we start with the fire? What can you tell me about the fire?'

'Oh now,' says Mr Barry, while his wife twists a solitary glove between her hands. 'The fire. Well, we were in the church hall, see, and then someone called fire, so we all ran over. Mr Protheroe, I think it was, wasn't it Zipporah? Yes, Mr Protheroe. So, we all ran, which was a shame now, the timing.

Miss Perry, the elder one, you know she's got a beautiful touch on the piano. Well, she was playing the piano, in the hall; Mendelsohn, was it Zipporah? Mendelsohn, yes. Lovely piece, so delicate a touch she has. And I was just thinking the piano needed a tune, the high A was a bit flat...'

'The, ah, fire?' suggests Jones.

'Och, yes, the fire. Well. Are you alright dear? Excuse me could we have a tea for Zipporah, she's... it's been a trying few days... thanks. Oh, me too, yes why not, why not. Lovely. Diolch.

Now, the fire. It was Ty Merched wasn't it, burning over there. We could see the smoke from the hall. Yes, definitely Ty Merched. Is there a biscuit? Lovely, *diolch yn fawr*, Young Williams. Umm. Ty Merched. Lizzie's place...'

'I know what house it was, Mr Barry, thank you. I want to know what you saw when you got to the site of the fire.' Jones glances at Williams, but Williams is looking at a different portrait with uncommon interest.

'Oh! When we got there, why didn't you say? Sure, it was well alight. A lot of smoke, and the heat look you, we were well back on the lane, from the heat; I had a burr in my sock, troubling me; didn't I, Zipporah? I had to sort that out, next thing I saw, the roof had fallen in. John, that English hippy John, he let the hens out. I didn't know if he was allowed, all things considered. Yes. A lot of smoke.'

'And Myfanwy Coombe?'

'Who? Ah now you meant Myfanwy Thomas, now; she was born a Coombe of course, Lizzie's first, but married. Before Sarah Maud was born; nothing improper there. Old Eifion Thomas, up Cwm Giedd, didn't think he had it in him; apologies, my love, that was indelicate of me... Lovely woman, dependable, a great sadness. Great sadness... loved her home she did. So clean. Great sadness. Yes.'

'Did you see her enter the house, while it was on fire?'

'Ah now, I couldn't be sure that I did... I had this burr in my sock, you see. I mean, did she now? Or was she... I just don't know. Great—'

'Sadness, yes, I agree. But I don't understand, Mr Barry, why you have such a vague recall; surely this must have been the most...'

'Astonishing! Absolutely astonishing, yes. The last thing anyone would expect. Beautiful house. Lovely woman. Great—'

'Mrs Barry? Can you add anything, about the events you witnessed?'

Mrs Barry has been quite overcome by the policeman's attention and she finds she is unable to add a thing to her husband's account. She has been barely able to speak a word since Sunday church. They take a second biscuit each as they pass the tea urn on their way out. Jones again looks at Williams, who says nothing. The retired music teacher is next.

'Mr... Davies? What can you tell us; were you in the hall when the fire started?'

'Oh yes, splendid arrangement, they'd done such an excellent job with the Under Elevens Choir. All boys yes; girls that age, just screechy. Yes. Miss Perry was at the piano; good touch the woman has, good touch. Lovely bit of...'

'Mendelsohn, yes.'

'Mendelsohn? God no, du du du man it was Chopin! Have you no ear? Chopin. So then just at the 16$^{th}$ bar—the piano needs a tune; top A is flat—someone called our attention to a possible conflagration across the valley. Now, who was it... Mr Barry, I think. Yes. No. Mr Protheroe, yes. Anything else I can help you with?'

'Ah, well I really—'

'It's just that the bus is due, I'd best be off now. Glad to be any help. Thanks, no tea; I'll just take a biscuit if I may. Right. Bus,' he affirmed, though no bus could be heard.

Jones consults his notes. 'Mrs... Davies next? Same family?'

'Not recently. There are a lot of Davieses round by here. This is Davies the Fridge's wife'

'OK, ask her to come in.'

A small boy appears at the door before Williams reaches it. 'Mam says to tell you she's sent me instead; busy she is.' The boy clambers into a chair, wipes his nose on his sleeve, hitches up his socks. 'She says can I have a biscuit please.'

'Williams?' says Jones, joining his assistant by the window.

'Sir?'

'Williams, what the fuck is going on?'

The afternoon wears on, the biscuits diminish, and the bald facts stay as bald as an egg. No-one mentions the vicar. The way they see it, no harm done; this is a secular investigation.

-oOo-

Out and far away, John and Mich, and the woman known as Blodeuwedd but of uncertain appearance—her raincoat does have exceptionally large pockets—are moving towards a common focus. There is a drawing in; there will be another memorial, a singing and a gathering and a drawing in. Soon.

-oOo-

It's dusk, and rain has roared up the Swansea Road, sweeping away the heat of the past few days, clearing the sooty air. Lizzie and her smaller family are settling. They shift lopsided round the bright empty  house, unsure of themselves and their places. Lizzie is reminded of the Grimms' tale of the bird and the mouse and the ... she forgets; something about changing the roles in a happy household, and disaster follows. She thinks to look it up, remembers where the Grimms' Fairy Tales book sat on the bookcase nine decades; and now gone.

Yet she can still feel the pages, the worn green cloth cover, in her fingertips' memory.

Unlike the furniture here, which is wrong to the touch. The beds, the light switches, the number of people, all is wrong. She is wrong.

John and Mich arrive with the end of the storm, bringing simple gifts; cider for Sarah Maud, a book and pencils for Jenner, and new eggs and a newspaper for Lizzie... that Myfanwy would have liked... Jesse, on duty at the bus, has sent a bone for Smalldog.

Lizzie bustles about, awkward in the strange space, looking in cupboards for a sugar bowl that never lived here, for the tea caddy burnt to crumbs. Sarah Maud cradles the cider bottle, leads them across the wet grass and down to the river. Lizzie is troubled by the smoke of their cigarettes lingering by the door, but when she climbs into bed (all wrong the mattress, the blanket; a wrong picture on a wrong wall) she's comforted by the murmur of their voices over the sound of the river flowing fast, here where the channel narrows though rocks. Late and long and later still, they talk. She has fallen into a deep sleep—a lake, an ocean of sleep laps over her—before Jenner slips out the side door, Smalldog running ahead in excitement, to meet a woman of uncertain appearance. A quarter moon rises over an unfamiliar horizon, to soothe this unsettled house.

Just before dawn, Sarah Maud farewelling her friends at the front gate, greets Jenner returning. Smalldog goes to sleep on the doormat. They linger in the garden, touching each other's arms as they talk. There is much to be recovered but little that can be hurried.

'Do you want I to mother you now, bach? You're not childish anymore, yet still my only.'

'No, Mam. No more than I need to mother you. But I'm still and always your only.'

The rebuilding needs time. Not much is said in words, and none of it carelessly.

# Chapter 15

# Dydd Gwener the second

Lizzie, past volition, past valence, cannot see to put a foot in front of the other. Dreaming, she struggles to breathe. She calls, holds out a desperate hand to catch at her daughter.

*Take me with you.*

Only, Myfanwy's not listening. Myfanwy has withdrawn, pulling the fabric of herself away, leaving Lizzie holding threads and tatters in her hands.

*Do you know, can you see how I am unbalanced now? Where are you...?* There is a thought, in Lizzie's head, how Myfanwy had quietly chaffed the long years under Lizzie's rule; there is another thought that Lizzie had overlooked, undervalued, her reliance on Myfanwy. There is a thought that sees Myfanwy for the first time and cries that this is so late; there is another thought: *'don't be so indulgent, you had your times and made your choices.'* Patches of thoughts layered one on another. Lizzie is unstitched by grief.

Breakfast: possibly breakfast will bring something. Change has become as constant as the sunrise. But breakfast must be prepared in this kitchen, sharp and bright with Laminex and a neat white electric stove as wrong as a stove could be. Lizzie snarls at the toaster, just as Jenner walks in. There is shop-bought bread in the cupboard, doughy and white and as unsatisfying as an half-kept promise. Jenner feeds the toaster, fills the electric kettle and plugs it in.

'Do you like this place?' asks Lizzie carefully. There's a shingle on the gate that reads 'River Cottage'. A house name with no history, a nothing name. An English name.

Jenner considers before she answers. 'Ie. We needs to be here, now. We needs a place with our own front door.' She looks for plates, mugs—mugs! —knives and butter. Shop jam.

Lizzie flutters her hands by the skirt of her unfamiliar dress; she cannot feel in this place, this time is suddenly not her time. Her skin, joints, muscles are waiting for familiar clothes, heavy boots. She has no weight in this polyester and jersey, these ridiculously light shoes. All this loose fabric that catches at her when she walks: "easy care" said the labels. *Pfft. Care is never easy...*

Jenner pours tea, passes the mug—mug! —to her. 'Toast it is, Hen Nain, there's no porridge yet.' She sits in a chair opposite Lizzie.

Lizzie picks up the milk bottle, tilts it askance; she pokes at the toast with her index finger. 'I don't know where I am, cariad.' The house is too quiet. It holds no story. Electric stove! Myfanwy would have liked to live here...

'This place will be fine, Hen Nain. Really. It will.' Jenner sips her tea, watches Lizzie mimic her, until their mugs are empty. 'We have no need for more. Really.' There's a pause, then Jenner picks over the words carefully, as if separating out chaff from blossoms.

'It's gone now. All that past, and the things we kept, and loved, and forgot. You're here and Mam and me, we're all safe. And, well, Mamgu, you know she chose that. She thought to protect us; and, well, to be in her world forever. We are special this family, and Mamgu, your firstborn, was the domestic one, the person that the house lived through, more than any; she belongs there with those stones and roofs, separating her would be like cutting the heart from a living lamb.

'You know this! I saw it; you knew and you understood her. We all did. Hen Nain, you know who we are. You know you're not like this, either; Myfanwy—' (here Lizzie winces at Jenner's discarding of the familial) '— made choice. You too, Hen Nain, you be strong. You're old, I knows, but this is old land. It holds us, and those others you love.'

'You don't know it, Jenner; you're but a child for all you're clever. Don't stop me from my grief, cariad. Can't I mourn in my way?'

'Well, but you're not mourning; you're complaining about the bread...'

It was true that Lizzie has slept better than she had for years, woken to a lightness in her joints that she put down to... that she has, in fact, chosen to ignore.

'Guilt, Hen Nain; we don't need guilt. Look at the harm it did. Mamgu don't need guilt anymore.'

'How do you say these things, Jenner? What do you know?'

'I been quiet a long time, Hen Nain, Lizzie bach, cariad. But we got things to deal with, and quiet I don't do no more.' The simplicity of vision. 'Mamgu is gone, Ty Merched is gone, like a river, isn't it. Come and walk outside?'

The trampled grass and ransoms on the riverbank smell of sap and greenness where the cigarette butts and empty glasses of last night's visitors lay drying in the late morning. Lizzie baulks at the homespun symbolism of Jenner's philosophy. 'It's not like a river, not at all! You don't know...' she begins to tremble with frustration and anger, censuring the swear words between clenched teeth. 'You're too young to know,' she finishes, exasperated.

Jenner faces away, downstream. 'I saw her, Hen Nain, after the fire. I saw her through the fire and during the fire. And I saw her after the fire. All of them, all the dead ones and the old ones, the attic and the pantry and the hall ones, from the sheds and the well and the far field past Mam's garden, they all just lifted up their heads. The house is done, its stories are rewritten now, the things that strung them—us—down are all gone. They're all gone.' Jenner kisses her great grandmother's hand, holds it firm and smiles at Lizzie, eye to eye; they are the same height now and Jenner will grow to be tall. 'The house's stories are ended, but we're not, Lizzie bach... There it is, then. I'll see if Blodeudd has any porridge we might borrow?'

Sarah Maud joins them at the house door. She hugs her grandmother carefully, as if she might break. Lizzie ruffles herself thoroughly.

She is still angry. 'There it ffwcing isn't' she would say, if only she didn't love this child so much. If only she is allowed to be angry. If only Myfanwy were there to cwtch them, cushion them from each other so they didn't jounce and rub... but Myfanwy walked into the fire.

Lizzie needs the anger, to drown out the wailing in her head. There's a crying baby somewhere and Lizzie suspects it's herself. Her belly feels so empty, or no, watery, like sea tides on the turn. Her hands... she's empty, and she's wailing, and she knows this feeling and she hates it. But here, where no sheep or garden wait, there is nothing to do to fill her hands.

'There's nothing to do!' There's nothing to want... 'I wanted to study medicine. Only, they wouldn't have it. And then, I married for love and that made everyone cross again.' And then, Myfanwy; came too soon, too soon... *did you need to be there so quickly my girl, in the house before I was ready...?* Myfanwy walked into...

Later, through the day, Lizzie finds herself down at the riverbank, forgetting how she got there. The water folds on itself in ribbons of glass, colours of moss and deep tannin, sounds of murmur and ruffle. The rocks flicker a colour palette of golds and browns and blues. Small birds, 'yellow-legged dippers' to the English, 'White-breast of the Water' to the Welsh, bob and splash from the water to their under-bank nests with beaks full of nymphs and bugs for the unfledged brood.

Lizzie is still awake at midnight. She hears John and Mich leave, though she didn't remember hearing them arrive. She hears Jenner return, though she never heard Jenner go out. Lizzie suspects that Jenner and Sarah Maud are pressing down their awakening desires—for movement and growth and a bigger horizon of their own—so they can allow Lizzie her little grumbles in comfort. She hates the idea that she might, by selfishness, have incited their kindness. And she's right in her guessing: with everything so changed, so new, their grief is unframed. Their future is waiting.

Lizzie once trimmed her desires to fit Ty Merched and its occupants, to her belly and the baby inside it, and she knows the weights of things: desire, loss, love; self, other, resentment; love is the heaviest. Lizzie knows anyone can have desires, make plans; that's the easy part. But as she looks for her accustomed anger, to rise it up as a shield before her again, it slips through her thought's fingers and scampers away chuckling.

And she feels the old book, the *Materia Medica*, has returned, a fixed point in this dimensionless house. Somehow, Jenner has her book again. Our book. In the dark, Lizzie can feel old Elizabeth is smiling. Lizzie doesn't need plans that fit the new house, for the new house doesn't fit her...

As she comes carefully down the unfamiliar stairs, Sarah Maud and Jenner are leaning against opposite door posts in the hall, whispering slow and quiet.

'I can't sleep,' says Lizzie. 'I'll put the kettle on.' She smiles, an open, honest smile, and Jenner and Sarah Maud relax, grinning in response. 'Oh, by the way...' Lizzie turns into the kitchen and fumbles for the unfamiliar light switch, '... was a woman I thought I saw going out the gate by here, in a raincoat. Such large pockets. It's not raining, is it?' She pauses again as water rattles into the kettle '... you could keep a forest in those pockets. Or the stars...'

# Chapter 16

# OTHER DAYS

There is another memorial in the village, in the chapel hall and without any vicar, on a damp summer's day. The choirs and soloists and the brass band; Elder Miss P at the piano (Mr Barry has had it tuned, the morning) and Younger Miss P reading from a book of poetry in her giggling lilt. Myfanwy would have been touched, even though she distrusted poetry. Contained grandeur is there: songs heard as if through a window looking out over Panteg, melodies that catch a breeze off the ocean. Words are read that Myfanwy—always anxious to be accepted, always uncertain—would have been surprised by. Unlikely rhymes: if not tender at least encompassing and kind. Myfanwy was known to them all, in one way or time, and the selections make them feel like children at a party, like flower seedlings tucked in warm earth beds, like a stove gleaming on a snowy afternoon.

And without a priest, look you! This ancient idea that the women have revived, modified: threnody for the well-known, saga of homely battles, litany of schooldays and sweethearts, is... well, it's fun. You can hear people thinking to themselves 'I hope I die to such a treat.' And sitting up straighter, as if they just might.

'The thing about Myfanwy, see...' say the neighbours, one by one, almost confidentially: 'it's not common knowledge about Myfanwy, but...'. Lizzie and Sarah Maud see that Myfanwy knew things they didn't: connections, and birthdays, and the small but valuable rewards of moving through a close community without intending harm. Jenner sees that room will be made for her in this place, should she want it, out of respect for Myfanwy.

Zipporah sees that, while looking down on someone can make you feel better, looking them in the eyes makes you feel best. And the rest of the village, even Jem Jenkins, are finding the change is ...well, let's just say no-one missed any vicar. There was sky, and breeze, and the seasons wheeling across the high grey mountains and the vast grey waters; certainly, no-one missed that vicar.

Maris has had several attempts at the brandy cake recipe, and variations on the theme sit glistening on the trestle table along with the cups and spoons and jugs of milk. There are no photographs propped by the tea things, for nothing suitable remained; certainly not the photo of Lizzie's birthday that the newspaper had used.

Did it matter that Myfanwy's considerable years had been so confined: home and cleaning and all the unliberated baggage of her generation? Depends on what one considers important.

No; it depends on what Myfanwy considered important.

Lizzie sits to one side, with Sarah Maud. Jenner organises the performances, the readings, the ending. Jenner has the village in the palms of her hands. *'Cysga'n dawel'* they sing; 'sleep quietly.'

-oOo-

Then there is another time. Jenner is leaving the valley and the house in the sunshine, and her small family. She'll cross the

Black Mountain with their blessing as she would have gone anyway without it; but this is best. She will leave her prison cell manuscripts at the house but has packed up the *Materia Medica* and will take Smalldog to live with Blodeuwedd, that woman of uncertain appearance ('young' doesn't fit her; 'timeless' seems accurate but disquieting), to learn and study, and to teach. Still and always, Jenner will search for her own place; find where she can fit her anachronistic skills into the world, where she can fit herself in this time and in times to come. Lizzie has confided in Old Blodeudd, counting over the different points that make up her anxiety, for the girl is so... different: only ten still, and missed so much school, and seen too much for young eyes; way too much. Lizzie dares not say what she feels most, knowing how deeply the binds of affection can cut into young wrists.

'Happen the girl needs to go... or she never will,' Old Blodeudd suggests, cautiously rubbing Lizzie's arm. 'She's not for the village school now. And that gift she has!' Lizzie knows the truth of it but, still, the threads of her love are stretched thin.

Sarah Maud is working. Sarah Maud has been up to London with John and Mich; the galleries startled her, made her shy and keen to come home, but gave her things to think about. She has made a Memory for her mother, in the yard at Ty Merched, from the fallen stones of the old house: a place of strange rooms opening onto the sky, stones mortared with coloured clays, baskets of polished wood and wire, aproned and frocked in flowers, the walls filled with niches and tiny figures; objects from the ashes, metal and glass, a shard of pottery with a fragment of harebell still visible. While it's a sad and debatable truism that art (and people) improves through anguish, Sarah Maud is now in such deep connection to herself, that the work she produces, from hiraeth, from old and new loss, is actually very fine: distilled by fire, trimmed of foggy sentiment.

The sheds are being rebuilt for a workshop. Her name, connected with so much news, has raised interest outside the valley, and Sarah Maud is responding to this external validation with erratic commitment as her inner ghosts are laid, revive, are laid again; slowly the space they consume in the graveyard of her dreams gets smaller. There's a woman coming from Cardiff to speak to her.

And Lizzie has been working. In her land agent's office and at the solicitor, checking and redrafting, and signing over. At the door she puts on the old attitude along with her new hat and tidy coat. An imperious tiny bird of a thing in pastel plumage—though she still insists on trousers, having no patience for those synthetic skirts the store manager tried to push on her—she makes her way through an altered world of bus travel and Swansea streets and shop tea. For she won't have the agent coming to the house; she insists on the privacy of the office, the anonymity of crowds.

She makes frequent trips to Swansea now, just a note to Sarah Maud on the table. 'Don't wait tea for me' or 'Meet me at the 3.17' or 'Shall I get us a fish at market?' make her granddaughter, great-granddaughter, smile.

'What do you do all day down there?' Jenner asks.

'Nothing needs me here...' she looks again at the clean surfaces and light cupboards, the... appliances. 'It's a city now, there's new! There's a lot to look at. And I have made a friend at the tearooms.' Lizzie replies opaquely. They think she means shops, clothes, books, another eccentric old woman at Marietta's for the 2-shilling cream tea. Sarah Maud and Jenner swap a smile behind her back.

-oOo-

The note reads 'Don't wait tea for me.' There's a breeze in the kitchen windows this bright autumn day, and the note paper is casually held to the table by the ruby necklace. Lizzie has undone the clasp at last.

She has caught the bus as usual, nodding to the regular fellow travellers. She nods at tree and flower and crying child, studies the ugly new roundabout and the war-stained relict church. The sky is unusually huge: wide and heavy and shielding. She considers the street rubbish, how someone had a thing in their hand and then just let it fall. She feels lighter, with the ruby necklace gone; history-less, ephemeral, as if she could be just let fall.

The land passes before her as a strip of moving film and she the stationery watcher. But the film has been double-exposed, and she sees more than just the world outside: forest and mine overshadow house and warehouse, canal barges slip beneath the highway, cattle markets and slag heaps and army camps and circuses and tramways all shift about, sinking and rising behind a foreground of bungalows and schoolyards, weeds and carparks and advertising hoardings. New cement, old brick. People running and frozen in place, men carrying axes and books and coffins, women carrying gunpowder and banners and babies. The overlaid images are familiar, the reality is not.

Lizzie watches out the windows as the road winds down to the sea, and film and window images merge, blend, become one again at the end of the Gower where the endless tides cross and the timeless cliffs stare west, always and only ever seeing day's end.

She's tired now, elation in abeyance, and she waits on a bench as the bus moves off. The breeze here is stronger, damp off the sea behind her; it chills her skin at neck and hands, a cool stroke on her cheek. A loose hair catches across her lips. There is no-one in sight, the other few passengers have gone their ways to pub or house. *Yes?* She enquires of herself.

*Yes.* Drawing a deep breath of conviction, Lizzie leaves the bench.

The path from the clifftop village down to the beach is swept clear of sand, although the autumn has brought few visitors; but it's steep and uneven, the new walking stick is needed. She is in no hurry. In one hundred years, what's a few more minutes. Lizzie steps carefully amongst the heather roots and dune grasses, falters over a thin gutter of wild watercress crossing the path and laughs quietly at herself and her habitual fussiness as she reaches the flat spread of sand. The tide is out, the shore seems to reach over the curve of the horizon. Lizzie momentarily loses her balance, sways and peers around at the cliffs ranging away on each side, the huge weight of the ancient land piling and pressing in behind her, the vast animal of the ocean breathing before her. A bird pinned on the dome of sky watching, like a god, this crumpled and emptied and self-discarding woman. 'Crccck' calls the gull, 'craaack'.

Lizzie hears again the crack of a carved wolf's head on a man's jaw and, remembering, straightens her back, lifts her head into the lightly stinging wind. *Ffwc, yes, I did that.*

'Yes, I did...' she yells into the wind. The gull dips one wing and spirals around the sky. Following it with her eyes, Lizzie spins, wobbles, spins; the horizons flicker before her, cliff sky sand sea cliff sky sand sea cliff sky sand sea, until she falls feather-light and painlessly backwards to the sand. She lies breathless and elated. 'Ffwc, I did that.'

'Language now, cariad!' William bends low to take her hand.

'Oh, I must look a fright in these hideous things, bach!' She's brushing the sand off the polyester jacket, shaking the ugly little handbag from her wrist and flinging it away. The jacket too.

William's eyes: blue-grey-black. William's smile: wolfish, hungry like the new moon. William's hands: cool, softer than a man's hands should be. Lizzie covers her face with her own weathered hands, to hide her wrinkles, her age, her naked need for him.

He takes her hands into his own, kisses her: eyelids and cheeks and mouth. They walk west, and west, and west. Lizzie lies back in her bed of waves beside her beloved.

The gull flies on.

-oOo-

So, dear reader. Murders, suicides, a house destroyed, a police station *eaten;* remember to keep your small dog healthy and watch where it shits. But then, look you: Watcyns rots at the bottom of the prison; it's a comfort to know that not all turds are in the wrong place...

The sounds of sheep and hens and geese are gone from Ty Merched; only the hedgerow birds and forest birds chirrup and hunt. For the first time in hundreds of years, no wood has been chopped in the yard, or straw piled into the lofts. The gate stands ajar, and Sarah Maud's little truck comes and goes with her tools and thermos; she has grown into herself and holds her head high and gentle. Her diminished family and the lost years visit her dreams; friends are close by. Mich brings her babies to play by the river garden on fine Saturdays, and over tea—not cider, look you—they talk. Sarah Maud runs drawing classes in winter, laughs with her students over gossip and biscuits. The occasional visitor pauses by Myfanwy's Place to discuss a commission, or a day long laid to rest. And there's a surprise: Sarah Maud has become firm friends with too-clever-to-marry Maris Protheroe at the shop. They like each other. They don't bother to figure out why; they just do.

The Ty Merched gate stands ajar and yet no creatures will escape, for none are penned in.

Local lads now grown tall bring their children a-piggy-back in fine weather and tell them garbled stories of witch-children and mad priests.

The place that was Ty Merched, the place that was the house of women, doesn't mind; soft things will come and go, hard things as well given enough frost and sun. Sarah Maud works on, mangling the words of a folk song and laughing quietly at herself. And will be here, with the old grey cat or a new grey kitten, when Jenner returns, and goes, and returns; all in good time.

The moon landing? Well, that's an easy story; they went up, they came down. How interesting could that be? Du, they weren't even from the valleys.

# Acknowledgements

I spent many quiet afternoons ambling the heath and long-buried pathways of Panteg where the red kites and honey-buzzards hunt, or practising my vestigial Welsh in the cloud-hugging Capel Gwrhyd graveyard: the occupants closer than most to their nominated God, sleeping now where black-faced sheep graze on farm and farmer alike.

I have set this story in the valley that planted the idea, high in the folded hills above Pontardawe, paved with the crumbs of Bronze Age villages and scarred by the ghosts of occupation: the clumps of brick that were once a school, the rail links no longer needed. The community in *Red Gifts in the Garden of Stones* is fictional; you can read my story of Lizzie's birth, *'Gwennie and Elizabeth'*, online at pamswanborough.com

But up the back of that real-life, pocket-handkerchief sized graveyard is a stone that lists the members of a family where, for a while, four woman outlived all the menfolk...

From musing over tombstones in windy sunshine to proof-editing in a record-breaking Australian summer, has been a fairly indirect ride, and way too slow; life happens. That said, excellent people have been nudging me in roughly the right direction with patience and skill.

Firstly, the land and people of South Wales where I made dear friends, and found just the nicest workmates and neighbours, and fabulous stories: of wise women and family herbals and other secrets. And, not to be ignored, the dead and departed, with their Brythonic and biblical names.

Staff and friends of RMIT PWE 2020-2021 even the ones who wrote swear words on my marking sheets (you know who you are, FSN, and I love you for it); thanks, it was a hoot!

Grateful thanks to Lee Kofman for her guidance and suggestions, and generosity with her time; and more so for assuring me that the raw work was actually worth more effort.

Special thanks to Rebecca Fletcher for wise and relevant editorial support, and being able to laugh when all about us were unfunny. Thanks to Jim McIntyre for encouragement and for being someone I might (and do) rant at. Thanks too, to the many beta readers who gave their time and invaluable feedback.

Always I am indebted to my endlessly supportive sister, Sue Mooney, and my family and friends.

Finally, notably, thanks to AE who never reads anything and thus delivers the most provoking incentive ever known.

-oOo-

I've made a Pinterest 'mood and info' board and a Spotify soundtrack: Radio Myfanwy... If this sounds fun (it was fun to make!) jump to the publisher website at Twofeathers.press and click on the link to '*Red Gifts in the Garden of Stones*', look for 'Reader Resources'

You can also sign up to my mailing list for release date of the follow-up, and/or leave a comment.

And there's a link to the Goodreads page if you'd like to leave a review or ask a question.

I hope you have enjoyed my book, let's chat anytime.

Pamela Swanborough started writing in 2019, winning 'Best Regional Writer/ runner-up Best Fiction' in the GMW Emerging Writers' Competition, Writers Victoria 2019, and completing an Associate Degree in Professional Writing and Editing at RMIT in 2021.

Pam is interested in almost everything, and her writing explores imbalance, the fragility of life and environment, age and memory, and fluid identity. She works in literary/speculative fiction and lyric non-fiction. She has short stories published in Australia and the USA.

Born in Melbourne, Australia, Pam lived in the UK for many years. She currently lives in rural Victoria on the unceded land of the Eastern Maar, and is working on further writing projects while renovating a crumbling ruin with which she feels a natural affinity.

*Red Gifts in the Garden of Stones* is her first novel.